Sherwood Green

By Don Hayward

Second edition

© 2023

Also by Don Hayward

Collapse
Book One of After the Last Day
ISBN 978-1-7752459-2-6 (Soft cover)

Under Shadows
Book Two of After the last Day
ISBN 978-1-7752459-4-0 (Softcover)

The End of shadows
Book Three of After the Last Day
ISBN 978-1-7752459-5-7 (Soft cover)

The Seventh Path
ISBN 978-1-62137-949-2 (Soft cover)

Journey's End
ISBN 978-1775-245933 (Soft cover)

Murder on the Goderich Local
ISBN 978-1-62137-993-5 (Soft cover)

Return
ISBN 978-1-7752459-7-1 (Soft cover)

RoH –Alien Legacy
ISBN 978-1-7752459-8-8

Echo of the Whip-poor-will
ISBN 978-1-7752459-1-9 (Soft cover)

High Falls
A pictorial history
ISBN 978-1-7752459-6-4 (Soft cover)

Author's word

Sherwood Green is a work of fiction. Any resemblance of the characters to real people, living or dead, is coincidental.

I conceived the story to give one answer to the question: "What would it look like if someone tried to act on the idea of covert extreme environmental resistance?"

The author is neither advocating that effort nor arguing against it. The reader must draw their own conclusions. Sherwood Green examines this question in a readable way.

- D.H.

Contact Don,

https://www.danddhayward.ca/

haywardon@gmail.com

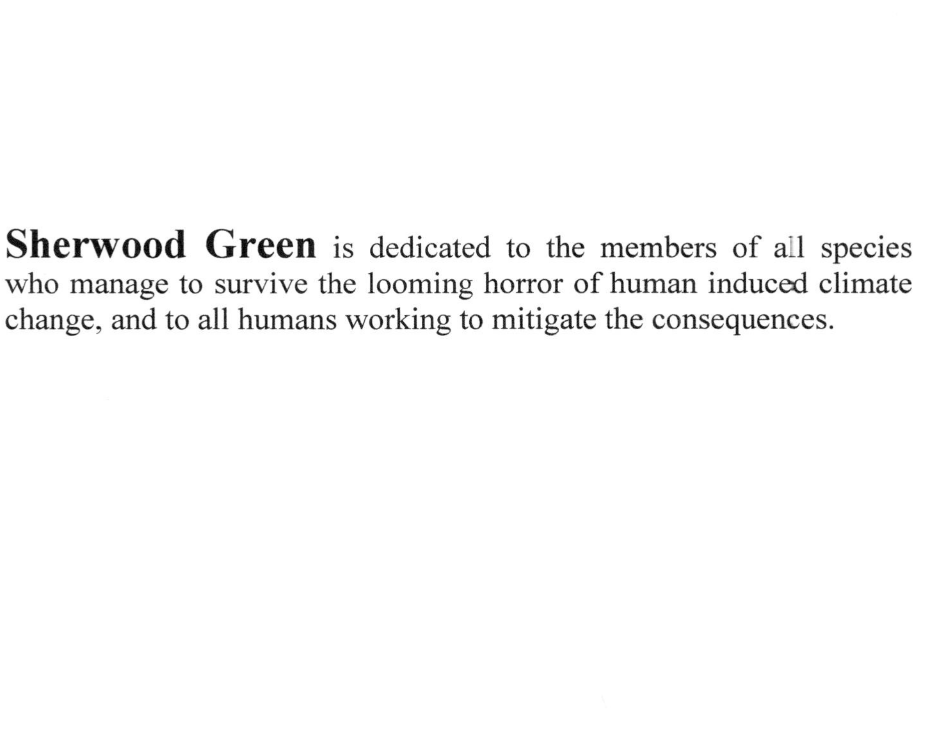

Chapter 1

She pressed her black clad body into the doorway as a parade of two pumpers and an aerial ladder fire truck screamed past. To the east, billowing smoke and low, scudding rain clouds reflected the red glow of flames devouring a huge lumber yard.

The stream of emergency vehicles ended. She resumed spraying messages on storefront walls and windows. Light drizzle soaked the ground, reflecting the light of a wasteful cobra street lamp and floodlights of the car lot across the wide street. The dealership lights died.

Two men dressed in black jumpsuits and balaclavas hurried between new cars, smashing windows, splashing diesel fuel into the interiors and pouring fuel on the ground, connecting the vehicles with a flammable stream. They placed plastic bottles of gasoline beneath fuel tanks. One man tipped a twenty litre container of gasoline sideways up the slight grade above the parked vehicles, making a stream of explosive liquid that found its way beneath them all.

They smashed the plate glass of the display room door and rushed inside, spreading diesel oil about the sales offices. Time was short. The power failure may not have killed the alarm system.

The pair fled, igniting the oil on the display room floor and in the cubicles with gasoline bombs as they rushed from the building. More gasoline fire bombs exploded amongst the shiny new cars. The raiders scaled a back fence and ran through a parking lot to a nondescript, newer model car.

The spray painter sat behind the wheel, stripped of her disguise. The men deposited their clothing, smelling of gasoline, into a plastic bag. She eased the car into the quiet industrial street and away from the mayhem as flames shot from the dealership. She drove onto the freeway and headed downtown where they abandoned the car on a dark street near where they had stolen it.

Twenty minutes passed before the dealership fire drew a response. Gas tanks exploded and flame breached the roof of the main building. A few vehicles had burnt out before the first fire vehicle arrived. The four-alarm blaze at the lumberyard had stretched the forces thin. Only a distant pumper company could respond, but the fire overwhelmed it. Two more alarms went out, but by the time adequate forces arrived, the fire had won.

Most of the media had covered the first fire. They diverted a handful of disgruntled reporters from that spectacular blaze to the smaller event. Jos Amiel later thought of his good luck in witnessing the public debut of Sherwood Green.

As the flames died, the small group of reporters in the street lost interest and tried to find a fire captain for an on camera segment and an excuse to leave. Jos checked his notes, but his cameraman grabbed his arm.

"Look at this!" Walt exclaimed.

Someone had sprayed the words, *Stop Murdering Whales–Stop killing the planet - Support Sherwood Green* on the building across the street.

"Who the hell is Sherwood Green?" Jos wracked his brain. The name had never been in the news. "Maybe he's an eco-freak who's in jail. I'll check later."

The tired reporter got five minutes with a fire captain who acknowledged the fire was arson.

"There's a strong smell of diesel, and someone set fires under each of the vehicles. The Fire Marshal will have to confirm it. The destruction is so widespread only arson could have done it."

The reporter pointed out the graffiti on the walls.

"Same thing on the far side of the building," the fireman yawned. "No doubt in my mind."

He wandered off to oversee the dousing of hot spots. Jos set up the opening shot of his report with the gutted dealership as a backdrop.

"I am reporting from the burnt-out ruins of the Fukushima Automotive Corporation dealership on Grand Ave." Jos made a quick nod to the rubble behind him. "Eco-terrorists torched the place."

Walt chuckled, but kept on shooting. Over Jos' right shoulder, the partially destroyed sign of the dealership had only two letters left. The fragment read, 'Fu'. The report would go viral on YouTube.

Jos spotted leaflets scattered on the ground. The pamphlets detailed the reasons for the attack and linked this fire to that of the lumberyard. A bold headline on one page proclaimed certified forests were the green washing of timber companies. The pamphlets denounced corporations as environmental criminals. Jos kept a copy, hoping to convince his producer to let him chase what would likely be a much larger story.

The general reaction to the arson at the car dealership came in an exchange on a radio talk show later in the day.

The host engaged in diatribes against what he called *the racist, unwarranted attack upon a Japanese business disguised as environmentalism.*

In the mix of denunciations of "lefty freaks" and "commies", one caller fired the opening shot of a propaganda war.

"You have it backwards," the man said. "It is an environmental resistance that the media are trying to twist it into a racial attack."

"Look, idiot," the host shouted. "How can you be so stupid not to see the racism? I wish you young, ignorant ones would grow up."

"You certainly seem to know a lot," the youthful voice said. "For instance, you seem to know who pays your wages and whom to keep happy."

"Are you claiming I am paid off?" The host screamed into the microphone, and gave his engineer fits as she tried to keep the volume under control. The accusation came close to the truth. People had called Bert Boyce an intellectual prostitute. He resented the label.

"I'll have you know, when I was younger I marched on Queen's Park against gravel pits and dumps and my grandkids help clean up the Parkway every spring."

"You're a genuine hero." The caller chuckled. "You wouldn't give up your SUV and walk or take the subway. You're just putting plaster on a cracking planet."

The caller's calmness upset the host. The kid exceeded the usual gang of back scratchers who called in to agree with Boyce's rants. He found foolish argumentative types pathetic and usually destroyed them.

"Are you the arsonist?" Boyce changed his tactics, and hoped he could turn this into an exclusive and get kudos, maybe a broadcasting award.

"You're all arsonists," the caller threw the comment back, "every time you burn gasoline, use palm oil, take out a loan or flip on a light switch. You're burning the planet. We destroyed a few cars that won't add to the disaster."

Boyce realized he gave the caller a platform to make his case. The boy did a good job of it.

"Look, you're a racist." He returned to the attack. "You ought to be in jail, you racist twerp."

Years of practice taught Boyce that personal attacks against intelligent callers usually made them to hang up. His regular audience cheered when he insulted anyone who questioned their biases.

"Where are you calling from, you *bleep-bleep?*" A three second delay allowed the engineer to remove vulgarity. It was routine for the show.

"From the site of the next defence of the planet, and Sherwood Green will not rest until we save the planet, until we destroy industrial civilisation, until we destroy the financial elite in Toronto." The voice remained calm.

"Get a job you *bleeping* twerp!" Boyce hung up, launching a long, expletive filled diatribe against the caller and all environmentalists and racists. The phones lit up with supportive listeners. The rest of the programme became a festival of self-congratulation.

"I work at the Canuck Car Company." The last caller of the day began, "and though I don't agree with these fire-bombing commies, people ought to stop buying Jap cars. It's a country stealing our jobs and won't buy our stuff. Remember, they killed our boys back in WW two."

Boyce spent a few minutes agreeing with the caller before signing off. He ignored that racism.

Within the hour, they turned the tape of the exchange over to the police. Lawyers for the radio station monitored the controversial talk-show ever since the lawsuit after Boyce libelled someone with money. The caller had made a threat, and the law forced them to alert the police.

Investigators heard traffic noises on the phone call. Forensic experts tried to mine the background sounds for clues. They decided the caller used a downtown payphone. The police found a manifesto of the new group glued to a phone booth with condensed milk. The phone booth was in a surveillance video dead zone, frustrating the police.

They added extra patrols all over the central city. Police set up a stake-out near the phone booth. The police harassed all young people who deviated from the police idea of normal as they passed through the surveillance. They extended carding beyond the usual non-white targets.

University students frequented the downtown and made it impossible to sort out the strange from the threatening by the way they dressed.

Sherwood Green had glued the manifesto to lampposts and walls. Police pored over hours of video from security cameras, trying to spot a notice being put up. Off duty constables were called in to help, but the task overwhelmed the downtown Division 52. They harassed and investigated every kid in a hood or with long hair. The police force felt a sense of urgency. The caller had warned there would be another attack.

The evening news displayed dozens of images of suspects. Television news eventually reverted to showing a few extreme suspects and asked people to check photos posted on the internet. The fires made exciting images, but no one bothered to discuss the issues. The Stanley Cup final round distracted much of the population.

Chapter 2

Jos Amiel swung his feet onto the cool hardwood floor and fumbled for his incessantly ringing cell phone. It was his most important tool and most enslaving technology. It was only three in the afternoon. Normally, the reporter would not wake until six, preparing for the night beat at TorontoNewsNow.

"Rise and shine, little boy, there are things happening with our guy Sherwood. We're famous." Walt was excited.

"What?" Jos stumbled into his kitchen and poured a mug of stale coffee. A minute in the microwave and it might get heart pumping again. He wanted a proper coffee from Starbucks beside the studio.

"Our report went viral on YouTube. People loved the F.U. in the background. The comments from Honda and Toyota drivers are priceless. Get moving. The cops called a news conference at headquarters. I'll meet you there."

Jos checked out the YouTube feed on his smart phone. The attention thrilled him, but also disappointed. None of the comments mentioned the content and professionalism of the report or Sherwood Green. Everyone laughed over the accidental subliminal swearing. He saw why old hands thought the audience lived in "zombie land". Still, this was a feather in his cap. Recognition and popularity were important to his career. Quality journalism could still impress the producer, but did not attract viewers.

Police reporters chatted in the comfortable surroundings of the briefing room. Many more, including Jos Amiel, milled about on less familiar ground. They had always held late night briefings in the lobby.

Jos could credit part of the interest to himself. His coverage of the overnight fires had been the only one to highlight the Sherwood Green terrorist angle. The other media had featured video of the spectacular lumber fire and played catch-up while pretending they were the first to break the news.

A handsome police sergeant strode onto the stage accompanied by a late middle-aged cop wearing a tailored uniform. The Sergeant spoke.

"Ladies and gentlemen, I'm Sergeant Stanton, and this is our new Deputy Chief, Frank Langstaff. Join me in congratulating Frank on his promotion."

The applause was polite but hardly enthusiastic. The old hands on the police beat knew Langstaff, and most did not like him. Everyone saw Langstaff as ambitious and not too smart. Jos had only seen him on television.

"There'll be cake in the lobby to celebrate Frank's promotion." Stanton was a press representative because of his on camera good looks. Polling showed that his type of spokesperson gained public trust. Women had given a strong positive response.

Broadcasters chose most on air television personalities for the same reasons. They had hired Jos Amiel despite inexperience because of his attractive on camera presence and ethnicity. Amiel was smart, competent and a hard worker. He considered himself idealistic, hoping one day he would report big stories and make a difference.

When they needed trust, networks presented older less visually appealing people of both sexes. These were no less self-absorbed than the good-looking ones, but even the biased, lazy, incompetent ones who simply read a script appeared wise. The public trusted the opinions of their favourite personalities.

"Frank's promotion was the original purpose of this meeting," the sergeant suddenly looked serious, "but we had some disturbing racist attacks last night. The force wants to assure the public we take it seriously." He paused dramatically.

"There were two acts of racist, terrorist arson last night. We are uncertain if they aimed the major attack at the lumberyard, but the racist incident at the Japanese automobile dealership is disturbing. A group led by someone named Sherwood Green committed these atrocities."

"How do you know?" A reporter shouted.

The open-ended, unfocused question allowed the spokesperson to ramble, outlining the bare facts of the previous night's fires. Some reporters did not know the details. Jos wondered if some of his fellow journalists watched or read any news.

"Who's Sherwood Green?" A reporter from The Star called out. "We've never heard of him."

Who is Sherwood Green would be the headline of this reporter's piece on the attack and become everyone's question.

"We don't know." The policeman said. "We're certain he's not a member of an environmental group."

How are they so sure? The police have spies. Jos thought.

"What are you doing to get this punk?" The print reporter called out.

Like the police, crime reporters had formed a view of the world in black and white, a place of "the good guys and the bad guys... heroes and punks". This was not surprising. A reporter's success, and their job, depended on the flow of inside information from officers. As in professional sport-reporting, no one who rocked the boat lasted very long. The simple conflict, between good and evil, attracted audiences.

"We have the recordings from every surveillance camera where we found posters. We've seen people of interest. One of them is Sherwood Green."

"How serious is this?" Jos asked.

Sergeant Stanton flashed the young reporter a disapproving look. He did not enjoy having a newbie in his sessions. They asked odd ball questions. He leaned over to whisper something into Frank Langstaff's ear. "Deputy Chief Langstaff can answer that question."

"Jos, isn't it?" The older officer smiled in the well-practiced manner of a politician. "That was an excellent report you did about last night's events, although I wouldn't be so sympathetic to terrorists." A critical shadow crossed his face.

"They have put me in charge of the investigation. The Force takes this seriously at the highest levels. We fear we have a nut case on the loose and want to apprehend him before someone gets hurt."

"Are you sure Sherwood Green is a person?" Jos asked. He understood it simplified the problem for the police if they could focus on one individual with a few groupies, like Charles Manson. No one in authority wanted the public to think there might be a large group. An organized threat would cause panic and encourage copycats.

The F.B.I. in the U.S.A. had been effective in arresting individuals and small groups, portraying them as domestic terrorists. Most of these had been young people, high on drugs or with mental health issues, voicing their upset with a system they thought had failed them. Security agents tricked such people into sounding like terrorists.

"We are sure." Langstaff did not smile. He nodded to a uniformed constable standing to one side. "Sheila will distribute a photo of the person we think is Green."

The constable handed out a press release with a blurry image of a young white man with a short cropped beard in a hooded sweat-jacket.

"The photo is from a camera at Bond Street and Shuter Street near to where a phone call to a local radio talk show originated. We think it was Green, probably not his real name. There's no trace of anyone named Sherwood Green."

"We have asked for copies of all videos and still photos from last night's crime scenes. When we know more, you'll be the first to know. I want Sherwood Green to know," Langstaff glared into the cameras, "I'm your worst nightmare. I'll get you. Thank you. Enjoy the cake."

"Did you get any useful footage?" Jos asked.

"It's boring stuff, but some will run, especially the answer to your last question. Frank's last bit was dramatic. He stared into my camera, more like a politician than a cop."

Jos' smart phone jingled. A tweet appeared. "Saw yr rprt, wnt 2 mt re Sherwood Green."

Jos quickly replied.

"Walt, I have to go alone." Jos said. "It's at the Tim's on John, so I won't be far. I'll catch up in the bullpen."

"I saw your report." A man in his twenties with long-haired and a reddish-brown beard slightly out of control approached Jos. He wore a perfectly fitting plaid flannel shirt and designer blue jeans that made Jos think the man was a student in designer dress-down mode.

I'm a lumberjack, and I'm okay... Jos smiled to himself.

"Your report was enlightening." They sat at an isolated table. Jos wondered if he should buy the guy a coffee, but the man and offered. The fellow was not short of money.

Not a student, Jos decided. *He wants something.*

"Why did you call me?" Jos hoped for an inside source. From his appearance, this person could be a radical of some sort. "Are you a member of the group?"

"Nope, although I wish I was. That's why I called you. You seemed sympathetic to Sherwood Green in your report. I thought you might have been told ahead of time and why you got there so fast. Can you put me in touch with Sherwood Green?"

"If I sounded sympathetic, I didn't mean it."

This was the second person today who suggested he was pro-terrorist. Jos was happy covering an interesting story; it had all the promise of being something larger, but Jos tried to be neutral and factual.

"My producer sent there me," Jos was defensive. "I didn't slant my report."

The man looked disappointed.

"I tell you what," Jos smiled. "I'll be working on this story. If I get a line on them, maybe I could introduce you. I would expect some information in return. Agreed?"

"Okay," the man seemed disappointed. "My name is…"

"Hold it!" Jos exclaimed, a little too loudly. Other customers glanced his way. "No names." Jos scribbled his personal number on his business card.

"If you call or text, just say it's Tim's friend calling. Don't leave a number. Use a throw away cell or a pay phone. I am at work most evenings except weekends, so check in once in a while. If you contact Green, please let me know."

"Are you sure you aren't one of them?" Tim's friend looked hopeful. "You do this conspiracy thing well."

"I never heard of these guys before last night, but I know how things work. We can find everything on the internet. If you join Sherwood Green, you'd be my confidential source. The cops might ask me about you. Don't contact me on the web. If you ever meet this guy, never refer to it electronically, or on the phone."

"I rely on anonymous sources. If I don't know the name, they cannot squeeze me under oath. The new security act doesn't give us reporters much protection."

"Okay, I'll call." The man left the donut shop.

Jos stared after him, somewhat bewildered. The tweet had arrived shortly after the police news conference, and it was a puzzle about how the man had known about his personal Twitter account nick. Only his network account linked publicly to his name.

Damn, I am acting like a terrorist. Do I tell the cops? The first guy who accused me of being with Green was a cop. Is this guy a cop, too?

I won't call him, but if the guy is legit, then he'll contact me after he connects with Green, and I'll get the story.

"There's no time to shoot an intro for the news conference footage. Jill will ask your question on the news cast before the bit plays. We're off to a bar." Walt seemed happy at the prospect.

"What the hell?" For the second time, Walt denied Jos a few moments to get what he considered a proper coffee at Bucks. "What's that about?"

"Sheri arranged for you to interview Bert Boyce, the talk show host who got the call from the Greenie. We're meeting Boyce at the Brass Hat."

Walt relished the idea. The place was a strip club noted for biker gang connections, drug dealing, and the best looking strippers in town. The sign advertised "French and Russian Girls" in flashing neon.

"I know, Boyce." Jos was less than thrilled. "He's a racist. Will he talk to me?"

Jos was the son of a single mother who was a refugee from Haiti. He was Canadian born, but his black skin reflected his ancestral home. The talk show host had been in trouble with media watch dogs several times for racial innuendo while pretending to be anti-racist.

"Waaaas yah want, again?" Bert Boyce had been in his favourite club since finishing his show earlier in the afternoon. He was on his third round of whisky chasers. A large-breasted waitress in a skimpy costume knew him well. She kept a close eye on him, ready to supply his needs. Boyce was a careless tipper after a few drinks. The man leered at the girl and then turned back to them.

"Speak up, I don' have all day." Boyce was well on his way to being drunk, but Jos thought he was still alert enough. The drunk refused to go outside for video, so Walt had little to do but enjoy the gyrations of the strippers.

If only one could actually dance. He thought.

"We heard you had a call from the terrorist." Jos wanted to get out of the place. He didn't mind the girls, but the burly bouncers made him nervous. Anywhere where dealing hard drugs was dangerous, although the small-time punk gangbangers would never tangle with the bikers here on their turf. The odour of legal marijuana drifting in from the girls' dressing rooms added to his jitters. Jos grew up in the public housing projects of North York where he had seen real danger. The driving beat accompanying the dancers distracted, and the music was as plastic as the girls.

"So they sent their fucking little black boy." Boyce slurred the words and leaned towards the reporter. His breath stank.

"You from fucking Alabama?" The man laughed and swigged his beer.

"I'm Canadian," Jos tried to control his anger. "My parents came from Haiti."

The man leaned closer as if imparting a secret, "You folks from there sure have it bad. Not good enough you fucking kill each other, but God sends fucking quakes and storms to finish the job." He laughed again.

Jos gripped the table. He wanted to curse Sheri for setting up this insulting farce.

Boyce blurted out, "Yur here 'bout the fucking commie creep phone call." Sheri had briefed Boyce while he was still sober.

"That little fucking asshole thought he could beat me." His eyes flashed. "He made me hang up, ME ..." his voice rose loud enough to fight the stripper's music for attention. A bouncer edged closer. "The fucking jerks are supposed to hang up on me. I'll get the little commie, asshole!"

Jos saw an opening. "Who do you think the guy is?"

"It was this Sherwood Green asshole himself." Boyce slurred. "He sounded like the fucking leader."

This was flimsy evidence, but Boyce was so full of himself only the leader would call him.

"So, you agree with the cops?" Jos wanted the disgusting man's impression. He regretted the question as the man leaned forward with his foul breath.

"Listen, I work with the fucking police. I was one once, you know."

Jos said that he didn't know.

"We work together," Boyce glanced around as if remembering bikers, drug dealers and other people who might not like the police surrounded him. "I help them get the fucking Commies, whackos and Nazis and that crud."

It takes one to know one. Jos kept silent.

"I have a bunch of regular callers who are total fucking nut cases." Boyce's eyes went sad, as if he realized, through his alcoholic haze, it added up to his work being pathetic. "It's valuable stuff for the cops."

Boyce fell into mumbling incoherence. Jos could not coax any more from him. He and Walt left the noise behind. Night fell. The sounds and neon lights of Yonge Street were paradise after the oppressive dive.

"Remind me to kill Sheri for arranging that mess."

He had learned one useful thing. Boyce was a police stooge, and another person Jos must treat carefully.

Amiel was not aware the police used Boyce's right wing, racist contacts as weapons against demonstrators. There was nothing like a good street fight between rival political groups to cover police intervention. Illegal riot suppression a few years previously had mixed results. The police wanted to avoid more black eyes, although most people supported their attacks on demonstrators.

Another fire happened that night at a Fukushima dealership. It erupted about three in the morning, far out in suburban Vaughn and firemen mopped up as Jos and Walt arrived. Destruction was as complete as the previous night, but unlike the night before, police everywhere, stopped Jos and Walt and examined their press passes.

"It is the same as last night." The York Regional police commander said. "The dogs followed tracks to that parking lot." He pointed to a nearby strip mall housing a muffler service and a donut shop, "but we lost them. It looks like they took a car from there. We arrived minutes after the alarm went off and cordoned off the whole neighbourhood. We had everything locked down tight but no trace of the punks. I think they're local and hid in a residential garage. We'll be going door-to-door tomorrow."

No one knew the arsonists had used time-delayed fire bombs to ignite the blaze and left the area before the alarm sounded. The device they used was a German invention from the first world war using a combination of sulphuric and picric acids. The Fire Marshal puzzled over the confusing chemical traces and concluded they came from the lead-acid car batteries.

With no video of flames and explosions, Jos filed a tame report. None of the rival outlets had anything better. They tied in the race for the audience. Jos' references to Sherwood Green in his report drew a discreet call from Frank Langstaff to Jos' boss, suggesting they not name the terrorists. Sheri would never ignore the boss, but later in the day when the newspapers' front-page headlines asked, "Who is Sherwood Green?" She convinced her manager that the need to ride viewer interest outweighed the wishes of the police. Giving the threat a name made it personal for the viewers. Sheri assigned Jos to follow Sherwood Green.

"File exciting reports and don't spend too much money." Sheri said.

Walt stayed with him as a videographer. Sheri had offered the job to others, but the story was not big enough to attract senior reporters. Jos was now on day shift, although the story would require him to rush to any terrorist event day or night. He happily considered how to approach the story as he drifted into sleep on the second morning of Sherwood Green's war against Toronto.

Chapter 3

Jos allowed himself four hours' sleep to reset his body clock to daytime and struggled awake at noon.

Food had been an important part of his upbringing. His mother taught him how to cook traditional dishes. This love of cooking persisted, and Jos could prepare delicious scratch meals. He ate his share of junk food but thought he restored balance through his own cooking. Jos enjoyed an asparagus, mushroom and chicken creation while he scanned the news. His report from the previous night compared well with the rivals.

Satisfaction lasted until the end of his meal, when the enormity of his problem took hold. To justify his special assignment, he would have to do more than file reports from the scene of an attack. He needed an angle to make his work stand out. He required a deeper approach beyond reporters' tricks or good luck. Hard work did not frighten Jos, but where should he focus? He remembered the words of one of his journalism professors.

Sell the news. It must attract the audience, she said, *but you have to sell yourself to your bosses, add something they can't get from anyone else. You need both to keep a job. If you want to tell what you think is the truth, make it interesting.*

Jos had scoffed at her cynical advice. Now he needed more of it. He dialled the university's main number. After hitting twenty keys on his phone pad, he reached Debbie Franklin's answering machine. He glanced at his watch. She would be in a lecture. Jos left his number.

He had always respected Professor Franklin's advice. He had taken her course listed in the syllabus with the sub-heading: *Do you pander to public taste and opinion or do you mould it?*

Jos had not attended her course about media and advocacy. Those lectures had focused on how to separate reporting a cause from supporting it. Jos hated violence and found arson upsetting. He did not support Sherwood Green, but Jos had to understand them.

Remember, propaganda is a fight for the power of words. His political science professor had emphasized. *Only people can give words power. If you control the words and definitions, you control the power and the people. The best device is to co-opt your opponents' words and turn the power against him, just like in jujitsu. Be on guard for the counter thrust. They try to control you.*

Amiel pondered these words as he sipped his favourite brew at Bucks. The police and the media had attached the labels of racist and terrorist to Sherwood Green.

Considering that, Jos thought, *how would Sherwood Green turn those words back onto his critics? Are they racists and terrorists or, as they claim, environmental resistors saving the planet?*

"Jos Amiel?" Professor Franklin's unmistakable Vancouver accent recalled hours of lectures and seminars. Jos explained his assignment and outlined his need to make his work significant and appealing. Franklin had a full schedule, including a dinner with some financial patrons.

"Come up to my place at nine. I always wanted a one-on-one with you. Bring your notepad and two pens."

"Two pens and a notepad" were Franklin's standard admonition for her students. She did not use her follow up line, "Having no notes is no excuse in class or for a journalist."

Widespread rumour said Debbie Franklin had slept her way into her job. As a student, she had seduced her lead professor, the other Professor Franklin, and after subverting his marriage, married the man. When he had transferred to the Toronto school, he found a job for her in the same journalism faculty. Despite this less than professional route to the job, Debbie Franklin was an outstanding teacher. Her students loved her, and the university found her good looks and wit useful in fundraising. She had a high rating in student evaluations.

Her students had given Professor Franklin's the nickname: 'Doctor Shorthand'. She was the only one of Jos' teachers who insisted on good note taking, and the only one who checked notebooks.

The crucial factor in a student's graduating from her course was a personal visit to her office with their notebooks. Franklin would examine the notes and then hand them back, asking the student to read their recordings of a random lecture. The woman would then discuss, from memory, the accuracy and incisiveness of the students' notes. Anxiety always made this session an ordeal, but it was actually a gentle way to succeed. The only ones who ever failed had too few or no notes at all. In effect, she had mimicked a story meeting between a journalist and editor. In a mockery of a puffed up American ex-president, she would let students know they passed by standing, pointing at them and shouting: "You're hired!"

The exam was easy in comparison. It was a take-home assignment about some controversial current social issue. Jos' class had to write an opinion moulding piece dealing with homeless street people and panhandling.

Jos stood at Franklin's lobby door, searching for the code to their unit. He was nervous, even though he had gotten on well with the professor. His mother raised him to be excessively respectful of authority figures. This had handicapped him somewhat in school. His older sister, with her cynical attitude towards authority, had helped ease his anxiety. Old fears were surfacing on Franklin's doorstep.

Debbie Franklin was a stylish woman in her late forties. She wore a bright pink, form fitting sweater and short skirt. The colours complimented her professional length blond hair. She was not a tall woman. Excessive high heels enhanced her elegance.

Jos sat in a plush leather chair as she placed a plate of cheeses, a variety of high-end crackers, a bottle of wine, and two large glasses on the low living room table. She slid Jos' notebook and two pens to one side. Her eyes smiled as she touched the objects. The room reflected Debbie's elegance, decorated with expensive furniture, authentic Persian rugs and deep red walls offset by cream trim. Professionally framed works of art adorned the walls. A series of black and white photographs of well-known Canadians attracted Jos' attention. The portraits reminded him of Karsh. Debbie noticed his gaze.

"I took them myself." She seemed proud of her work. Jos could see why. "I went to school with a couple of them, taught a couple and met the rest here and there." She poured some wine and continued, "Unfortunately, I never slept with any of them."

Jos paused at the innuendo, but said nothing. Debbie served a wonderful sparkling red wine designed for informal occasions. The label on the bottle said, *Jip-Jip Rocks Sparkling Shiraz* from Australia.

Debbie spread cream cheese onto two crackers and offered one to Jos. The taste mixed perfectly with the wine.

"I saw your report," Debbie opened the conversation. "It's a big story."

Jos nodded, unable to speak with his mouth full of cheese and crackers. He felt foolish.

"It's a change from gang shootings or the antics of your neighbour's cat." She smiled broadly as Jos blushed at the reminder of his more insipid stories.

"I hate the mealy feely stuff, anyway. There are too many graduates making a living on that bullshit. I was afraid you might turn into a Chuck Ford. Ford's pandering to the lowest common denominator pisses me off." Her bluntness reminded Jos of her lectures. Debbie sipped her wine. "So, what do you need to talk about?"

Jos opened his notebook. He had only one question.

"I need to know how to approach this. How do I present it? My boss has a bias against Sherwood Green, but I want to pin it down, tell the story as I find it." It hardly seemed important enough to interest Professor Franklin.

"Do you want to just present the facts, keep your bosses happy, or do you want to do more?" She cut right into his confusion.

"I want to do more. I want to help people understand what's going on. What are Sherwood Green's motives? What it means to all of us. Do they actually have a point?"

"You always were idealistic, Jos. I had you marked down for someone who would either be a big time journalist, or you would quit in frustration. I was right."

Debbie touched his hand and poured more wine. She leaned back on the couch and regarded Jos with a searching look. Finally she said, "This is serious journalism, real investigative stuff. I would suggest you explore the story from the reaction and impact on outside society at large, from the point of view of the established environmental groups and from Sherwood Green's deviation from the main-stream tree huggers. Help the public understand this organization. Scientists aren't supposed to ask why, but journalists must. It's too easy to call them terrorists."

Jos scribbled down the gist of her statement.

"Sort out everyone's bullshit. That's the actual job of a journalist, and keeping your boss happy." Debbie chuckled. "It's the hardest job you'll ever have. The establishment will want to stir up hate for Sherwood Green."

"You don't have any contacts in the environmental movement, do you?" Debbi knew the answer. Jos partied as an undergraduate and had not taken part in any serious extra-curricular activity.

"One thing really makes me sad. All of you young people are better trained, technically, than journalists ever were, but your knowledge of the world is shallow."

"My mother told me lots of stuff about her own life. Lots of kids never had that." Jos was defensive.

"I met your mother. She would be a brilliant writer with the struggle and experiences she suffered. You don't need to suffer, but you need to get out and experience the world. You do that as you cover Sherwood Green. This story is going to be big, unless they catch them tomorrow."

Debbie shared the last of the wine. Jos let his glass sit. His head was already a little confused. He would wait until they were through.

"Where do I start? I can't just go up to Sherwood Green and say hello."

Debbie pulled out a campus newspaper and pointed out a large advertisement.

"The Anti-Whaling Coalition is meeting Friday night at Hart House. They have a big time speaker from the campaign against whaling. Start there. I'll e-mail a few more ideas and maybe a contact or two, and I support some of these outfits even though they never seem to accomplish much." She paused. "I'm almost cheering for Sherwood Green. You know how to make contacts. Try to pick these anti-whaler brains. Sherwood Green mentioned whales. Maybe someone from there is an arsonist."

They finished the wine and emptied the cheese tray.

"They don't feed you as well as they used to at these dinners." Debbie seemed sober but laughed loudly.

Jos rose to leave. Over two hours had passed. He didn't want to overstay his welcome. Professor Franklin had given him a lot of ideas and encouragement. Debbie took his hands in hers and looked into his eyes.

"Remember to follow your instincts, too."

Her eyes were demanding. She kissed him.

Jos did not remember how they reached the bedroom, but they were naked and on the bed, kissing wildly and exploring. Debbie was indeed a beautiful woman.

"What about your husband? Won't he be home?" He managed the question between their urgent kisses.

"He won't be home for hours." Debbie's mouth demanded. "He's off with his own bit of fun, joy for him, more for us."

Their lovemaking was hot and wild, physically satisfying. Every rumour he had ever heard about his former teacher was true. She was wanton and wild. Once he overcame his surprise, their passion was free and fulfilling.

In her orgasm, she cried out, "Yes, my little brown boy. Yes!"

They finished together. Her words stirred memories in Jos. He had made love with white girls who had cried out in the same way the spent and panting Debbie had done. As his passion subsided, he remembered his theory.

Those girls wanted to affirm their anti-racist ideals by sleeping with men of other races. Jos once discussed this with his worldly sister. She agreed, but suggested the women might have been angry at their fathers. She said he shouldn't worry, especially if the sex was good, but she added, "Don't marry one. You can't build a life on that."

Jos lay in his middle-aged lover's arms, feeling warm and secure. Wonderful memories of childhood flooded back, and he drifted into a contented sleep. It had been a long day with little rest.

His cell phone jerked him awake. It was Walt.

"There are two more fires going on right now, one near the second one and another way east of the lumber fire."

"Meet me at Second Cup on Church." Jos slipped the phone into his pants pocket.

"That was wonderful." Debbie's voice came softly from the bed as Jos slipped on his shoes. "Any time you want advice, you can call me lover boy." Her tone was seductive, but serious. "We don't need to fuck if you don't want. We can just discuss your assignment."

It reassured Jos she had not said "make love". Whatever had happened between them, it had not been making love. He eased out of the darkened room. Debbie was already slipping off to sleep.

"Good night, boy." Mr. Franklin's condescending voice from the darkened living room startled Jos. He froze. He could make out someone on the leather couch. Jos instinctively checked his distance to the door.

"I hope you had fun," the voice continued, "and you left some for me."

The sarcasm was thick. Jos hurried out. He heard laughter as the door closed.

What kind of perverted relationship do they have? What kind of perv am I?

Jos made his way to the all night coffee shop thinking about Debbie's advice and the questions she raised.

Walt was waiting.

"You made it quick." The camera man was only half done a small coffee and a crueller.

"I was just around the corner." Jos felt embarrassed.

He waved at a couple of gorgeous drag queens sitting by the window, enjoying exposure to the street. Jos knew them well, having spent many slow nights sitting in donut shops contacting the night-time population. He knew many of the street people, prostitutes, and others. The pair smiled back and waved. These cross-dressers were not selling sex but out for a fun time. Jos enjoyed their wit, humour and knowledge of the city. He wondered what would happen to those two if Sherwood Green achieved their goal of destroying industrial civilization and another angle that he should document. His producer might love the sexual titillation of transvestites. These two would be insightful and attractive on screen.

Walt set up, and Jos called to the fire captain in charge of the latest fire. A police officer appeared and shooed the fireman away.

"Reporters can only talk to the police. The firemen are off limits. They're too busy." The constable shoved between Jos and the crew working the smoldering ruins.

The arsonists were as ghostly as the night before.

"We don't know how they ignited this fire. I hear on the radio it's the same in North York. We have a dragnet out. We'll catch them." The cop's optimism was unfounded. There was no trace of the terrorists, although the police had a shootout with a drug gang at a roadblock. A cop suffered serious wounds, and two drug dealers were dead.

Jos and Walt found graffiti and a few posters. Sherwood Green had a new message.

Sherwood Green is not racist. All races of the world, but especially non-white races, are being ground down and destroyed by the capitalist elite through their corporations. These companies are the true racists, turning people against each other. They are destroying the natural world and no one will survive. Wake up, people.

The Japanese people have suffered environmental collapse as much as everyone else, if not more. The prefecture where the headquarters of Fukushima Motors used to be located is now a nuclear wasteland. That one disaster threatens all of our health. Wake up, people!

It is the large corporate interests that are killing the whales and polluting us with radiation and carbon. Even the masses who support them are their victims. We will destroy these industrial corporations. Wake up, people!

"I thought we were off the night beat." Walt yawned as he drove the network SUV up to Jos' apartment building.

"Me too..." Jos returned the yawn. Walt sped off with the rising sun glinting from the garish depiction of the network's most popular and trusted on camera personality.

Maybe, one day, it will be me. Jos hoped.

Jos' reference to the police media restrictions disappeared from his broadcast. His summary of the anti-racist, anti-elite comments of Sherwood Green remained. The producers knew the populist message would play to their audience. The shootings were the bigger story.

Jos Amiel drifted off to sleep, comforted by a lingering image of Debbie.

Chapter 4

Amiel's latest report was another hit on YouTube. It was network policy to only post video to the TNN website. A user nicknamed 'Friar Tuck' reposted their video stream. Jos feared Sheri would blame him.

Jos confronted Sheri, upset she had censored his clever bit on the police control of the media, with the awkward expression of their police handler.

"The police asked us not to broadcast anything about their operations. That's why I cut your comment about the management of the media. No conspiracy. It's reasonable."

Sheri Stein was more concerned with advertisers and access to police than a more complete story. She would not admit to submitting to official censorship.

Jos had to play along. As a citizen, he hoped they would catch the terrorists. Still, he was confused. He forced himself to focus on the major theme, the spectacular appearance of violent, pro-environment, anti-industrial terrorism. Police censorship and manipulation were not important to his employer. Jos convinced himself of the reasonableness of the situation. The terrorists would have to be caught before they hurt someone.

Jos wanted to protect the planet. He had covered environmental initiatives such as kids planting trees and groups cleaning up the Don River, but he did not support terrorism. He remembered his mother's admonition that "the end does not justify the means".

This Sherwood Green thing is new, exciting and good for our careers, but someone is going to get hurt.

Sheri quashed his idea for a documentary, saying it was premature. Stein had her own plans. When the time came for an in-depth documentary, she would work with a more experienced reporter who would not need baby-sitting. She imagined a significant production with a Gemini prize and promotion or a job at a national network.

Jos saw what Debbie Franklin had meant. The media were superficial with more concern for the popular, spectacular and titillating. Jos's career was an important consideration. When he got this job, he had been starry-eyed and naïve, savouring the public recognition, the glamour and the rewards it brought to his social life. The stardust had blown away. Jos recognized the shallowness of his education, scolding himself for not having taken the world more seriously. He was more the actor than the writer.

Jos's conflicted feelings for authority stirred some guilty satisfaction with the terrorist attacks.

Am I actually cheering for Sherwood Green? Jos concluded he only wanted more attacks to advance his career, but did not want his way of life destroyed.

Sheri threw him a bone. Jos became the face for a news segment called *Terrorism Toronto*. She showed him the glitzy introduction with quick cuts of Jos talking to the camera, along with fires, police and emergency vehicles racing down the streets, and the face of Frank Langstaff fading in from the mayhem. The hard-driving, base-filled music evoked urgency. It would be the third item of each newscast.

Jos would provide a report each day to follow the introduction. Other outlets copied it, but TorontoNewsNow led in exploiting the arson. More attacks would make it easier to fill his time slot. The public would soon associate Jos with Sherwood Green.

Jos covered the event sponsored by the Canadian Anti-Whaling Coalition. Good video footage and contacts would be a bonus. Sherwood Green had not attacked during the day. Jos needed something for the next episode.

When they arrived and began setting up, the organizer, Diane Arsenault, demanded they not film inside the meeting. Jos' argument with Diane attracted Bill Meeks, the keynote speaker.

"It will be good publicity," Meeks said, smiling at the camera. "It will help to fundraise."

Jos recognized Meeks' help as self-serving. Not all politicians sat in parliament. Meeks' career depended on publicity. Contributions to his cause meant more trips and perks. He had a good life, travelling all over the world for high appearance fees. Not all of this money found its way into the coffers of the Oceans Defence Fund.

Bill Meeks was middle-aged, pudgy, with longish greying hair coifed into a politician's style. He meticulously trimmed his greying beard. A deep navy-blue, roll-necked sweater hung down over the beltline of a pair of flared khaki trousers that appeared to be sailor's canvas but were expensive, soft-cotton double-knit. Mountain Co-op designer hiking boots completed his look.

Meeks appeared as a seasoned sailor wanting to save sea creatures, a man of the sea fighting for the life of Moby Dick. In fact, even though the organization had several vessels around the world harassing whaling ships, Meeks had seldom been at sea. His had last taken a brief ride out of Halifax harbour, a media event, as they shadowed a Norwegian whaler into the open ocean. He became violently seasick and ended his sailing career. The coalition had hired him for marketing and fundraising. Meeks did the job firmly rooted on dry land.

The audience filled the large room, eager to hear the famous champion of the natural world and echoed Meeks' styling. Men had beards. Many of both sexes wore khaki shirts with Tilley hats tucked into shoulder loops, bush pants and hiking boots. They fit the cliché of rich, middle-class environmentalists.

A handful of ordinary looking people and students made up the audience. A lone male heckler at the back of the room in a white shirt and tie was the president of the *Student Forum for Good Government.* He thought all activism should be illegal. He interrupted Meeks' presentation several times, vehemently attacking special-interest groups, nearly coming to blows with a radical student who said corporations were special-interest groups. The confrontation made for an exciting video, but Jos doubted Sheri would air it. The fight might find a place in their documentary.

Diane Arsenault introduced herself as chairperson of the Toronto chapter of the Canadian Anti-Whaling Coalition. She originally came from Montreal but moved to Toronto to inject leadership into the stagnant chapter. Toronto provided members and money.

Diane had built a dynamic group of dedicated people. She was in her early thirties with dark brunette hair hanging shoulder length, framing a make-up free face highlighted by piercing brown eyes. She wore a coordinated blouse and skirt. Her appearance was of elegant professionalism.

Arsenault was competent and self-assured and worked as a freelance computer software consultant. Her expertness in the world's largest business software system guaranteed constant work. She could have had a comfortable lifestyle.

Her idealism and dedication to saving the planet reduced her to living in a simple apartment.

Meeks launched into his slick presentation filled with humour and anecdotes. He described the plight of the large sea mammals in graphic detail.

"… and that, my friends," the speaker smiled benignly over his audience, "is why we must continue to lobby for international reforms to the anti-whaling rules and support financially the Oceans Defence Fund."

Applause rose from the packed room. Forty-five minutes had passed quickly. Heckling and hostile questions from the radical conservative student mingled with friendly questions. The speaker handled both with experienced smoothness. The audience's hostile response to the heckler allowed Meeks to remain calm. Jos thought the meeting was a bust until Sherwood Green popped up.

"Can you comment on these latest fire attacks in Toronto against Japanese whaling?"

Up to this point, Bill Meeks had relaxed behind the table, responding quietly to the questions, but he leapt to his feet, and his face became animated with anger.

"This Sherwood Green guy," Meeks shouted, "is a threat to us all. He's a racist using the environment as a cover for his Nazi, eco-fascist activities. He'll destroy the work we have done in raising awareness and funds to carry on the fight. It'll hamper my work. People will harass environmentalists. I hope the cops catch him soon."

Jos thought the applause sounded less than enthusiastic. Meek's answer disgusted Diane.

"If I can interject," she said, "Many people in the environmental movement are reaching the conclusion advocacy and nonviolent protest does not work. It won't save doomed life on the planet."

"We're making great strides." Meeks glared at his host. "This threatens all of my work!" He repeated his vilification of Sherwood Green.

Arsenault ignored Meeks and asked several leading questions about the state of the environmental movement, prompting audience members to talk about their own misgivings. Some were confused. Several people supported radical resistance.

She pre-arranged some of this, Jos thought.

Jos' suspicion deepened when Diane Arsenault used the expression "Wake up, people".

Has she read the posters or heard it on television? Jos wondered to himself. *Perhaps she had a hand in it from the beginning. Perhaps she's part of Sherwood Green.*

The idea excited Jos.

People asked who was Sherwood Green and how could they get in touch with him. Diane denied knowing, but she dropped a bombshell.

"While we still support protection for whales and all species, most of us in the Coalition will help Sherwood Green in any legal way we can through a separate organization. If you want to support those aims and believe direct action is now the only option to save the planet, you can join us. We will set up a legal defence fund to help if they catch Sherwood Green."

"I have to warn you the police will go after us. Laws and due process have never protected people if the elite want to suppress them. We will see similar attacks."

Cries of "you're crazy" erupted, intermingled with shouts of "I'm ready". Some shouted abuse at Arsenault. Bill Meeks moved to the far end of the table and glared towards Diane.

The meeting collapsed into uncontrolled debate, ignoring the sullen Meeks who, for once, had nothing to say. Eventually, Diane thanked everyone for coming and directed the audience to the table where Meeks would sign his latest book, *Excitement at Sea: The Continuing Saga of Ocean Defence.*

She pointed out the Sherwood Green Support Network table that held membership forms and information.

The tables attracted equal amounts of attention. Many people wanted to hobnob with Meeks and have their photo taken beside the famous man. Walt shot filler video.

Jos explored the room, looking for people to interview and waiting to chat with Diane Arsenault. Photocopied Sherwood Green pamphlets filled the table. A banner lay on the table with words written in Lincoln green, *Wake Up People–It is time to act!*

Activity at the book table ended quickly, and Bill Meeks packed up unsold books. Jos interviewed him, and Meeks enjoyed the spotlight. Jos' question about the Fukushima fires resulted in a vehement repeat of his earlier attack. Meeks felt satisfied. Jos had allowed him to advertise his next two speaking engagements, one of which would be to the Empire Club business lunch. He glared disgustedly at the crowd around the competing table and muttered, "no one at the Empire Club will support Sherwood Green". Before he left, Meeks confronted Diane.

"You're done with us, you stupid bitch. We had a good thing going. I'll get you." Meeks huffed away.

Diane refused an on-camera interview. Her group did not have a media policy or spokesperson. She accepted Jos' business card with his personal cell-phone number handwritten on the back.

Arsenault's distinct Quebec accent intrigued Jos. It reminded him of his mother, who would never lose her French influenced Haitian accent. Jos mentioned the man who wanted to join Sherwood Green.

"I do not know who Sherwood Green is or how to get in touch. We've had e-mails from Sherwood Green sent to the Coalition address, but always after the fact and from spoofed e-mail addresses. If this guy wants, he can join us. They might recruit him, but they know more about us than we know about them."

"Can I see the e-mails?" Jos asked.

"I'll tell you what; they're attaching documents, parts of a manifesto, to their messages. If the group agrees, I'll get them to you, but I'm not sure they're for the public."

Jos' and Walt's cells rang with the news that a blaze had broken out at a Fukushima dealership east of the original attack. It was not yet midnight, and that surprised Jos.

Diane watched Jos disappear through the doorway. *He's nice and seems sincere. Maybe I can recruit him. A media contact would be useful.* Diane remembered an old friend who had abruptly left the Coalition. She had cared for him, but he said he had more important things to do with his life, and it had been many months. She turned to chat with potential recruits.

With the newest fire and the meeting, Jos easily filled his Terrorism Toronto segment. Sheri highlighted Bill Meeks' anti-terrorist statements; however, she allowed Jos to say that the Toronto chapter supported Sherwood Green. She had not allowed him to air the split in the environmental community, and Meeks' diatribe energized anti-terrorist viewers.

Chapter 5

There was a lull. Several days passed, and *Terrorism Toronto* could not report any new excitement. In desperation, Sheri allowed Jos to rehash the anti-whaling meeting and the debate about destroying industrialism. Jos replayed David Suzuki, the patron saint of Canadian environmentalism, denouncing the reliance on corporate business solutions to climate change. He had said it was "absurd" to think the process that caused the problem could solve it.

The episode stirred public anger with personal attacks on Suzuki. The old man, living out his days in his west coast paradise, could not respond. It improved TNN's ratings.

The Ontario public television network used its premier talk show, *Table of Content,* to stage one of its super-balanced panel discussions. Unable to locate anyone to defend terrorism, the host used the Suzuki video.

The live discussion featured Professor Samuels from the University of Toronto economics department, alongside

Winston Bayer, who had written a book about potential climate wars. David Jones, the leader of the provincial Green Party, sat with them. Jones expected to be elected to provincial parliament in a district brought together in a fight against becoming Toronto's garbage dump and a victim of urban sprawl. The progressive media helped him. Bill Meeks joined via a video link from the deck of a boat in Halifax harbour.

A debate did not materialize as the guests all took anti-resistance positions. Bayer predicted climate conflict, but it would be between states. "The puny efforts of the public have never, and never will, accomplish anything. The failed so called Arab Spring a few years ago proves it. There will be no class war over climate change."

Professor Samuels added, "The world economy is too big to be destroyed on purpose, especially by attacking a minor economy like Canada's."

"What about the persistent financial crisis?" The host asked. "It's an ongoing problem and makes us vulnerable."

"It'll recover soon," Samuels replied. "Everything is cyclical, and the recovery is underway." He lacked conviction. "We have a sound business plan for restoring the economy and the environment by creating jobs with growth through green business. We disagree with Suzuki's view."

David Jones of the Green Party could not bring himself to attack Suzuki, his green hero. "Thousands of jobs are being created by green corporations."

"Does that include filling sandbags?" The host smiled mischievously.

"Disaster response is a last resort," Jones flared. "We denounce violence. It's dangerous and counterproductive. The police need to move swiftly and catch these terrorists."

Everyone nodded.

"I want to add," Meeks chimed in from his boat safely moored in calm water, "that this risks destroying everything we gained over the past forty years."

The host played the devil's advocate. "It seems the climate is in worse shape now than ever, and there really are two hundred species a day going extinct."

"We're on the cusp of a breakthrough," Meeks retorted. "I apologize for the terrorist support group you have in Toronto. They broke away from us. They never fit in and are a bunch of losers."

"What makes you think there will be a breakthrough?" The host prodded. "Paris turned out to be a sham." Meeks and Jones remained silent.

"Is the political arm of the environmental movement in damage control?" The host persisted. "Aren't you just desperate to distance yourselves from extremists? The terrorists claim you have achieved little."

The discussion was open to e-mail responses. Most supported the guests; however, a solid ten percent supported violent resistance. Everyone had avoided naming Sherwood Green until an e-mail arrived that turned the discussion to the Fukushima attacks and Sherwood Green.

"I have an e-mail, supposedly from Sherwood Green," the host interrupted Professor Samuels' lecture on some obscure detail of the economy.

"This is of a scoop on our part." His controlled voice disguised his excitement. He had provoked the enemy into a response.

"We can't verify its authenticity, but we believe it's genuine."

"What does it say?" Bayer did not hide his enthusiasm. Real or not, this sensation would be publicity for his books. Meeks felt the same.

The host put on his reading glasses and paused for a dramatic few seconds, carefully studying the paper. He glanced at the camera and then read.

The police and taxpayers' money are being used to protect the interests and property of the rich. 'To Serve and Protect the Rich' is the real police motto. Wake up, people!

The host wondered if he had put too much dramatic emphasis on the last phrase.

It is not about Fukushima Motors or Japan or only whales. It is about the planet and its survival, and the end of industrial corporate destruction of the planet.

It is about the two hundred species that become extinct each day. Canada should quit NATO and stop supporting the American Empire. It is not about that empire, but the imperial actions of the worldwide corporate banking elite that make nation states obsolete. We will destroy their empire by destroying its financial heart. No longer will their global factories enslave the workers, poison the environment, and impoverish the helpless. No longer will two hundred species a day die merely to make the elite richer while toys divert the rest of us. Destroying industrial civilization is the only way to save the planet. Wake up, people!

Canada is small in the global scheme of things, but we will do our part. There will be more blows for the planet soon. The people of the rest of the world are doing their part. Look to Syracuse, look to Athens, look and act. Wake up, people!

"So, gentlemen, what do you think?" The host stared at the paper, trying to understand how anyone could believe it.

"Who the fu-bleep do these ass-bleep think they are?" Bayer exploded. "They are stupid. If they weaken Western economies, more ruthless people will take over."

"These guys are crazier than Suzuki." Samuels spoke with a condescending chuckle. "They don't understand the benefits of capitalism and the technology it has created." He waved his cell phone at the camera.

"But is Suzuki on the right track? Is Sherwood Green right in concluding there is no other option but to destroy industrial civilisation?"

In the outburst of competing voices, the Green Party candidate raised his voice above the din.

"Mr. Suzuki didn't say that. Only Sherwood Green says it." The man paused. "Our party's platform shows a logical alternative. People need to elect us."

Winston Bayer rolled his eyes. Samuels smirked at Jones. Meeks sputtered in support. The host looked directly into the camera. "How long will that take if two hundred species are becoming extinct each day?" Then turned to the Green politician. "How much life will be left by the time you can accomplish anything?"

"We have a great programme." Jones repeated his mantra.

The discussion collapsed into a debate whether the claim of two hundred species extinctions per day was correct. None of the participants were biologists or experts in any scientific discipline that might answer the question. The trio tried to outwit each other.

Between the witty remarks, the host wondered, "Were Syracuse and Athens historical references? Millennia ago, both cities were places of learning." Everyone said they had visited Greece and Italy. No one answered the question.

The reference to Syracuse and Athens intrigued Jos Amiel as he watched the TVO episode. He logged into the TNN internal Web feed, searching the international news services for references to Athens and Syracuse, Greece. There was nothing.

No reports of terrorism, simply the ongoing street battles in Athens, the backdrop of their economic collapse. He remembered Syracuse was in Sicily, still nothing.

Was the reference just a generalization? Jos thought. *Was it meaningless? It's not Sherwood Green's style to confuse their message.*

Jos was an experienced Internet user and removed the reference to Greece. He found a dozen links about Syracuse, New York State and Athens, Georgia.

He looked at a live Syracuse report. At first, he thought there was a glitch. Everything was black. Suddenly, a reporter appeared on the screen, his face lit in ghoulish fashion by a handheld flashlight shining from below.

"There's not much light in Syracuse right now, folks. A massive explosion has knocked the electricity out. There wasn't much fire, but the authorities tell Big Ten News someone destroyed the high-voltage feeds. It'll take all night to repair the damage."

On-camera floodlights suddenly lit the man who blinked in the sudden glare.

"Ah, that's better Frank. I looked like an Addams Family uncle." He laughed at his own joke.

"There is no official word, but workers found this pamphlet near the blast. It's from an outfit called," he giggled, "Green Side Up." The cameraman laughed as the reporter brandished the paper.

"I know it sounds silly, but this damage is no joke. It might be an international conspiracy. ISIS might be involved. In the message, they claim they are acting in solidarity with someone called Sherwood Green in Toronto, Canada. Apparently, there is eco-terrorism up there."

The American media mostly ignored international events unless there was a connection to the USA. An American citizen being killed or hurt was usually required for any attention to international news. They had ignored the events in Toronto.

Jos switched to an Athens feed. The events there were much less widespread but more spectacular and reactions more emotional. Someone had set fire to the University of Georgia football venue, Sanford Stadium.

CNN, Atlanta, coverage showed the old part of the stadium in a spectacular blaze, with flames shooting high into the air.

Someone had torched the grandstand. Dating from 1929, this part of the structure contained old, dry wood. The sprinkler system had malfunctioned. CNN emphasized the arsonist had knowledge of the stadium and its weaknesses and discussed the potential role of ISIS.

The blazing structure lit on-camera interviews of weeping cheerleaders, cursing football players and an angry school president. No one mentioned pamphlets or Sherwood Green, but from the e-mail sent to TVO, Jos assumed a connection.

Sherwood Green knew of these attacks before they happened. He planned to cover this angle in the next Terrorism Toronto episode.

Jos' piece on the Syracuse events excited Sheri and TNN paid for a direct live link to the original reporter, allowing Jos to ask about the Sherwood Green connection.

Canadian media were always eager to highlight any references to Canada in foreign reports. This was especially true of news from the USA. Although cynics constantly referred to the Canadian inferiority complex, students of history pointed out, through the rise and fall of many empires, ambitious people in the colonies craved recognition from the imperial centre. Sheri bragged these events had "put them on the map".

The international connections of the eco-terrorists concerned Jos more, and he set up regular exchanges with his counterpart in Syracuse. The man did not know of the connection to the University of Georgia.

The US media had not known of Sherwood Green, but the FBI was aware. Their cooperation with the RCMP ensured that some information had flowed over the border. Sherwood Green had a high-alert status within the American federal police who always looked for international threats. Many FBI agents believed most terrorists entered the USA from Canada, as did the American public at large. To the American police, Sherwood Green reinforced that mistake.

Undercover agents searched for any reference to this Canadian threat. Robotic spy programmes had analyzed billions of internet searches and social media posts for Sherwood Green references. They compiled a long list of people who had used either or both words from the vast database at Clarksburg, West Virginia. An army of analysts connected names to the Syracuse attack.

There were dozens of people to investigate in Syracuse. The agency detained an English major at Syracuse University. The unfortunate woman wrote a thesis on English folk tales and had the misfortune of searching for 'Sherwood Forest' and 'Lincoln green' in her analysis of Robin Hood. Her arrest received wild media coverage, with a "perp" walk staged for the reporters. In the end, they quietly released the poor woman with no fanfare and a tarnished reputation.

Many followed in her footsteps during the chaotic days after the attack, but the FBI charged no one. The FBI distrusted intellectuals and believed the terrorists were university students.

Jos' contact passed on information from the FBI that there were recriminations within the agency. The Syracuse attack had surprised them, and the FBI brass purged the local field office "to cover their own asses." Jos' contact said.

In Athens, Georgia, no one had found terrorist pamphlets; however, despite the local authorities blaming a deranged arsonist, the FBI terrorism branch took control of the investigation.

The population of Georgia worried mostly about the fire hurting the University of Georgia Bulldogs football season. CNN spent hours discussing the options for the location of home games. The inferno had destroyed all the team's equipment and much memorabilia, but appeals for financial help raised millions. A teary-eyed reporter summed it up. "They might have gone to a bowl game."

With no recent attacks in Toronto, Frank Langstaff called a news conference to claim the police had contained the terrorists.

Jos' cell phone rang.

"Are you going to Langstaff's news conference?"

"Yes, I sure am. Who are you?" Jos and Walt were about to leave for police headquarters.

"Never mind that; let's just say we have a mutual acquaintance." Jos did not recognize the voice. "There's something you should know before you go."

"What's that?" Jos did not like anonymous callers, but during his career had received many good tips in this way.

"They left lots of pamphlets at that last fire, but the force made sure you guys found none."

"Can you get me one?"

"Can't take that chance, buddy. There's more." The caller paused. "There is a pattern to the fires."

"Yah, I know." Jos was sarcastic. "They're all Fukushima dealerships."

"Not that!" The caller snapped. Jos regretted his sarcasm.

"The locations form two lines that intersect just about at Fukushima Canadian Headquarters."

"Is Langstaff going to announce that?"

"No, he's keeping a lid on it so he can stake out the place. He has already sent a team from the ETF there. Frank figures this will make him chief. Langstaff is a power-hungry jerk who knows the game. He would be a disaster for the force." The caller hung up.

Jos wondered how to get Langstaff to reveal the police theory. The cop ignored his question, asking if there had been a pattern to the attacks. He then asked if they had involved the Emergency Task Force. Langstaff glared at Jos and made a stumbling denial.

Langstaff's discomfort convinced Jos the caller was right, but Sheri would not allow him to use anonymous information on air. If he could get corroborating evidence, it would be sensational. Another scoop.

Walt suggested the solution. In a clever video sequence, Jos took a large map of the metropolitan area and performed an on-camera analysis, concluding the Fukushima headquarters were under threat. It excited Sheri who then suggested the military phrase, "Fukushima headquarters are in the crosshairs."

Jos contacted Diane Arsenault and got copies of the Sherwood Green pamphlet the police had suppressed at the last fire. He read parts of it on air to support the theory of the pattern of attacks. *All vehicles are a threat to the environment and we must destroy them along with corporations that build them.*

The item caused a sensation and forced Frank Langstaff to make a public show of strength by stationing uniformed officers at the building. He revealed the ETF had been in place for days, ignoring his on-air lying. He now hated Jos.

After a few days of sensation and anticipation, nothing happened. The police waited impatiently and the mob of reporters and camera crews surrounding the Fukushima Headquarters trickled away. The calm frustrated Sheri and she told Jos, if there was no new action soon, he would be back on the night beat. She said, "These guys are one-shot wonders. They fear the police."

Fortunately for the young reporter, an attack on a Fukushima dealership occurred in London, Ontario.

Sherwood Green's Goldstein Brigade took credit. It was enough to entertain the public and satisfy Sheri.

Jos received a surprise call from Debbie Franklin. She had not returned Jos' calls since the first torrid encounter.

"Hey big boy, have you figured out the riddle in the London attack? I watched your bit about it and hoped you would understand." She was teasing and seductive.

"Do you know Goldstein?" Debbie became his teacher.

"Who's Goldstein?" Jos suppressed his lust and tried to focus on the question.

"You don't know, do you?" The playful tone returned. Jos tried to recall if Goldstein had been on the news.

"Who is he?"

"Why don't you search the Net for it?"

"I did, but didn't see any news for that name."

"You won't find it in the news. Here is a hint, 1984."

"What does that mean?"

"You read little, don't you?"

Debbie hung up without saying goodbye. Frustrated, Jos searched for Goldstein and 1984 on the Internet. He was astounded. Goldstein was the invented enemy of the repressive state of Oceania in George Orwell's novel, 1984. The message was obvious; Sherwood Green had declared itself an enemy of the state and knew they would be the target of hatred by the propagandized masses.

Chapter 6

"So, now you know about Goldstein." Debbie Franklin smiled across the little polished wooden table of the coffee shop. That Debbie still felt the project worthy of her attention cheered Jos. He knew his motives were not all professional and tried to ignore his sexual desire. Debbie wore a plaid skirt and an expensive, clinging pink angora sweater that highlighted her breasts. She looked like a first-year student on the prowl.

Still looking good in pink, Jos thought.

It reminded Jos of the television comedy series "Happy Days." He glanced around the Bucks, thinking about the 1950s hangout depicted in the old TV show. Like the fictional eatery, this one served mainly students; however, the similarity ended there. This pricey place catered to the high-income student population. Many students frittered away their loan and scholarship money at the campus pub. In this place, expensively dressed young people stared at laptop computers or phones, tweeting or chatting online or perhaps doing actual school work.

This crowd could afford the five-dollar lattes, taking advantage of the free Wi-Fi, the comfortable couches and polished rosewood tables. Racially, they reflected the diversity of the city and the large number of international students who contributed to the university's cash-flow. No one looked out of place except perhaps Jos in his more affordable workday casuals.

"You got me reading the novel." Jos tried to focus. "What message is the Goldstein Brigade sending?"

"They are teasing us." Debbie reached out and touched his hand, aware of the effect of her own teasing. "I think they're idealistic students, power tripping and trying to show they're smart."

"They seem competent." Jos sipped his latte and wiped the foam from his upper lip with a monogrammed paper napkin, hoping his skin colour hid his blushing cheeks. "Their methods have the police baffled."

"They'll trip up and the cops will get them, but their weak point, where you can get to understand them, is through their public supporters. Sherwood will get caught, but you'll get good stories and make a name for yourself."

Jos sighed, "I guess the industry is all about that and not the actual story. I'm as ambitious as anyone, but can't I succeed by being an excellent reporter?"

"I am not saying to sell out." Debbie looked annoyed. "But it's good for your career. If you can't tell the complete story, do a documentary later."

"Sheri downplays that idea. I already presented an outline. She called it premature."

"Is that Sheri Stein?" Jos' boss had been another of the professor's brighter students. "I think you should be careful of her. Sheri's ambitious and not above stealing good ideas like your documentary. How do you think she got where she is?"

Debbie had the experience to recognize another schemer. Jos did not think Sheri used sex like Debbi had, but Debbie saw the woman's activities more cynically. "Stein plays the game with no care beyond her self-interest."

"I know the system sucks," Jos said. "Everyone is out for themselves, the cops, the media, the banks, schools…" He looked at Debbie. "Even environmental leaders just want to play the system for good jobs." Jos sipped his coffee. "I want to get ahead, but I want to do good work."

Since Sherwood Green unleashed these attacks, it forced Jos to think a deeper than doing his job, collecting his pay, and having fun.

"I don't want to destroy the system, maybe help improve it, but do something. I don't understand Sherwood Green wanting to destroy it all. It will hurt them too?"

"You're caught in the middle, Jos." Debbie winked.

Diane Arsenault appeared beside their table. She had entered through a side door from the darkened street. Diane held a thick wad of leaflets.

"Hi Jos, I saw you through the window and thought you might like one of these." She placed a pamphlet in front of the reporter and slipped another to Debbie.

"I've left the Coalition." Diane sat down at the table without waiting for an invitation. Debbie assessed this newcomer. "They forced us out. Resistance is bad for business." She chuckled. "We've solidified our group and are ready to support Sherwood Green. He'll need legal help soon, I think."

"That's what I think." Debbie interjected, drawing Jos' attention from Diane. "The cops will get him."

Diane examined Debbie. She assumed that this middle-aged female was one of Jos' workmates or his boss. Arsenault did not like Debbie's siding with the police. Jos made the introductions.

Careful, Diane and Debbie thought at once. *I have to be careful of her.*

"I thought you would like this new pamphlet. We received it by e-mail today. The city removes their posters. It's harder to get the word out. You mention Sherwood by name on air and that helps. Anyway, our work makes it safer for the underground… but not for us." She laughed in a friendly way as she stood to go. "We get a little abuse."

Jos noticed Diane had a red mark on her cheek, the result of an altercation handing out leaflets at the subway.

"We're fundraising."

Jos handed Diane a twenty-dollar bill. Debbie made no move to follow suit.

Diane went from table to table, dropping a leaflet at each and saying a few words. The response was mostly hostile, but one young Chinese man gave her a fifty-dollar bill. She slipped quietly out the way she had come.

"Is she your girlfriend?" Debbie did not sound jealous. "You were quick handing over the cash." Debbie seldom parted with anything without receiving back.

"No." Jos' reply was more forceful than he intended. "I want to strengthen my relationship with Diane's group. The donation was part of the effort."

"Interesting..." Franklin looked thoughtful. "I wish I could join her, but I can't risk it."

Debbie reached into her leather hand-purse. "I have a student who might be interested. Here's his name and cell number." She handed Jos a sticky-note with a name and phone number written in red ink.

I wonder if the guy is one of Debbie's lovers.

Her hand disappeared into the purse once more and extracted a plastic hotel room-key. Debbie slid it to Jos.

"It is a quiet night. I can think of a way to make it livelier." She smiled, "room 2016 at the Hyatt."

Debbie left with a seductive smile and without waiting for an answer. Her young stud would accept. She was good in bed.

The police car eased up to the temporary traffic barrier, blocking two centre lanes on Bay Street. A trestle with luminescent orange cross-hatching and flashing amber lights protected the rear of a large white service vehicle parked at an open access cover between the streetcar tracks. Amber strobe-lights reflected from storefront plate glass. The track blockage was unimportant. The line ran up Bay Street between King and Queen as a detour. At two in the morning, there was little traffic in the financial district.

A constable approached a young flag-man. The unnatural amber flashes distorted the men's faces. The worker had a full red beard and shoulder-length hair. He wore heavy white coveralls with green reflector stripes. These shone in the headlights, turning him into a cartoon stick-man. The open top buttons of the coveralls revealed a dark blue T-shirt with the logo of the University of Toronto. Tinted glasses made his eyes yellow.

The young man appeared bored as the officer approached. His calm hid nervousness. They carefully prepared Jake for his role and had meticulously planned every detail of his appearance. Jake had lived in a safe house, growing his beard as a disguise and rehearsing his role as a Toronto Hydro contract worker.

An ex-Hydro employee forced to resign for publicly complaining about safety violations by corrupt subcontractors had coached him. He taught Jake most of the administrative people's names and titles, as well as on-the-ground supervisors and workers, anyone who might be familiar to the police or public. Jake's backup line, if asked about anyone he didn't know, was, "I am the new boy. That's why I get flag duty."

The logos identified them as a subcontractor to Toronto Hydro. They contracted maintenance out after massive layoffs of full-time Commission employees. It was common to see unfamiliar vehicles bearing the names of many companies. Nothing about the crew that blocked the two centre lanes of Bay Street seemed unusual.

"We're always notified." The cop was officious.

"Let me check." Jake went to the truck and retrieved a written work order. He flipped through several pages until he came to the list of authorizations.

"It says here we notified 55 Division." Jake showed the page to the officer.

"That explains it." The constable laughed. "We're 52 Division. No one forwarded it to us."

"Typical office fuck-up," Jake laughed. He took out cigarettes and offered one to the constable. He declined and spit some over-chewed gum towards the gutter.

As the officer returned to his car, he glanced over his shoulder and said, "We'll be around. See you later."

"Okay," Jake replied, "but we are cleaning a couple of substations tonight and will be down on Wellington later."

The car sped off. Jake heard the radio requesting backup. There had been another shooting in the entertainment district. Jake threw away his cigarette and focused on the dark hole in the street.

Twenty minutes later, three figures, dressed like Jake, emerged from the opening. Two had matching beards and long hair. The exception was a tough-looking woman with a rather outrageous tattoo on her left cheek. This decoration was a temporary paste-on and would disappear by morning. By noon, three clean-shaven, well-groomed young men and a rather pretty woman would be on the streets.

At four in the morning, the access cover on Bay Street flew high into the air and clanged into the gutter. Bright blue flame shot through the opening. In seconds, acrid black smoke poured out, filling the canyon. The explosion echoed up and down the street.

At the College Street control centre, panel lights changed from red to green and then white as breakers opened to isolate the new fault. A raucous klaxon demanded attention.

Pagers and cell phones around the city roused key personnel from sleep. Sirens echoed as several fire stations scrambled trucks.

The crews had been on the scene for only a few minutes. The fire captain discussed a plan of attack, watching the billowing smoke and waiting for the electrical experts to make sure the power was off. Two blocks away, a similar explosion added to the confusion.

In the second blast, the heavy cover flew sideways onto the sidewalk, instantly killing Amalia Garza, a night cleaner returning from work in one of the bank towers.

Police, fire crews and Toronto Hydro-Electric staff swarmed into the downtown and everyone expected a third blast. It would be a long morning for everyone.

Every bank headquarters and all other office buildings within a 10-block square went dark, including the stock exchange. At the exchange, backup generators kicked in. The trading day was only hours away; investors needed futures data and overnight trading deals had to be recorded.

In the complex world of international finance, the Toronto exchange was a contracted 24/7 operation service provider for several smaller exchanges spread around the planet and a vital hub for energy trading. The diesel generators ran for a few moments at full power before their output declined. In an hour, their ability to generate electricity approached zero. The last fuel delivery had added gasoline to the diesel oil.

The sabotage of the generators became secondary because one fire had burnt through fibre optic cables connecting the financial district to the outside world. The few surviving satellite links could not handle the required data volume, and it isolated traders and customers in remote parts of the world from the global system.

The explosions did not seem to be related to terrorism. Jos did not feel guilty being with Debbie while these dramatic events were happening. He sat in his living-room watching the noon news with detached interest. The Toronto Hydro CEO held a news conference and blamed the incident on a technical-sounding "cascading equipment failure." It would be at least a week before they could complete repairs, and the blast had damaged one substation so severely they would rebuild it completely.

Jos picked up his cell phone and realized he had turned it off. This was a sin for a reporter. On the text screen was a curt "turn on your damned phone" from an unknown caller.

Before he could set it down, the phone shrilled

"Sleep in, buddy?" The anonymous voice was familiar.

"Yah, I guess so." Jos' yawned.

"You'll be hearing a bunch of bullshit about last night. Don't believe any of the crap they are saying. Sherwood Green blew the hydro and Frank is hot on the case. He's fucking ecstatic and believes he'll arrest someone soon. A scout car from 52 checked out a contractor working on the first site about two in the morning, just a couple of hours before the blasts. They got an excellent description of a suspect, a young guy, red beard; probably a university student from his clothes. They've distributed composites throughout the force and to the Provincial Police and Mounties. Langstaff thinks it is only a matter of time."

"How do you know all this?" Jos wanted confirmation.

"I said before, no questions. They are placing agents in environmental and student groups. Talk again."

The line went dead. Jos called Sheri, outlining the information. She repeated her position: "No unnamed sources. We don't want lawsuits. Find another way."

By the following day, confirmation had come in two forms. First, an e-mail arrived at the Toronto mayor's office, the head of the Hydro-Electric Commission and the media. It claimed Sherwood Green had blown up the electrical vaults. Police efforts to trace the message ended in the City Hall Library, where they had video of a suspect. While the authorities denied a terrorist attack caused the explosions, they treated the message seriously. Dodge claimed the messenger was a sensation seeker. Jos thought otherwise.

Better support for the terrorist connection came via a contact Diane Arsenault provided. Jos did not know the tip had come from Sherwood Green.

A retired system construction engineer for the electric commission would talk on camera because putting the blame on a poorly maintained system sullied his legacy.

"I replaced the old equipment with a modern installation that could handle many times the load on Tuesday morning." The man fidgeted in the glare of Walt's camera lights. Jos soothed him.

"How many years did you work for the THC?"

"Thirty-five years and worked up from a substation maintenance manager to the head of design and construction. The system is old in many places, but downtown was not one of them. We completed upgrades two years ago. It was strong and protected by the latest tech. She wouldn't fail on her own, especially in two places at once."

"The design put capacity way above the load demand and there are, or were," he corrected himself, "modern breakers and flash detectors and so forth that should have shut it all down if there was a load fault. Since none of those devices worked, it can only mean someone disabled them and the first blast was not electrical." The man leaned back in his chair, confident he had made his point.

"So what could have caused it?" Jos wanted a simple answer. He received it.

"Terrorists claim they bombed it and I think they did."

He stood by his conclusion, conveying honesty and authority directly into the camera and satisfying Jos. This would make a great last statement on air. He did a summary of the man's engineering credentials and finished with Sherwood Green's e-mail.

The audience was enthusiastic, but Jos had upset the network owners.

"How can we be credible journalists if we don't report the truth?" Jos glared at Sheri Stein with defiance that had not shown before. He had basked in the glow of personal satisfaction when Sheri summoned him to her office.

"The truth is relative." Sheri Stein leaned forward and rested her right hand on top of her cluttered desk. "These people are crazy and we should not give them credibility. We're not the propaganda arm of Sherwood Green."

"We can report the facts and information without it being propaganda." Jos fought to remain respectful. "The news should be separate from our opinion. I agree, these people are dangerous and the cops should get them, but I'm a reporter, not an advocate for anyone, including our owners."

"They pay our wages." Sheri thought that summed it up. "This terrorism thing is good for business, but we have to walk a fine line." She paused for a moment, then said, "Here are my orders."

Sheri handed Jos a printout of an e-mail from the owner of the network, or at least the man who represented the group of private capitalists that ran a far-flung media conglomerate. The key sentence in the e-mail was simple: "Say nothing to support terrorism."

"That seems more like a comment than an order." Jos handed the paper back to his boss.

"Coming from him," said Sheri, carefully tucking the paper into a folder. "It's an order."

She was happy the boss knew her name, but in this situation that was a danger if he wanted to fire someone.

"I'll err on the side of caution. Take it to mean we repeat nothing that will spread their twisted message." She paused again and then added, "I like you, Jos. You're an excellent reporter and work hard. I have seen no bias in your coverage, but this guy does. He owns a lot of papers, television, and radio. I enjoy working in this industry, and it would be hard to find a job if they fired me. Make it exciting without spreading propaganda."

"We will not mention Sherwood Green by name on air unless it's the police speaking. Refer to them as 'the terrorists'. We won't read any of their propaganda on air." The interview ended. Her orders were explicit.

Chapter Seven

Late morning sunshine of a warm June day streamed through leafy trees onto greening turf. The glorious morning contrasted with the sadness of a small group gathered at an obscure cemetery. Amalia Garza, innocent bystander and unintended first casualty of the environmental resistance, was being buried in a pauper's grave. No one had claimed her body.

"I take it Sherwood Green couldn't be here." Jos said.

Diane Arsenault scowled at Jos' flip remark. Once again, he regretted his smart mouth. "I'm sorry. I really felt for Ms Garza." He did not want to anger Diane.

"We all do," Diane replied. "No one wants casualties, especially innocent ones. Joe and I are not here to apologize, but this woman deserves some respect. She had few friends and no family here." Joe seemed about to cry.

"Are those her friends over there?" Jos pointed to several people standing near the freshly dug grave.

"They're from a Mexican café Amalia went to. They paid for the flowers on the casket."

A plain wooden box sat on stays over the open pit. They had scattered fresh roses on top of the bare wood. A small Mexican flag stood beside the flowers.

"I don't know the men with the priest." Arsenault nodded. Beyond the grave, two men in expensive suits chatted with the priest. One represented the Canadian department of citizenship and immigration and appeared bored. His would confirm that Ms. Garza was dead and buried. Her file could be closed.

The second man, from the Mexican consulate, watched everyone. He had the official title of "Secretary for Trade and Development." His worked for the Dirección Federal de Seguridad, or DFS, the Federal Security Directorate, the Mexican secret police.

Beyond a few trees, a man took pictures. Walt noticed the photographer, but when Walt turned his camera towards him, the man hid his face.

The priest from a local church that served the Latin America community in Toronto's west end presented brief service. He intoned the standard Roman liturgy for burial in English, repeated in Spanish, and that satisfied Amalia's half dozen friends from La Tortilleria restaurant. Two workers, who had waited respectfully beside their backhoe, stepped forward and gently lowered the box into the ground.

There were no tears from her friends, only profound sadness. The government men quietly left.

Diane paused with Jos and Walt. "We will organize our group today. I'll send you a press release."

"Our network won't cover it." Jos was truly sorry. "I would like to get it, of course, and everything else you issue. I hope to do a documentary sometime."

"If Sherwood Green is successful, there won't be a 'sometime'." Diane smiled. She and Joe left.

Jos and Walt headed off with the little crowd to their favourite eatery for an informal wake and to hear the story of Amalia Garza.

Mayor Dodge sat back in the plush chair and surveyed the people around the teak conference table. With lunch done, it was time for serious business.

The mayor was a tall, thin man with sharp, hawkish features. His long nose protruded at an odd angle, the unfortunate result of a schoolboy encounter with a soccer ball. His lanky frame made him appear underweight and posed a challenge for his tailors and image spinners. Clothes never fit properly; however, his dishevelled look and unique face endeared him to voters. His imperfections gave him the common touch.

Dodge's lack of good looks had taught him early in life he had to work hard to make friends. This skill made him a success in politics, where hearts and emotion, likes and dislikes of personalities and image were overriding factors sweeping logic and wisdom aside. Dodge possessed intelligence and knowledge. Once the fickle public tired of him, he would have no problem resuming his role as a corporate manager in a media conglomerate.

Everyone at the table shared ambition and self-interest. There would be no misunderstanding of motives. Dodge had yet to decide on the strangers, but his Chief of Police Heron and Heron's deputy, Frank Langstaff, both had intelligence to match their ambition. Chief Heron was about to retire and had become annoyingly honest.

Deputy Commissioner Hardy of the Provincial Police reflected the Premier's penchant for appointing non-career people to head his police force. The man was astute, ambitious, and cared for the welfare of his officers. He had gained respect from an organization that resented outsiders. If the current government won the next provincial election, the Premier would name him as Commissioner.

The Security Intelligence Service's man was arrogant and a mystery. The American, the FBI terrorist expert, might be a problem.

She was a looker, as his son would say, and her presence had enlivened the lunch table. Frank Langstaff had flirted. Agent De Cruze had a long record of undercover work and a list of terrorists and potential terrorists on her arrest record. De Cruze was also brave, having been the point agent in a raid that had led to the arrest of two native terrorists holed up with hostages in a house somewhere in North Dakota. She would be part of the team and not a flunky. Dodge recognized professionalism in De Cruze. He knew Americans usually took more than they gave, but she would help track down Sherwood Green.

The FBI desperately needed information about the terrorists. The mayor's staff mentioned the embarrassment the FBI had suffered in allowing two surprise attacks in one night, and the Bureau did not want to make more mistakes.

"Gentlemen, and lady," Dodge smiled at the woman, "I am thankful you are here. We have a serious situation spanning international borders," he nodded at De Cruze, "with major economic impact and one death." Dodge avoided using the name Sherwood Green.

"I thought these hydro blasts were equipment failure." The CSIS representative asked Chief Heron.

"That's for public consumption. If we acknowledged the terrorists had attack, it would give Sherwood Green too much credibility." Chief Heron shot a questioning glance towards the mayor. "I think we should make it public and use this girl's death to stir up anger."

Langstaff risked disagreeing with his boss. "The public doesn't care beyond enjoying the fires on television."

"Who cares what the public thinks?" Mayor Dodge felt safe enough to disparage the voters. No one took minutes. "My backers want us to get these guys. They don't want publicity, and the Bay Street power cuts hurt them. If the incident is terrorist-related, insurance won't pay. Toronto Hydro needs that insurance money and the banks as well. Fukushima has had to use its own money to repair the damage and the lumber company declared bankruptcy. Their insurance had a terrorist clause. We must call the hydro attack an accident."

"That's a mistake. We should exploit this Fernandez woman's death." Frank Langstaff risked arguing with the mayor.

"Garza," Chief Heron interjected, "her name was Amalia Garza. They buried her this morning. We aren't even sure she wasn't a terrorist. Mexican security had an agent at the funeral." Heron produced a large photograph of two men in suits talking with the priest.

"I talked to the Mexicans. The Garza name has some radical connection back there, but they had no file on her."

"We have a jacket on Garza." De Cruze reached for a file folder. The FBI had done its homework.

"A network that supports illegals guided Garza from Texas to the Canadian border." The agent sifted through the thick file. "We know about each step, but until now paid little attention to Garza. We had more interest in the organisations, but now think that the network has connections to this terrorist group, and Garza has some significance we don't understand."

"How will you find out?" Mayor Dodge was eager for a breakthrough. His question raised a horrified look.

"Don't ask about our methods," De Cruze said.

"What's our plan?" Dodge turned towards Heron, trying to cover his indiscretion.

Frank Langstaff spoke up. "We have several initiatives. A constable saw one terrorist who carried out the hydro blasts. He gave us an excellent description."

"How could the cop not have guessed something was going on? He should have arrested them then. What idiots do you have on the force?"

"We have the best," Langstaff fought the urge to shout at the mayor. It would not be good for his career.

"Constable Kowalski was in a flying squad at the summit last year and arrested dozens of troublemakers."

"They all got off. Some police work."

"They were off the streets for two days and caused no more trouble. That was our intention." Chief Heron knew the actions were illegal. The courts had convicted one cop, but he had never paid a fine or served any time.

"Kowalski's the only one who has seen a terrorist. He's now on my squad."

"We expect an attack on Fukushima headquarters. We think they have big egos and will show off, and we will make arrests soon."

"The operation is expensive." The mayor worried about the budget, given declining tax revenue and equally broke governments in Queen's Park and Ottawa.

Chief Heron upset Dodge again. "Charlie, we'll have to submit a supplementary request."

"We have close tabs on this Sherwood Green Support Network." Frank changed the subject. "We hope to get them on conspiracy charges. Maybe they are the terrorists."

"How close?" Once again, the mayor violated the rule against asking detailed operational questions.

"VERY close." Frank smiled knowingly. He hoped to sit down in private later with Deputy Commissioner Hardy, the CSIS man and the FBI, to coordinate the spying efforts.

The mayor stood and turned to the police chief. "Bill, keep me informed. I have another engagement. Thank you all for coming. Do what's necessary to end this siege."

No one thought the mayor exaggerated. Sherwood Green had attacked his city. Dodge left the professionals to plan a defence. In fact, defence was all that was possible. Except for the new support network, they had no target to pursue.

"We have agents in all liberal groups." De Cruze gave the impression of preparedness. "We sifted through their reports. Central Intelligence is working on the Mexican end. We always fear that Mexican cops are on the take. They have the Zapatista problem and think Garza's death was not coincidental. She links Sherwood Green to the Chiapas rebellion. The Mexicans have a source in the café that Garza frequented. We are now screening their old reports to see if we missed anything."

"The Zapatistas are a political movement, not an environmental guerrilla squad." The CSIS representative spoke up. "We're convinced it's Indians behind this,"

He passed several papers around with a list of names and a poster from a native band that declared war against whites who had stolen their land. Rumours of native armed resistance to the west coast pipelines had stirred federal action. They had informants inside those groups.

"We track everyone on that list, and we have details to share with the FBI, through proper channels, of course." He meant the National Security Council. He made it plain he did not deal directly with ordinary police forces. As head of the Ontario operations of CSIS, he considered this meeting a courtesy call to people at lower levels. The minister responsible for CSIS felt pressure from the White House and had ordered him to attend.

Everyone had inter-jurisdictional biases and resented sharing control with other forces. Frank Langstaff, who had struggled with the terrorist reality for some weeks, felt only he understood that lack of cooperation would hurt the work. He had successfully coordinated with surrounding regional forces, but he wanted to break the case and get the glory.

The last exchange dashed any hope of easy cooperation. It was hard to get anything out of the unrepresented Mounties, let alone work through the entitlement of the Canadian intelligence agency. Frank's network of undercover officers had grown, limited by his budget. The other agencies would not share information unless he could return the favour.

"So far, we've only been concerned with Toronto." D. C. Hardy opened a folder. "The cross-border and London attacks show this thing spreading. If Toronto had not pulled out of the Provincial anti-Terrorism Section, things would be easier. Our people could not take part in Toronto."

"That was before my time." Heron responded.

"We think it's an American organization," De Cruze said, "but we're puzzled that they attacked Toronto first instead of better targets in the States."

"Maybe it's the other way around." The CSIS man resented the American insult. "Perhaps Syracuse and Athens were copycat events, and the London thing, too."

"More likely they just tested things out here in your fair city. It would be easier for them here." De Cruze said. She did not hide her sarcasm.

"This is a terrorist threat you have finally imported from Canada." The CSIS man played his trump card.

Langstaff sighed. The conversation had deteriorated.

"We need coordination, not acrimony." D. C. Hardy agreed with Frank. "I think this thing is going to spread fast. We need to be prepared no matter where the terrorists are from. Can we agree to share all the information we have?" Hardy glanced at the De Cruze and Langstaff. "Anything that you uncover in the USA involving Canada would be helpful, and we will send you all we get. You have greater resources. We would like to know about any suspects. Agent De Cruze, what are your thoughts?"

"The native connection's interesting," De Cruze said. "But it doesn't fit the native M.O. They usually focus on defending ground, a reserve or sacred site. I'm not convinced there's even a philosophical connection between the perpetrators in the USA and those here. We have no evidence of an operational connection."

"Except," Frank Langstaff interjected, "the sender of the e-mail TVO received had advance knowledge of Syracuse and Athens."

"Yes, that is a hint of coordination." Agent De Cruze retrieved her copy of the message. "

"The e-mail came from a City Hall Library computer." Frank Langstaff reminded the woman. "They used a stolen library card. From the video, we think it was a woman disguised as a male, who changed in the washroom before leaving. We counted males and females entering and leaving and they didn't match. We know what the male disguise looked like, but do not know which woman it might have been. Two or three almost identical women came and went. None used a card."

"Damn," De Cruze exclaimed, "can't you get photo ID on your library cards up here?"

"What for," the CSIS man laughed, "to stop cross-border reading?"

"So far, we have one female suspect we can charge for using a library card that isn't hers to send a legal message. That will grab the headlines." Frank laughed.

"Gentlemen," Patricia De Cruze said. "There's a higher-level data source I cannot talk much about. I'm hoping it will trace any messages. We're scanning for keywords." De Cruze consulted her smart phone. "So far, there's no result. They may have used landlines, the black web or something as primitive as regular mail."

She consulted another paper. "We are running a data search for border crossings for anyone from Toronto who mentioned going to Syracuse, or vice versa. The demographics should narrow that down."

"There were two student-exchange events between Syracuse University and the University of Georgia. One was a basketball exhibition game. A lot of busloads of people went from New York to Georgia. The other is more interesting. Delegates from Athens attended a, Students for Peace conference in Syracuse. We have the list of attendees. So far, there has been no loose talk. We have alerted agents in all schools and hope to catch another attempt before it happens.”

“We want to keep this hush-hush. The see conspiracies everywhere and want us to arrest Arabs and foreigners. There’s the possibility ISIS is involved, but they usually try to kill and create terror. They have never attacked without intending mass murder. Speculation would stir up the politicians and things would become complicated. We like quiet behind-the-scenes action we control.”

“Conspiracy theories have always worked to distract the public from the actual game,” the CSIS man observed. “There’s one blaming Fukushima Corporation for staging the attacks to increase sales.”

“Yes, it has always kept the whackos busy in the States.” The FBI agent had firsthand knowledge. Ongoing psi-ops efforts fuel many dead-end conspiracy theories on the Internet. “My boss calls Internet conspiracies, rock-turners, exposing all the weird political bugs that crawl out, and it’s easier to watch them.”

“We have too many suspects,” Frank sighed at the daunting task. “We’re sure one is Sherwood Green and hope our undercover guys nab him. That will probably be how it breaks open.”

“We analyzed Sherwood Green’s statements,” De Cruze said. “They think Canada is simply a consumer country and a resource exporter and not an industrial superpower. We predict they will continue to attack the financial services sector in Toronto, but they will also hit transportation and energy infrastructure to disrupt things.”

“That won’t get them any fans,” Chief Heron commented.

“They don’t care.” The CSIS rep spoke quickly. “If you read their stuff, and this green resistance manifesto garbage, they don’t care if the majority hate them. They see this as a non-political act of saving the planet and not a popular movement. It makes them more dangerous. The attacks on the car dealers sent a message to environmentalists that asking for change won't work. Electric cars won't save the planet, having no cars will."

"Yah, those three authors of the original resistance rant are at the top of our watch list." The FBI agent smiled as if she were a cat about to pounce. "They are squeaky clean, but we're thinking we might drag them in on conspiracy to commit acts of terror charges."

"We're downplaying any mention of Sherwood Green or their propaganda." Langstaff looked satisfied. "They want publicity and others might copy them. We're counting on them recruiting." He smiled, as if privy to some inside information. "The only weak link is controlling the internet. We can't stop the spread of news there."

"If it becomes necessary, we will take steps to control the Internet back home." The FBI agent did not elaborate.

"I am assigning more people to PATS to coordinate for Ontario." D. C. Hardy passed out a list of names and contact information. "They are in Orillia and are available 24/7. I would appreciate it if they gave us any information of any terrorist attack right away. The Premier gives this top priority."

They agreed the PATS group would become the information processing centre in Ontario. None of them would follow the protocol to the letter. Everyone wanted the glory of being the agency to break the case.

"One last question." Patricia De Cruze had not yet packed up. "Where are they getting their money?"

No one had an answer.

The similarity between the Toronto attacks and the London incident struck Langstaff. It convinced him Sherwood Green had committed that crime. His first request to the Provincial Police was for traffic-camera analysis of the 401 highway near London on the night of the attack. Hopefully, the computers could pull most of the plate numbers. The information to check was growing. It would be Hardy's problem and expense.

The Sherwood Green Support Network held its first meeting at the University of Toronto at the same time as the city hall meeting. SGSN wanted to create the impression Sherwood Green attended a university and to feed the public bias. Diane did not know the makeup of Sherwood Green, but thought the deceit was useful. The resistors seemed to be more sophisticated than simply a collection of undergrads.

The room, a jewel of Hart House, had woodwork finished in quarter-cut oak with lead-glazed windows and large paintings from Canadian artists that included a Group of Seven scene of the Ontario wild in autumn. Diane was unaware the building was a tribute to the founder of an agricultural equipment manufacturing empire that once dominated Ontario industry but had faded into bankrupt obscurity. The place symbolized the agriculture and industrialism, causing planetary destruction.

"Let's get going." Arsenault glanced about the room. Eight activists sat at the oak table. "Only use first names. Joe, Melissa and I will have your complete information. We'll be the weak link in any police investigations. There will be lots of attention from cops."

Arsenault let this sink in. She rubbed the healing bruise on her cheek. She watched for signs of wavering. Her anti-whaling friends were all solid. She did not know the recruits.

One of the new people was Joe's girlfriend, Stevie Grey. Diane hoped Stevie had joined out of commitment and not because her boyfriend was a member. The young girl seemed whimsical, dressed in a garish shirt and skirt. She had piercings, tattoos and her hair was a rainbow. Joe said Stevie was intelligent and thoughtful.

If Grey worked out, Arsenault hoped she could be a path into the counterculture. Even though refusal movements such as the hippies of long ago had been ineffective, the fact they rejected industrial culture raised possibilities. Hopefully, Stevie would recruit more.

The young newcomer, Joel Phelps, was a greater unknown. Jos Amiel had given her Phelps' name, a student suggested by Debbie Franklin. Diane's suspicion of the university teacher put on her guard. She had interviewed Joel over the telephone. His answers seemed somewhat vague. In person, he wanted to blend in. His major at the university, 'Modern Cultural Anthropology', was so esoteric few could know if he was genuinely studying. Diane hoped he would be trustworthy.

"Okay." Joe took over. "This is not a democratic organization in the sense we might think of democracy, and this is not a founding meeting. The Sherwood Green Support Network already exists. The three of us are the coordinators."

He paused, waiting for objections. No one spoke.

"There won't be regular meetings of the entire network. When the three of us need guidance, we will call a meeting. We encourage everyone to give us their ideas and to discuss things informally with each other. Everyone is free to quit, but we three are open. If anyone leaves, we would appreciate it if you talk with us first. We are human and will make many mistakes. Please point those out to us. The SGSN is, like Sherwood Green, not trying to convince anyone. It's not a popularity contest. Their aim is to destroy industrialism, and ours is to support them with legal activity."

"We have decided on this less than democratic structure to avoid what happens to most lefty outfits. Debate paralyzes them, or they end up with too many objectives. Obviously, Sherwood Green is an illegal resistance force. They will be called terrorists, and our role is to give whatever above ground help we can. Our only objectives are to raise money for legal costs and to give them above ground help in propaganda."

"Of course," Diane interjected, "if a large enough number of you demanded a meeting, we would comply. We'll try to hold retreats out of town for rest if the fight lasts that long."

Diane noticed Stevie wincing. She was a city girl. Diane wondered if Stevie really understood the implications of a Sherwood Green success. Her urban lifestyle, with its artsy groups and superficial counter culture rebellion, would vanish into a struggle for immediate survival.

Joel piped up. "So, what will we be doing?"

"Well," Joe replied, "the immediate, essential effort is to spread Sherwood Green's message that the media suppress. It's dangerous for the resistors to do public work. They risk getting caught. An above-ground group can do it with less risk. We'll distribute these," said Joe, lifting a large bundle of pamphlets.

"What about me designing some?" Stevie was creative and eager to contribute.

"We encourage everyone to submit anything for consideration. Anyone can create and distribute their original material or art. If you want to put SGSN on it, we must see it first. Remember, this isn't an effort to convince the masses. The majority will hate us. It is an effort to tell the truth about the death of 200 species a day and the destruction of the planet by the industrial elite. We'll be countering propaganda."

"Won't the establishment lie about us?" Joel's question sounded like a statement.

"Of course," Diane responded, "but it won't matter in the long run. We aim to support the attack on industrial civilization. The elite's propaganda will make it rougher on any resistors if they catch any, and on us, too. We must accept the risk."

Melissa spoke, "That leads us to a second major aim. Our fundraising, besides paying for printing and Web access, will be for building a legal defence fund to support anyone arrested, us, or Sherwood Green resistors."

Melissa was a lawyer. Legal matters were her job. The woman had recruited a couple of idealistic lawyers to remain on standby. A famous established attorney also volunteered to help. He did not support the end of his privileged lifestyle, but loved publicity.

"How will we raise money?" Joel was eager. "Will we funnel some to Sherwood Green?"

"You are full of questions," Diane smiled, but Joel's suggestion of an illegal act made her uneasy. "Each will donate whatever we can spare. Everyone donating should be working. If any of you are on welfare or living on student loans do not, I repeat, do not donate any of your support money. It could discredit us and the cops could use it against you. It's a big enough risk just to be a member. If possible, get a job and pay your own way."

"Whenever we hand out material, ask for a donation and invite people to join. Tell them exactly what we will use the money for. We might go door to door in friendly neighbourhoods, collecting empty beer bottles and money."

"To answer your second question," Diane stared at Joel, "we will not give one cent to Sherwood Green."

Melissa spoke up. "It's a crime to aid terrorism, and they would charge us. We can't do any good from jail. We want to avoid fighting the police directly. They are just the paid thugs of the establishment, and the exploiters are our real enemy."

"How do they get money?" Joel asked.

"That's none of our business." Diane's cut him off.

"We might encourage people to join Sherwood Green." Joe's statement aroused interest. Joel Phelps made a note on his phone.

Diane hastened to add, "We have had no requests from Sherwood Green, and we have no way of getting in touch with them."

Arsenault knew that wanting to become a resistor would be the reason some joined the SGSN; however, the police would know all SGSN members, or possibly police informers, and of no interest to Sherwood Green.

This was an unstated purpose of the support group. Watching them would divert police resources down a blind alley. She surveyed the room, wondering if one of those present was actually a Sherwood Green fighter. Maybe her fears about Phelps were wrongheaded. He could just as easily be from the resistance as the police. More likely, he was just a student wanting to help. Based on her experience with the harmless whaling movement, with eleven people at the table, one was a cop. She knew the OPP ran the Provincial Anti-Terrorism Service and PATS were watching just about everyone. The Mounties had similar efforts, and likely CISIS did too. It was a wonder they were not bumping into each other in the dark.

"Do they communicate with us?" For the first time, Stevie thought of herself as a member of the SGSN.

"I've received e-mails from someone claiming to be Sherwood Green, with copies of their pamphlets and a manifesto." Diane lifted a small pile of paper from the table. We're reworking the manifesto into public handouts.

"The manifesto states their aim is to end industrial civilization. There is no detailed plan for what would come after. They say any hope for the human species will learn to live in harmony with other species and the physical processes of the planet. How it will happen is not foreseeable and not ideological."

"Destroying civilization will mean a horrible loss of life and suffering," Joel said. "Millions will die."

"That is a possibility," Melissa said. "Perhaps we could learn to localize, live more simply and decline less painfully, but even if we don't tear down this society on purpose, a massive decline in human numbers will happen. All species have more hope if we do it sooner, not waiting for nature to kill us."

Most of the attendees nodded. Joel looked shocked. Diane thought he might leave. He remained, with a dark look on his face.

"We suggest," Joe said, "that people get out of the cities to the country where they might survive."

"We can't all do that." Joel said. "There's not enough land."

"Maybe not," Joe agreed, "but few will take our advice. Perhaps we'll wake people up."

"Do they have a detailed plan? Where will Sherwood Green strike next?"

"Read the Green Resistance manifesto." Diane held up a copy. "I will e-mail it to you. They outline a target selection process that lets a resistor decide on strategic targets with the goal as the destruction of industrialism and its hierarchy of sexism, racism and privilege. We should avoid attacks on people and minimize accidental deaths. Terrorism is not the aim."

"Like the Garza woman." Joel seemed sceptical.

"I feel sad it killed Amalia Garza," Diane admitted. "She was on that street because she worked for cash slave wages. Her boss had a big contract with one bank, and he got rich exploiting illegal immigrants. The bank received cheap work, and no questions asked. The media have ignored that story."

"Anyway," Joe added, "we won't advocate violence, but explain if industrialism doesn't stop, most species on the planet will die, including ours."

"Sherwood Green," Diane added, "defines Canada as a consuming nation with a resource base and providing financial services. It should not surprise us if they attack consumerism, including retail, warehousing and transportation, as well as the resource industry and its infrastructure, especially fossil fuels. That means the highways and more automobile-related attacks. They have already staged an attack on finance."

Stevie piped up, "Why did they hit small car dealerships?"

"They singled Fukushima out because of the whaling connection." Diane leaned back into the hard leather-finished chair. "But it was more a signal to the environmental movement such as the Anti-Whaling Coalition. They say the game has changed and our old methods of politely asking don't work. The biggest criticisms of those attacks have been from people like Bill Meeks who exploits the current stalemate. Their first strategic attack was on the financial district. Capitalism was the target. It was quite a statement."

"Why is the city saying it's accidental, even after Sherwood Green owned it?"

"I don't know," Diane admitted, "but I bet it has a lot to do with money."

"It's about insurance." Melissa added. "Terrorist clauses would get the insurers off the hook. There are millions in claims. Actually, I think one way to attack finance and capital would be to maximize insurance claims. No prediction, but perhaps we will see lots of incidents that don't appear to be attacks but cost lots of money. It would depend on the actual target. If you want to bankrupt a drilling company, make it terrorism. If you want to weaken the financial industry, then stage accidents."

Diane distributed stacks of pamphlets and the members paired up to hand them out at the subway entrances.

"Fill out fundraising report forms accurately with the amount collected. Hand over all the money to me. I will document expenses and pay if we have agreed ahead of time. We won't pay for any other expenses. We're in this to win. If Sherwood Green wins, money will be worthless."

"Only accept cash, no cheques. They create a paper trail. The Network runs on cash only and postal money orders." Joe handed out the forms.

"Joel, you come with me," Diane walked over to the new recruit. "We'll go to the St. George station to work the rush-hour crowd."

Diane wanted to satisfy herself he was not an agent. She did not tell any of the recruits they would accompany leaders until they had earned trust. As they left, no one paid attention to the people lounging in the shade on the grassy island of the Hart House traffic circle. Universities were an excellent cover for activists and informants.

Chapter Eight

Diane Arsenault sat at a glass-topped table nursing a glass of beer. Her table shared an outdoor patio facing Spadina Avenue and cooled by a late afternoon shade. She chose a spot in the second row from the street to lessen the traffic noise, fumes, and dust.

In this unseasonably hot June, most patrons sought the air-conditioned interior. Arsenault's computer job meant many hours in air-conditioned buildings. She enjoyed being outside in Montreal style.

Sunlight reflected from a glass and chrome building on the opposite side of the wide avenue and glared uncomfortably, so she wore sunglasses. Diane mused about the unusually hot, dry weather. The city had declared watering restrictions, and they closed Lake Ontario beaches because of fecal bacteria.

A white van pulled up with a flash of reflected sunlight in front of a fire hydrant across the street. No one got out of the vehicle. Years of public protesting had taught Diane to watch for surveillance. She tried not to be obvious. Reflection from the plate glass storefront passed through the vehicle's dark side-windows. Diane saw silhouettes of three people moving in the back of the van.

A waitress appeared, checked on her drink, then adjusted the potted plants on the railing and disappeared.

"Hi Diane, it is nice to see you again." Jos Amiel had arranged for this interview to follow up on the SGSN. Nothing new had happened, making him desperate for something for his evening time slot. *Terrorism Toronto* had become an intermittent feature. Despite the death of Amalia Garza, he hoped for another attack.

"Please," Diane smiled at Jos, "move the plant on the railing over to the right? The glare from the street bothers my eyes. Turn it so the bushy side is the other way."

Jos adjusted the decoration and slipped into his seat. "It sure is hot. The street's bright. I hope that worked."

"It's fine, thank you," Diane said. The plant obscured the van.

"Things have been quiet. I wondered," Jos laid his cell phone on the table, "did your meeting go well?"

Before Diane could answer, the waitress appeared. Jos ordered a beer. As she left, the woman returned the plant to its former position.

Arsenault smiled, took out a pad and wrote a few words on it, passing the paper to Jos. It read, "We are being watched and listened to." He raised his eyebrows. Diane touched his hand and motioned with her thumb towards the street. "I saw your good piece on Amalia Garza."

"Her friends told a heartbreaking story, but it was uplifting too. I plan a piece on the crooked contractor and tie it to the attack. Her friends denied she was involved with Sherwood Green, but they know they did the explosion. They're sad for Amalia, but angry at the crooked contractor and the banks. They gave me lots of leads to other exploitation of refugees and illegal immigrants."

Diane had made a note on her pad. This hint led to her recruiting of several of the Mexicans into the support network. Many of the Mexicans were political activists who had fled to Canada for safety.

"The response to that piece surprised me. Most people were positive, sympathetic to both Amalia and Sherwood Green. It seems some like attacks on banks. Even Burt Boyce defended Amalia when some of his callers got more racist than he was. Some said, 'The wet back deserved what she got'. Boyce actually wants the contractor jailed. I guess drunken racists can have a heart."

"The meeting went well," Diane changed the subject and sipped her beer. "We'll have lots to do. City Hall panicked after the hydro attack."

"Yah, well, they still deny it was Sherwood Green. I can't guess why. The head of the THEC resigned last night, accepting blame for the decaying system. He could have blamed Sherwood Green and kept his job."

"They are covering it up." Diane glanced at the van and thought she saw it wobble. The sun no longer gave her a view of the interior. "Melissa thinks it's because they want to collect insurance. Terrorism voids policies."

"Makes sense," Jos finished his beer and thought of ordering another. It was a hot day. "They're hassling street folks, too. The homeless are being rounded up and dumped in the suburbs. They think some are lookouts for the terrorists. The official line is they are a security threat and they can look after them better out there, trying to make it look like they are doing something progressive."

Jos spotted the waitress hovering near the doorway and beckoned her over. Diane asked for the cheque.

"I know a better place." She winked at Jos. He wondered if Diane was another woman on the make.

Diane dropped some cash on top of the bill, leaving no tip, and hurried for the exit. Jos scrambled to follow.

"What's up?" he gasped as they hit the sidewalk. Diane led him across the street to a subway-bound street-car. The waitress, still in uniform, followed them into the car. Jos and Diane went to the rear. The waitress took a seat on the side bench behind the driver. She stood out in the almost empty vehicle.

"What are you doing?" Having his relaxing afternoon turned into a scramble annoyed Jos.

"We're being followed. Don't look up. Our waitress is up at the front, behind the driver. Stick with me and don't talk." Diane glanced out the back window. The white van ran a red light, following the tram north.

"There are three people in the white van behind us...no, don't look." Diane glanced at the front. The waitress had her arm raised, adjusting her hair. Her lips were moving.

"What do they want with us?" The police had never tailed Jos, and this sounded serious.

"Nothing, I hope," Diane smiled and sat back to enjoy the ride into the subway. "They had a bug in the plant you moved. They want to know what we're talking about. I had you adjust the pot as a test. The cop waitress up there put it back the way it was. The mike was in the pot. I'm sure the guys in the van were listening and photographing."

At the subway, Diane led Jos out the double rear doors. They ran down the stairs to join the crowd on the westbound platform. The waitress had not followed. A rush of air from the darkened tunnel announced an arriving train. The crowd pressed forward. Diane drew Jos back towards the wall, allowing the people to board the train in front of them. The platform cleared, and she headed back towards the stairway. As the whistle sounded and the doors closed, a passenger hurried off the train. The pair rushed up the stairs, through the concourse, past the boutiques and coffee shop and down the stairs to the eastbound platform as a train arrived. They scrambled on as the doors closed. A man wriggled between the closing doors. He had had no time to choose and so was right behind Diane and Jos; however, he scurried to the front end of the car while they walked calmly to the rear.

The last-minute passenger was the man who had jumped off the westbound train and their new tail.

Diane watched the green walls of St. George station come and go. When the train squealed to a halt in the Bay Street station, she led Jos off, joining a throng of other riders. She knew their shadow would follow along. They flowed with the crowd along the edge of the platform, but as the trainman blew his warning whistle, Diane yanked Jos back onto the train just as the doors slid shut. They left the man on the platform.

In the madhouse of the Bloor-Young interchange, they made their way to a north-bound train and rode it to the St. Clair station.

"We didn't really need to lose him," Diane looked back over her shoulder as they reached the sunlit street, "But it was fun… just a game. Everything I do is legal and open. The police have no real clues, so think all of us are terrorists. They will always follow us. Maybe you too."

"Do you think they'll find us?" Jos was excited.

"If they got to the TTC control centre cameras, I would guess they already know we got off at St. Clair. We might never spot them again, unless they are really careless. Most people would not have noticed them on Spadina."

"You're good at that. Are you a terrorist?" Jos asked.

"I don't enjoy being listened to when I want a private conversation," she responded. "There are some things I don't want them to hear. We can't be too high a priority yet. This team was good but sloppy, and there weren't enough of them. My move in the subway was too obvious. They should have had a back-up tail in the concourse. Next time will be harder."

"Here's the Sherwood Green statement." Diane handed Jos several sheets of paper stapled together. The cover featured a line drawing of a bear, reared up straight and clutching a rifle in its forepaws. Piercing eyes stared straight from the paper. This was the first hint of guns. It wouldn't be the last.

They reached Avenue Road and sat on a shaded bench. Diane spotted two surveillance cameras. This was an affluent neighbourhood of corporate managers, university professors, lawyers, and other members of the establishment. The cameras showed the elite's paranoia.

Jos read:

To all people.

If things do not change, the rate of species extinction of 200 per day will increase, and we will irreversibly destroyed the ability of the planet to support complex life.

All of us are guilty, but most of us are less so. It is those in control who are the real guilty ones. Their greed, lust for power and lack of empathy to other living beings, including their fellow man, make them and their lackeys sociopathic criminals destroying the planet. Those people who understand and do not act are equally guilty.

The ignorant and brainwashed majority must either awaken or we must discount them in the fight to save the planet.

The problem is not that decision makers do not understand. The lackeys have convinced themselves things are not as bad as they really are, or some technology will save the day. Most of them understand but have decided their interests lie in their own short-term gain and in service to their masters, the industrial corporate financial elite. Letter writing, petitions, running environmental candidates in the elite controlled parliaments and hoping to rouse the masses will change nothing. Asking politely has not worked. It is time to act with force against these powers. People will become either part of the solution or part of the problem. The more people who act will encourage more to fight.

The media are a prime tool in the distraction, deception and self-blame of most of the population. None of the corporate media are worth saving, and their message deceives their audience. Our job is to destroy the illusion of there being value in the present suicidal system of corporate capitalism.

Aim: To destroy corporate industrialism globally and to neutralize the impact of the human species upon planet Earth.

Targets: the elite and their safe havens; *the financial system industrial agriculture and the corporations and technicians who live off of its destructive activities*

infrastructure, but especially the energy and other resource extraction and distribution systems along with transportation and communication networks

petro-chemical industry

global trade and the long-distance shipping

the corporate media

corporate educational institutions, as these are the trainers for sociopathic group-think and compliance with the corporations.

the business of environmentalism including eco-tourism

the commercial operation of parks and natural reserves, including camping

the corporate entertainment industry, including professional sports and their support systems

frivolous consumption and consumerism

cities

This list is not complete but covers all the areas at the root of the problem.

We will attack targets based on their strategic value at each stage of the resistance. There will be no intentional killing of innocent humans or other species; however, we recognize resistance activity may harm both innocent and guilty people. From time to time there will be targets of opportunity. The aim will be the selection of targets that are strategic.

The army, politicians, the legal system and police are not strategic targets. Fighting the proxies of the elite is wasteful. We will harshly deal with collaborators and infiltrators, but we will avoid direct confrontation. Being arrested and becoming a hero does not help the cause. The aim is not to convince the public but to encourage action that will destroy industrialism.

Above ground supporters are necessary but not part of the physical resistance. We will have no direct connection with any of these groups. Supporters will spread the message with no risk to actual fighters. If they accuse anyone of taking part in resistance activities, these organizations will organize physical and legal support.

Cities are unsustainable collections of consumers. We encourage people to leave them and create more rural, locally sustainable groupings living in harmony with the natural world. Individual survivalists are not to be trusted, but above ground organizations should advocate and help in the orderly evacuation of the cities. The majority will not respond, but this will help the minority who heed the call. There is no guarantee these people will be better off than those who stay put; however, chaos, disease and starvation will be worse in urban areas. The human global population will decrease and will happen without great suffering.

We encourage people to opt out of the corporate economy. Using cash, barter and gifting will reduce the revenue the elite expropriate to run their repression. Reducing the income of the repressive public institutions, combined with the burden of more security forces, will weaken the elite. Refusing to take part in banking and other institutions will reduce the ability of the police to keep track of individuals. Above ground organizations should use that strategy, but egotistical agitators and actions are self-defeating and above ground organizations must avoid these types of people.

Sherwood Green is part of a global movement. Organized activity, well planned and executed with clear strategic objectives, is the most effective. There are many people worldwide engaged in this effort on their local battle-fields; however, as people awaken, if they cannot join an organization, then random acts against the industrial structure will help. Sabotage in the office or on the factory floor can be effective. Unfortunately, individual acts will usually result in arrest and punishment. Sherwood Green does not encourage anyone to take isolated heroic action. We are open to accepting sincere, dedicated fighters into our ranks. Joining an above ground organization will be safer, but even that will require sacrifice. As the fight intensifies, desperate forces will attack and isolate anyone labelled a supporter. Members of above ground organizations are likely to suffer from physical attack, arrested and, in many places, tortured and murdered. Only those who are prepared to risk and sacrifice will help save life on the planet.

This is not a debate, and Sherwood Green does not care whether the majority or even a significant minority support these actions. The planet cannot wait for consensus. The resistance movement is not planning to replace existing governments or economic organizations with any new ideological design. Halting the disaster is the only goal of Sherwood Green. What comes after will evolve from local needs and the people who survive.

Wake up people. No matter what the elite tell you, it is not your fault. You too can resist, be brave and act.

- Sherwood Green

Jos looked thoughtful. "Why attack entertainment, parks, and shopping? I see no value in these targets."

"Let's keep walking." Diane led the way south along Avenue Road. A small Honda had stalled in the right lane, and the driver had lifted the hood and talked on her cell phone. Horns sounded as impatient drivers forced their way past the stopped vehicle.

"The industrial culture that's destroying them has misled the majority into enslavement and dependency. Shopping and entertainment give the illusion of normalcy. Eco-tourism and cottage life in all forms creates the impression things are fine in the natural world while actually destroying habitats and eco-systems. That impression needs to be changed. The system cannot deliver the happiness people think it does, and distractions such as television, sports, movies and electronic toys are part of the brainwashing. People need to reject the system emotionally, so they can understand that it must die."

Her reference to death seemed morbid, but after reading the declaration, Jos evaluated his own life. Diane's splash of cold water jarred him.

"The list of targets is everything in the industrial world." Jos thought it was unfocused.

"That seems so, but most overlap a bit. Do you see why they might concentrate on Toronto?"

"Yes," Jos smiled. "It's the focus for the money behind these things in Canada. The three big cities; Vancouver; Toronto and Montreal should be the primary targets. Have there been any attacks in Vancouver or Montreal?"

"I don't know," Diane paused. "I'm a Quebecer. The focus there is always independence. Nationalism absorbs most of the radicals. I don't think separatists conceive of anything other than a corporate, industrial Quebec. Narrow nationalism won't be in favour of Sherwood Green, but the separation of Quebec would weaken the Canadian federation, and it might help the fight."

"It would allow the USA to take over Canada."

"As global resistance develops, there will be many disruptions of political and economic structures. Each one will represent a wobbling of the wheel of the apple cart."

"I think Sherwood Green has chewed on a big apple." Jos laughed, extending the metaphor.

"How does the support network fit in?" Jos had asked for the meeting just to ask this question. "Can you tell me a bit about your organization, on the record?"

"Everything's on the record." Diane smiled. "I'm sure the cops know all about the meeting."

Diane had used this meeting with Jos as a test. Joel Phelps was the only one who knew when and where she was going. The police were waiting. Phelps' was a spy.

"I am not sure how I can use any of this." Jos frowned. "My boss forbids any mention of Sherwood Green."

"We're gaining new members almost every day. The network has become a proper organization with several sub-groups. I won't use names." She touched Jos' arm. "The cops know, but I won't put individuals in the public eye."

"I head the propaganda effort, and we distribute literature," she nodded at the manifesto in Jos's hand, "press releases and so forth."

"Joe, whom you met at Amalia's funeral, runs the action group. They organize demonstrations. We'll try to avoid confronting the police, and we fear an infiltration by trouble makers and police provocateurs."

"Melissa runs the legal department and has lawyers to defend arrested members of Sherwood Green, or us."

"We three are in charge of membership."

"We're establishing the rural enclaves Sherwood Green proposed." Diane seemed excited. "We already have a rural property to turn into a resilient community."

"Could I visit?" Jos had seldom been out of town. His camp experience had been at an inner-city Christian mission camp for the underprivileged.

"You could not report its location, but you could mention its existence. It might encourage copy-cats."

"I would be discreet, but how do you make formal decisions?" Jos could not walk and take notes and could not find his cell to use. He could reconstruct the conversation later even if that would horrify Debbie Franklin.

"We leaders do the planning and decide, even if that seems undemocratic, but subgroups meet to decide how to carry them out, like where to distribute leaflets. It's crucial because when we hold a demonstration, we're all exposed to physical danger."

"There have been no demonstrations." Jos smiled, trying not to sound accusatory.

"The first one will be tomorrow, at dinner time in front of the 'Blue Schooner', the big one downtown. Seafood restaurants rely on industrial fishing, draggers and things that are destroying the ocean bed and stripping the sea of fish. We would rather the cops don't know beforehand."

"Walt and I will be there." Jos enjoyed conspiring. He enjoyed working with Diane.

"How is Sherwood Green organized?"

"Read, Green Resistance. We don't know how they work, but it seems solid and effective. No one knew of Sherwood Green until the first attack. That's how deep they made themselves. They don't seem to have cracks in their organization."

"How do you get messages? How do they recruit?"

"They send e-mail, but I don't know how to contact them. As for the second question, I'll pretend you aren't a cop." She winked at Jos. "They have been underground for a long time and have several people working together. I would guess they recruit by direct contact, but I have no clue how they identify potential fighters. People like me and you," she paused, watching Jos' reaction, "are too public. Our members would have to disappear for a long time and fall off the radar. The cops have my fingerprints and DNA, so I would never make a front-line fighter."

"What do you think?" Diane wanted to recruit him.

"I'm not convinced about this approach. Industrialism is killing the planet, killing us, but I don't think terrorism is the answer." He paused. "I'm caught in the middle, and although I hate the network owners who want me to lie and stir up hatred just to make money, I'm not ready to blow things up. I want to be neutral."

Diane looked disappointed. "I think the time for neutrality is gone." Jos' thoughtfulness encouraged Diane. They crossed Avenue Road and headed north. The Honda had left.

"I am going to catch that streetcar coming west."

Jos offered Sherwood Green's statement back to her.

"You keep it." She searched for her pass. "There's one in your e-mail. We sent it to every media outlet and the cops. It was a bugger getting Frank Langstaff's inbox."

"You know about Langstaff?" Jos disliked the cop as much as Langstaff disliked Jos.

"He's the face of the enemy. I hear he's a jerk."

Arsenault waved from the window as the tram ran an amber traffic light. Jos headed for the studio.

"Are you a fucking idiot?" Sheri Stein stood behind her desk, shouting at her young reporter. "We can't use that manifesto. They would fire me on the spot. The boss has already seen it and ordered not one word was to be quoted on air, not even to mention its existence."

Jos had expected a no, but Sheri's over the top reaction shook him.

"Calm down, boss," Jos smiled. He resigned to the censorship. "I figured you'd say no."

"This is bad for my blood pressure." Sheri, too young for heart problems, sat down and reached for her herbal tea. "I'm sorry Jos, but I got shit earlier today for your funeral piece on the Garza girl. When the owner saw it, he wanted me to fire you. I told him it was great journalism, and we can't fire a reporter for doing the job. It was Garza's friend's reference to Sherwood Green that sparked him off. I hoped to get away with it, never again."

It surprised Jos that Sheri had stood up for him, and he now had to revise his opinion of her. She was more complex than the self-serving climber Debbie Franklin had suggested. He wondered what Debbie actually thought of him. Jos wondered what Diane thought of him.

Amiel was angry when he left Stein's office, not at his boss, but at the corporation. It convinced Jos the public deserved to know about Sherwood Green. He wondered at the fear in the owners, who wanted to suppress the truth. Jos went to the copy room and ran off copies of the declaration. TorontoNewsNow was about to contribute informally to the SGSN publicity effort. Jos planned to leave copies everywhere he went: on tables at Bucks, on transit seats, anywhere no one or cameras would remember him. It would all be fun if he could only find his cell phone.

Chapter Nine

"Hello?" the female voice startled Jos. He had dialled his cell number countless times after he had lost it. The phone held his contact information. He needed it back.

"Who's this?" Jos demanded.

"Who's calling?" the female voice responded.

"Jos Amiel, you answered my cell phone." His softened his voice. He depended on the goodwill of this woman.

"What colour is it?" The woman asked.

"Blue, with a black protector. The ring tone is from Waving Flag."

"What's your password?" She sounded innocent.

"I'm not telling." Jos said. "I'll log on in front of you."

"Okay, I guess you are legit. Come to the Stein and Skillet on Spadina. Ask for Lori."

With the cell in his hand, Jos offered Lori a reward.

"Nope, thanks, we get these left here all the time and we try to help the customer. I leave mine places. It's nice to get it back."

It did not surprise Jos; and in Toronto, you had a good chance of getting a lost item back. Little things like this had convinced Jos that the city had good people.

"I called a dozen times, but you were the first to answer." Jos examined the cell. The call list was intact.

"I wouldn't know about that. I'm the opening manager. This was under the bar and on when I got here."

"That explains the low battery. Maybe it was too noisy for anyone to hear."

"At least I'll have a beer and a sandwich," Jos smiled at Lori and wondered if she was available. The ring on her finger told another story. Ironically, he sat outside at the same table he and Diane had used the day before. No white van appeared, and he left a large tip.

Jos deposited a Sherwood Green declaration on the railing with the paper held in place by the infamous potted plant. He left a copy in the washroom and in front of the fishbowl for the business card dinner draw.

I loved doing that. I feel I could enjoy the whole thing. Am I a radical?

Jos basked in self-satisfaction; however, the question upset him. He had invested a quarter of his life in his career. His family was proud of him. He was a star in his circle of friends. Jos risked it all.

I don't want to destroy everything. Jos crossed the street to walk back to the studio, b*ut things could be better. Perhaps Sherwood Green will shake things up.*

Jos tried to sort out the implications of Sherwood Green's statement. His conversation with Diane Arsenault had not eased his doubts. He glanced over his shoulder at the pub and wondered if Diane would meet him again.

Maybe Debbie can help me sort this out. Jos stopped in the shade on the south side of the street. It would be another sweltering day. He dialled his lover's number. He now thought of the woman as both a mentor and lover, but blocked out feelings of guilt. When he thought about the situation, he ended up remembering the good sex.

If someone offers you fine wine, never turn it down.

Jos trusted Debbie, and they could honestly discuss his doubts and sympathy about Sherwood Green.

Debbie Franklin opened the hotel room door and yanked Jos inside. She was alluring in the semi-darkness.

Their embrace was consuming. Debbie eagerly stripped the young man. Jos gasped as he laid his cell phone on the bedside table. The garish light from the view screen created an intrusive glow in the warm shadows.

"Do you need that thing on?" Debbie's frown hid in the dim light.

"I am technically at work and need to be in touch." He pushed the device behind the lamp as his lover embraced him from behind.

"Let's get it on, lover. I have a three o'clock lecture."

"I have to be somewhere too." He gasped as her demanding hands explored his body. They collapsed onto the bed. The phone did not ring. Jos forgot about it in his passion.

"You have a very esoteric major." Diane Arsenault walked beside Joel Phelps. They carried signs condemning the raping of the oceans and pleading for people to stop eating at seafood restaurants. "What made you study something so different?"

"I want to be a writer. I want to study modern society from a historical perspective, so I can write about it."

"Why didn't you take sociology?" Diane handed a leaflet to a couple about to enter the Blue Schooner. The man crumpled the paper and threw it at her feet.

"Fuck off, bitch, get a job!" His companion giggled.

"Jerks," Joel continued. "Sociology trains people to be welfare police. I want more."

Diane ignored the dismissal of sociology. There were few jobs for the hundreds of graduates dumped onto the streets each June.

"We got your name from Professor Franklin. Is she your teacher?"

Joel knew Diane tested him. He wished he knew if Franklin was a liability. "I took journalism as a minor to make my writing more readable." Joel got a smile from a young woman who took a pamphlet. "Maybe I could get a job at The Star, like Hemingway." Joel laughed. "Debbie spent a whole lecture on Sherwood Green issues. We should recruit her." He saw Diane's frown.

"She said she had some connection with you. I thought I could help, so I asked her to pass on my name."

Joel seemed sincere and either partly honest or an excellent liar, but Diane had proof Joel worked for the police. She waved at Jos as he arrived.

The crowded downtown sidewalk bordered a roadway filled with slow-moving vehicles. Police officers watched from a distance.

"Stay on the sidewalk and keep moving," Joe said. "Stay off the road or they'll charge you."

The demonstration remained peaceful except for noisy exchanges with hostile people. Others took leaflets; some stopped to chat. The major incident, if it deserved the term, was a loud discussion with the police. A sergeant arrived to take charge. He argued with Joe and Melissa, but the cop could not match the woman's knowledge of the law.

Constables stared gloomily at the demonstrators. It frustrated them at not having an excuse for action. Two members of Frank Langstaff's terrorist unit appeared, with one taking photographs of those who accepted leaflets. They got faces to attach to Sherwood Green and collected leaflets bearing activist finger prints.

Sherri allotted thirty seconds for a *Terrorism Toronto* segment, mostly showing Stevie Grey parading along the sidewalk, chanting and holding a large sign. Sheri thought the woman's garish dress and wild hair would discredit the radicals and make her bosses happy; however, her sign said Sherwood Green Support Network in large bold letters. Among Stevie's clearer shouts was "join us" and that slipped through the censorship. In his voice over, Jos only referred to the group as "terrorist sympathizers", but the video did the work for him. He relished this cat-and-mouse game. The clip circulated on the internet, and SGSN recruited more members.

Chapter Ten

The quiet ended on two fronts, but the police did not link the event on Cherrywood Lane to Sherwood Green.

Cherrywood Lane was a quiet cul-de-sac in the heart of suburban North York. An apartment building towered twenty-three floors at number 643. The structure's white ceramic coated brick facing shone as a ghostly pillar in the stray city light. Down the street, on the opposite side, a low red brick building housed the local youth centre. Young people engaged in a lively game of pickup basketball on the poorly lit asphalt court behind the centre. Their shouts raised calls for quiet from the townhouses on the next street where poor residents opened windows for relief from the June heat.

In front of the apartment block, a black SUV sat nosed into the visitor's parking. A guard eyed the vehicle from his lobby desk, making sure no one bothered it.

The security guard stirred when two slightly built black men emerged from an elevator, members of the Black Stallions had dropped off product and picked up boodle from street pushers. One man laid a fifty on the security desk. The guard pocketed the bill without comment. The payment was a face-saver for the guard, a token deposit on his loyalty. These young men were not above killing him if he betrayed them.

"See you next time, man." The young drug dealer followed his companion outside, and the guard returned to his newspaper now that The SUV was no longer his problem. He ignored the unchanging views from the security cameras. He did not see two figures rush to the SUV, and the solid front doors masked muffled gunshots.

A third figure appeared, dressed in black with its face covered. The attackers slipped large plastic bags over the two dead gangsters and deposited the bodies in the back. An attacker slipped behind the wheel while another took the passenger seat. At the curb, the third slid into the passenger seat of a Honda. The SUV headed towards Steeles Avenue. The Honda made a U turn and followed, and after a quick run to the Bathurst intersection, the pair of vehicles headed north, out of town.

A tenant smoking on his balcony six floors up looked for the cause of the popping sounds. He saw three people scurrying about a vehicle and watched it drive off. He called 911.

Walt and Jos worked late in the editing room organizing video for the documentary project. The police scanner crackled in the background.

"940 we have a 10-14 at 600 Cherrywood Lane, cross is Steeles." The police dispatcher's almost incomprehensible voice crackled from the speaker.

"940… are those kids behind the gym again and the call from the guy on Seymour?"

"10-4, 940 same citizen … proceed 940."

"I'll go have a chat with them. My 10-20 is Keele and Steeles." The male constable's tired voice carried clearly from the speaker. It was all routine and boring. The dispatcher's tone suddenly changed.

"940 what's your 10-20?" the calm female voice sounded urgent.

"940, Steeles and Bathurst, just around the corner."

"We have a 10-11, shots fired at 643 Cherrywood. Cancel 10-14 and proceed. Are you 10-12?"

"10-4 I am alone… proceeding to 643."

"Units 2032; 848 and 985 please assist 940 at 643 Cherrywood Lane. Possible shots fired. Plain clothes dispatched, 940… complaining citizen did not identify, but called from Apartment 606. Leave it to the plain clothes."

Jos thought it sounded like another drug gang shooting. There would be a couple of bodies discovered somewhere, and a vacuum in an organization would have to be filled. Retaliation was a given. In that area, the Knights and Black Stallions competed, and likely one had hit the other. Jos and Walt carried on viewing the video.

About 11:15, just as the pair was wrapping up for the night, the radio crackled in loud urgency.

"10-85, all units, we have a 10-17 in progress… Shepherd and Bayview ... fire dispatched. 1033 is on scene and declares Project Tom. Headquarters is dispatching. 1011; 918; 647; 2142 and 2546 respond to this location. Assist fire and protect evidence. Deputy Langstaff will take command."

Walt had his camera gear on his shoulder before Jos could secure the video recordings. Project Tom was the Sherwood Green task force.

"Doesn't hold a candle to the first one," Walt smiled. Jos scowled at the joke.

Someone had torched only a few cars and the building. The fighters had extinguished the car fires, but the fire crews struggled with the building blaze with several well-established fires. Police vehicles blocked the intersection and spread along the street.

Frank Langstaff was in animated conversation with uniformed officers. He had dressed casually and was in a good mood since they had found some evidence. This was in contrast to Sherwood Green's earlier clue free attacks.

Walt spotted graffiti on a building opposite the fire

"The writing's on the wall." Walt said.

"I'll ask Sherri to replace you." Jos laughed.

This fire was not at a Fukushima dealership. The franchise belonged to another Japanese company, Sun-Sun Engineering and Automotive. This was a struggling manufacturer, more at home building oil platforms than cars. Sun-Sun had been trying to get a foothold in the Canadian market, and the strange graffiti painted in garish bright yellow, not Lincoln green, raised questions.

"Stop the whales!" was the odd wording of one. Another was counter to Sherwood Green's message, *"Make cars in Canada."*

"I smell a rat." Walt panned the camera slowly over the graffiti and then focused on the fire. The flames had disappeared. Acrid smoke billowed from broken windows.

"I think we say this as a copycat, not Sherwood Green. I want to ask Langstaff." Jos headed across the street.

Langstaff loved to be on camera but said little. "We have found evidence that I hope leads to a terrorist. I have no more details."

In the greater scheme of things, the incident on Cherrywood Lane was more important to Sherwood Green. It was not the first such operation, but the violence was new. Sherwood Green's morality of not harming people did not apply to murderers. The harsh street court of the destitute neighbourhood had long before convicted the dead men. Everyone knew the murders they had committed and would have empathy for grieving families, but not the dead.

The SUV and the Honda headed north as the pair in the SUV fought to calm the adrenalin rush. Two corpses in the back seat did not help. A money filled hockey bag sat on top of the bodies.

"That was tough." The man in the right front seat gasped, and his stomach heaved.

"Hey don't throw up on me, man." The driver fought his nausea.

"Yah, I would leave my DNA all over this crate." The passenger took a sip from a water bottle. "I've done nothing like this in my life. These were bad dudes, but it makes us vigilantes. I used to believe in the law, but I guess we're right. The one punk killed the brother of a guy I knew. He ordered murders. The other guy would kill you for your coffee."

They had removed their ski masks and now looked innocent. The driver was white and clean shaven. It would not be out of keeping for him to own the dead men's Escalade. Their roles were purposeful. They did not want to be pulled over for the crime of driving while black. Police commonly harassed young black or Asian men driving expensive vehicles.

Everyone went by a nickname. The driver was Whitey. The rider was Sri Lankan ancestry, although he had been born in North York. His handle was Tiger, from his previous relationship to the rebel group that fought a long and bloody civil war in his parents' homeland.

Tiger had quit the organization, disillusioned by the tactics and racism of both sides in the war. Too many innocents had died. The Sri Lankan rebels had radicalized Tiger and made him a natural to help found the resistance. He led this money collecting cell.

They had dispersed all the original resistance founders into their own small cells. With four members, Tiger's cell was one of the larger ones. Most task cells only had three members, but, as in the successful Bay Street operation, they could combine two of these for special purposes. Tiger knew where to contact his three cell members and how to reach a contact in a cell at a higher level. He had known all the original founders but could contact no one but his coordinator. Three people made up the managing cell at the top that coordinated everything. All the cell leaders had last met a month before the first Fukushima attack to talk strategy. Everyone left that meeting ignorant of the tactical plan and it surprised them as much as the public when action began. Perhaps there was only one higher layer, but maybe more. Ignorance was safer.

Tiger's involvement began through a website that had since disappeared. It had been a blog discussing radical environmental solutions. A network of like-minded contributors had developed. In those days, the Canadian police did not take radical environmentalism seriously.

The blog led to casual meet-ups where discussions happened in off-line safety. Attendees only used first names and the wonderful flora of on-line monikers.

The blog compromised its owner, a university professor named MacDonald, with his identity attached to the website and every participant knew him. He identified potential leaders and guided them until they formed the resistance organization.

MacDonald had withdrawn from any contact well over two years ago. He concentrated on trying to radicalize his official students through an extension course on environmentalism. Under the guise of discussing competing views regarding appropriate action, he put such radical books as Deep Green Resistance on the syllabus. The sudden bursting of Sherwood Green on the scene had given him satisfaction. He believed Sherwood Green was his friend's organization, and once the SGSN appeared, he steered promising candidates to them. He looked forward to teaching the course in the next school year.

Tiger worked as a community organizer and found Whitey living on the street. During hours of discussions, sometimes late at night beside Whitey's rude street hovel, hot coffee steaming into the cold winter air, Tiger had realized his friend was good resistance material.

Whitey came to the streets after he flunked out of college. His father had disowned him. He was not an alcoholic or a drug addict, both of which would have disqualified him. The young man soon had a safe place to stay and new friends and purpose. Whitey and Tiger knew each other's real names, making them threats to each other if arrested. It was why they were in the same cell.

A black woman nicknamed Spike drove the Honda. She worked for one of the large railway corporations as a technician on the hazmat team. The others believed she had quit that job in disgust, but Spike still worked for the railway. She lied to reduce the risk. Her railway connection earned the nickname. Tiger would tease her, saying she was as hard as nails. Spike was tough.

Spike sought a radical group after being involved in a railway cover up of a toxic spill caused by a derailment. She could never make amends for that. Images of the discoloured vegetation and chemically burnt soil along with the floating dead fish in the little creek always motivated her. She knew the residents of the remote native community had never been told of the danger. The company and the government had fed them lies.

They discouraged personal discussions, and the members could only piece together each other's stories from isolated comments. Except for Whitey and Tiger, no one knew much about the others.

Tiger had cell phone numbers memorized, but they used coded messages disguised as sales calls on the phone. The codes set up rendezvous locations. Meeting places had codes such as "time share"; "world vision"; "Easter Seals" and "Food bank". The locations, restaurants, libraries or pubs, changed regularly, along with the code words.

The passenger in the car was the newest recruit. His nickname was Audio, a black man from Nova Scotia. His family had come as slaves with the 'United Empire Loyalists'. Audio had been told many stories of racism, suffering and hardship. His parent's had fared better by migrating to Ontario, but he was bitter.

Tiger wondered if Audio's emotions might make him unreliable, but his background had instilled a powerful motivation to change an old system. Audio worked as a car radio installer when Tiger met him. Audio had an intimate knowledge of hot wiring vehicles, even those with the latest security devices. Disabling GPS systems and other security circuits was another part of his expertise and made him a useful member. If he passed muster, Audio would move to another cell that needed his skills.

Audio brooded, but finally spoke as they crossed Highway 407.

"Did we have to kill those guys?"

Spike sighed. She didn't enjoy shooting. "Tiger knew those two. They murdered several people. The drugs they sold destroyed hundreds of lives."

"Maybe they deserved a trial." Audio stared out the window. Suburban wasteland retreated in the glare of sodium street lamps.

Spike glanced at Audio. She wondered if he was up to this kind of work. It must have been hard to help bag the bodies. Tiger had asked her to evaluate Audio. She would report this discussion.

"It must have been rough." She braked hard to avoid a sports car passing on the right and cutting in front into the left lane, speeding out of town.

"I hope the jerk in the Beemer doesn't attract the cops." She looked at Audio as they waited at a red light. "Do you think you can handle it?"

Audio stared back, "That isn't my problem. Punks like those give us blacks a bad rap. I felt nothing for those two. I enjoyed it too much."

It startled Spike, and Audio gave her something to think about. These assignments required action without hesitation. She decided they needed an open discussion of feelings, options and consequences before and after a violent operation. The technical planning that had gone into this job might not be enough. Spike also felt a mixture of disgust, fear and satisfaction.

"We need a group bull session."

"I think so." Audio became quiet.

The Honda turned off Bathurst onto King Road and then up Jane Street and deep into the countryside. Traffic moderately heavy traffic thinned and north of the Aurora

Road they saw no vehicles. Spike eased the car west to the end of a King Township side-road where it looped to an end in some trees.

The SUV stopped beside the car. They had no time to waste. Being with the vehicle increased their risk. Tiger pulled the weighty hockey bag from the back. Spike and Audio examined it carefully. They did not want blood stains connecting the stolen Honda to the SUV.

"I still think we should torch the Escalade." Spike hated leaving clues.

Tiger smiled at the thought. "We discussed it. The fire would attract attention too soon and wouldn't get rid of all the evidence, anyway. Make sure we've left nothing."

Spike persisted, "The guys who torched Fuck-U motors had a way to delay a fire. Too bad we don't."

"If you move to an attack unit, you'll get to use them." Tiger concentrated on the work in the SUV. "I've never been told how they do it."

Everyone wore gloves and Audio and Whitey searched the corpses. The fatal wounds were precise, small calibre shots to the heads. There had been little bleeding.

One of the dead men carried a handgun, while the other still clutched the small satchel of money they had picked up on Cherrywood Lane. They added it to the larger bag. The North York drug trade was lucrative. They left the men's personal effects, and the gun had probably committed murders. It stayed with the bodies. Spike locked the SUV and threw the keys into the trees, while the bag went into the trunk of the Honda.

Spike headed south on the 400, towards the city and stopped at a busy fast-food joint. She parked in a dimly lit spot, far from the surveillance cameras. Audio went to buy coffees. Spike and Tiger obscured the line of sight from the store, and Whitey went to work, changing the licence plates to the originals from the Honda. The plates they had used were genuine, for a matching car, registered to a fictitious person. The insurance and ownership papers given to Tiger from higher up were all genuine. They easily bought fake I.D. from the Hell's Angels who had infiltrated the police and the MTO. Once a fake driver's licence was in the Ministry of Transportation computer, they got everything else from Service Ontario and insurance brokers.

If the police recorded the information at a road stop, they would destroy the identification. Some of tonight's cash would buy identities.

They drove a few blocks, turned into a poorly lit side street and stopped behind a Chevy. Spike remained at the wheel while they transferred the hockey bag to the big car. She took the Honda around the corner and eased it to the curb where she had picked it up four hours earlier and left the key in the ignition. A specialized cell provided vehicles. She assumed they had stolen the Honda or changing plates would not have been necessary. She climbed into the Chevy's back seat.

After midnight, the team reached the safety of a small bungalow at the west end of the city. They rented the house using the fake identification and fraudulent credit card Spike carried. It was on land slated for condo development.

A broker, careless with details had handled the rental and had made a single call to a fictitious former landlord, Tiger, at a throwaway cell phone number. They used the address to create another phoney driver's licence, and the new I.D. got more credit cards.

Spike's phoney name had all of its addresses changed to the house. The place served for meetings and an overnight emergency shelter. Spike had her own place, under her real name, and did not live in the bungalow. No other Sherwood Green activists knew its location. All the cells had a similar safe house. They paid the monthly rental through the credit card and paid the balance each month using the on-line bank account set up with phoney I.D. Spike used the card occasionally to generate a broader profile of use, making purchases to set a precedent that would not raise alarms. If it ever became necessary to kill the fictitious identities and destroy the cards, she would max out the credit cards in a few cash withdrawals.

"We do not know how much is here." Tiger stared at the bag on the table and removed a pile of loose bills. This was fresh street money, and the dealers had not counted and bundled it. He counted out two thousand dollars and had barely touched the bag's contents.

"Put on gloves and run this through the washer's cold rinse cycle." He handed the bills to Audio. "We'll dry it on the carpet. I am sure there are drugs on it. I shake hands with druggies all the time so it doesn't matter, but you should stay as clean as possible."

Audio's face broke into a broad smile. Tiger growled, "I don't want to hear the money laundering joke."

It suddenly released the tension and everyone broke into teary laughter.

Tiger zipped up the hockey bag. "I'll drop this off higher up, and Spike, keep the two thousand operating stash somewhere safe."

It was late, and the team took the risky step of staying in the house until daybreak. They watched the late news and the first reports of the Sun-Sun fire excited them. Every member of Tiger's cell wanted to join an attack cell.

The four slept fitfully as the hours of tension and fear had taken their toll. None had ever killed, and the sounds of nightmares from one awakened them all, while, in their turn, they would disturb the others.

They found it necessary, over the following few weeks, to get together and discuss it all. In due course, the work of planning their next operation would displace this previous one from their minds.

Jos had an attack to report, but knew it was not the work of Sherwood Green. Frank Langstaff claimed they would soon arrest a terrorist. A tearful statement from the owner of the dealership followed the police interview. He said that sales had picked up and things looked positive.

In the afternoon following the attack on Sun-Sun Motors, Langstaff announced the arrest of Tony Sorda. Spray cans found at the scene held his fingerprints. He had cut his hand and DNA evidence confirmed him as the arsonist. Tony was a middle-aged, broken down alcoholic who had been in and out of jail. His several convictions included five years for torching an abandoned historic building that had stood in the way of developers.

"Sherwood Green is desperate if they hired Sorda to do the job. We have them on the run." Langstaff planned a "perp-walk," at Old City Hall court.

The case for terrorism crumbled as Sorda confessed at his bail hearing. He implicated the franchisee. The owner wanted to declare bankruptcy and hoped insurance would cover his losses.

Frank passed the case over to the arson squad and hid from the press for some time. He had not built his career on carelessness. He blamed the pressure of daily phone calls from the mayor. He would not make this mistake again.

As if to mock the police, on the night of the Sorda court fiasco, fire destroyed a Fukushima dealership well east of corporate headquarters. Sherwood Green had clearly done this attack, but it lay beyond Toronto police jurisdiction and involved the Durham regional force. The Ontario Provincial Police now had four different jurisdictions to coordinate.

Lost in all the sensation of the arrests and fresh attacks, York police found two gang members dead in their SUV. No one seemed to care about two murdered "bad guys" as no innocent people had died.

The next afternoon, gunfire killed two members of the Knights in front of a pizza shop, and the attackers fled in a silver Honda.

Chapter Eleven

Jos Amiel stumbled from the elevator and stared down the well-lit corridor. He headed right and soon leaned on his apartment door, fumbling for the lock. After a few tries, he succeeded and raised his arm in drunken victory.

Debbie's excellent wine had a lot of kick. They had shared a large bottle over several hours of loving and talking. She had invited Jos to her home. Debbie's husband was out of town. Jos felt satisfied and eager for his own bed.

Jos stumbled into the darkness. He slipped on crumpling paper, and he fell against the wall. He fumbled for the light switch and after several tries, retrieved a large envelope from the floor. Jos slumped onto his old chesterfield and fell asleep staring at the envelope.

His alarm clock buzzing in the bedroom woke Jos. Sunshine streamed through the window. He felt miserable.

Something fell onto the floor. Jos remembered arriving home, and the sealed envelope. He sat bolt upright and stared at the apartment door. The landlord had installed tight seals to keep smoke out of the apartments. No one could slip the package through so had opened the door.

Jos crept about his apartment, reliving old fears. He fought off the temptation to call 911, but held his cell-phone ready, finger on the panic button. He relaxed once he found all rooms and closets clear.

Jos cleared his head with a large cold orange juice.

He slit the envelope open and shook the contents, a stapled sheaf of papers and a single folded sheet of printer paper onto the wooden coffee table. The document had the Metropolitan Toronto Police letterhead. The title said Sherwood Green: Objectives and threat analysis, addressed to Frank Langstaff with a blacked out circulation list and marked *Confidential*. He saw an unsigned typed note.

From now on, this is the only way I will communicate with you. It is too dangerous now to call on your phone. You got too close to Arsenault, and they are tracking you.

Jos frowned and examined his cell-phone, but he knew of no way they could tap it and concluded the best the police could do was to hack his call list. He had no secret contacts. Jos thought the snitch was a cop.

They don't name you directly, the message continued, *but the media sources mentioned include TNN. Be careful.*

Jos decided he and Walt should copy their stuff outside of the studio. If there was anything he didn't want others to see, they could delete it from the network material. It would be illegal, but that didn't bother him. There were already statements from Diane and others to hide from the police.

Langstaff received this document today. Never refer to it. Only a few people know about it. It is clean, but burn it. If they discover you have a copy, they will look for me. I hope the information is useful.

Jos sipped his juice. He was eager to read the report, but thought about the motives of this nameless police renegade. The voice on the phone had not sounded like a rookie, and Jos thought he was a senior cop. Perhaps he was on that hidden circulation list.

Is he a supporter of Sherwood Green, Langstaff's job or has some grievance?

Jos' questions had no answers. The traitor cop might be a police sting. His apartment break-in upset him. He sipped reheated coffee and opened the document.

They wrote it in stilted jargon that detailed the attacks by Sherwood Green and said the electrical explosions were terrorism. The cover-up originated with the mayor.

The next pages analyzed Sherwood Green and the posters and pamphlets from them and the SGSN.

The police considered Sherwood Green an organization, not an individual; however, it advocated publicly claiming the opposite. They thought the public would hate a person more than a group. Jos recalled the Bernstein Brigade. The author estimated Sherwood Green had only six members based on the belief that more would have betrayed each other, and, so far, there had been no leaks, leaving the members of Sherwood Green unknown.

They speculated on how the terrorists got money, with the conclusion their public supporters must be funnelling money. They seemed enthusiastic that this might be the way to capture the criminals and arrest people supporting terrorism. The new Canadian terrorist law was a powerful tool to detain people with no proper trial.

A few pages talked about the Sherwood Green Support Network with a complete list of members and their biographies, although some names had no additional information. It disappointed the author none of the members had a criminal record. The paper listed bank account and credit card numbers. The language was contemptuous of Diane and her comrades.

It mentioned sources with few details, but it startled Jos with a reference to new infiltration and surveillance efforts and *several unnamed additional sources from outside the department.*

Not me or my friends, Jos thought.

They would interrogate the three leaders at the first excuse. The conclusion said that some of the support network members had to be part of Sherwood Green, and this would be the best way to capture a perpetrator. Getting this information would have required search warrants. Jos would let Diane know.

"There is a suspicious, close relationship between some members of the media and terrorist supporters."

Jos was not the only suspect. Several reporters of rival media organisations had filed balanced stories, but Jos now knew that they had him under surveillance.

The section on objectives and threat analysis reached the conclusion that: *"... they want to destroy all industry and the city of Toronto itself. There is every sign they want to avoid unnecessary personal injury. This distinguishes them from our traditional religious terrorists. Either the Garza woman was an innocent bystander, or she was a terrorist caught in her own blast. No link exists, but the FBI and the Mexican authorities are engaged. Several of Garza's acquaintances are now members of the SGSN."*

With the short-term threat they had too many targets to cover. Potential objectives filled several pages, with details of steps being taken to protect them.

The author worried about the transportation and energy systems, noting the inner-city attack showed sophistication with expert knowledge of the electrical distribution system. Some public had sympathy for the group because, *"... they only attacked foreign corporations and the rich."*

We conclude they will continue to attack Fukushima Corporation and the downtown financial core, but they are not large enough to threaten the city. The one attack in London was probably a copycat effort, perhaps by local racists. Toronto should implement extra visible police presence, and every Fukushima dealership and corporate facility should be under constant guard. This is our best hope for capturing the terrorists.

The last paragraph appealed for more resources, officers and money. Jos realized this was not only a briefing paper for Frank Langstaff, but a supporting document for a police budget request to the city. It was for the mayor's eyes. This would explain the missing names of informants and readers. He wished he had a copy of the appendix, *cost details to date.* The amount must be large.

Jos intended to call Diane. He sat for a moment with the phone in his hand, thinking about the references to surveillance and the warning from his unknown snitch. His memory of the dash through the subway with Diane decided the matter. He would call from a payphone and decide what information to pass on. Despite liking her, Jos was not sure he supported Diane enough to give her a copy.

Jos had little time to recover from his night of fun. The workday saw him thrust into the reaction to the latest attack upon Fukushima Motors. He enjoyed a fresh pot of coffee while watching the network morning show. It consisted mostly of empty chatter about celebrities and sports, but it had a segment called "Breakfast Hash," where they read e-mails, tweets and input from other social media on air. Apart from the inane fascination with the power of the twitter-verse, the content almost divided evenly between a celebrity's drunk driving and the attack on Fukushima. This trend continued in the call-in segment.

One woman, a Fukushima employee, said, "I work late and Sherwood Green might attack. I'm quitting."

Jos' cell rang. Sheri Stein wasted no time in greetings. "We have a Fukushima employee who just called in and says she is quitting because of fear. She'll be here at eleven, so see me at ten thirty."

Stein sounded harried and hung up. *She must be getting flak from above.*

Callers referred to Sherwood Green. Sheri had received angry calls from her boss.

"Here's a list of questions." Sheri slipped a typed page across her desk. "Do you have any to add?"

"I see I can name Sherwood Green." Jos said.

"Everyone else is doing it, and callers and tweeters are uncontrollable. If we don't go along, the public will go elsewhere. The sponsors will be happy at the ratings."

Sheri's comment reminded Jos news was a money-driven business and had to pander to the public.

"One more thing." Sheri hesitated. This was rare for her. "This chick seems like a bit of a flake and... racist. She heard you would do the interview and asked for Faye."

Faye and Grant were the two morning show hosts and popular for their light banter and silliness. The serious journalists sarcastically referred to them as Bimbo and Bobby. Jos had more sympathy. The two were well-trained television journalists, but jobs were scarce.

"I told her you were our terrorist reporter, and it was your show. Being on television and famous is stronger than her bigotry. Faye will show her around the station, and especially the celebrity wall."

The attractive woman sat in a comfortable leather chair as Jos eased into his own plush seat.

"What do you do at Fukushima Motors?"

"I work the evening shift in data-processing. We enter information into the business system."

"How long have you worked at Fukushima?"

"Three years, on contract."

"Did you start right out of high school?" The girl looked young, and it was a low-level job.

"No!" She seemed offended. "I graduated with honours from York with a psychology degree. I hoped to be hired full time, but that won't happen now. They have great wages and benefits, lots of perks, too."

"Why do you say it won't happen now?"

"Sherwood Green has made me quit my job."

"Why?"

"I work at night. I'm scared. There are cops everywhere. The company told us they would protect us, but the big shot hasn't been at the office in weeks. He's working from home. Coward! What if Sherwood Green kills us?"

Jos felt sorry for the woman. She had likely made it impossible to continue working at Fukushima. *Never publicly criticize the boss.*

"How do the other employees feel?"

"They're all scared. The higher mucky-mucks are all Japanese, so they have no choice." Jos caught a racist hint. He no longer worried about her lost job.

"Do you think Sherwood Green will kill anyone?"

"He killed that Mexican chick, didn't he?" Jos had not intended to relate the Fukushima attacks to the hydro blasts, but now he had an opening. Perhaps he could expose that terrorist attack, since the woman had planted the idea in people's minds.

"You think Sherwood Green did that one?"

"What else? I saw a report that said they did," the woman did not remember Jos was the reporter. "It isn't like she didn't deserve it. She was illegal and probably a terrorist. You know those Mexican drug-dealing murderers?"

"Her friends say she was innocent."

"Everyone can fake that stuff. They are lying to us about the whole thing being an accident. She didn't pay taxes, not like me. I was getting minimum wages, too."

"Well, she was getting less than minimum wage. A Canadian boss skimmed all the money."

The woman frowned. Jos marvelled at how widespread racism was, even if most people denied their racism. He recalled bigoted classmates.

Jos extracted more details about the fear and stress within the Fukushima organization and more racist hostility towards the Japanese managers. The camera captured a close-up showing her fear. Her face would become an iconic image in a new version of the *Terrorism Toronto* introduction. Faye took their guest to see the morning show set. Jos searched out Sheri.

"Great interview, Jos," Sheri was genuinely pleased. "I will cut the bit about the Garza woman out."

"Why?"

"Garza did not die in a terrorist attack, and it isn't part of the story. We don't want speculation, and besides, she was racist."

"I thought we showed it was likely a terrorist effort that blew the electrics; and the racist comments reveal her character flaws."

"The story isn't about her. We want viewers to be sympathetic. Her racism would reduce the impact."

"We know Sherwood Green did it." Jos almost blurted out he knew the police thought it was terrorism.

"Officially, they didn't." Stein handed Jos a sheet of paper. "Here's your opening for the interview."

Jos read over the typed script. "There is no evidence that Sherwood Green is racist. I can't read this." He tossed the paper onto the desk. The script implied that Sherwood Green was anti-Japanese and racist. The segment on Garza would not have fit that message.

"It doesn't matter what you think." Sheri rose to look Jos in the eye and pushed the paper back to him. "This came from above. The discussion is closed. I can get someone else. You can go back to being a night reporter."

The threat was real. It would end Jos' career.

"Jos, I agree with you, but…" her voice trailed off.

Jos' censored interview was mild compared to the vitriol that saturated the radio call-in shows. Racist and especially anti-Japanese callers deluged Bert Boyce radio show. One of the favourite racist conspiracy theories had the company staging the attacks to claim insurance and raise sales. The Sun-Sun Motors arson inspired this. The callers could not comprehend the insurance terms about terrorism or remember the Sun-Sun affair had turned into a disaster for the businessman.

One caller, a steward in the auto union, claimed, "Jap cars are costing us jobs." Although the auto union disowned the caller, they had begun an advertising campaign that was anti-Asian under the guise of "Buy Canadian." In the slick television version of their advertisement, an image of Canadian war graves in Hong Kong flashed briefly onto the screen and made the message clear. The ad sparked the vandalism of foreign cars.

On air, Jos asked, "Does Sherwood Green regret the racist consequences of these actions or was that the intent?"

He would ask Diane Arsenault the same question.

Chapter Twelve

Despite a rainy Thursday morning, a large crowd dressed in the corporate uniform of dark suit and tie and prim skirt suits, watched twenty demonstrators march in front of the main entrance of the largest Canadian bank, the British Trans-Colonial. The bank would announce record profits, and Emilia Garza had cleaned their building.

Placards criticized the bank's labour policies, and that most of its profit came from tar sands loans. With the rising price of crude oil, almost every company related to the industry had soaring profits. Several signs called for an end to industrial society.

Joe led the contingent from the Sherwood Green Support Network. Jos and Walt positioned themselves on the opposite side of King Street, where they could capture the complete scene. In fluorescent rain gear with the network and sponsor logos, they stood out from the watching crowd sheltering beneath umbrellas.

"This is boring picket-line stuff. All we're going to see is umbrellas." The problems the intermittent showers created frustrated Walt. He thought of the dozens of picket lines he had recorded, all looking the same.

A work crew used a ladder to reach the marquee above the entranceway to a posh eatery. After negotiations, Walt stood high above the street to capture high angle footage to intermix with street-level shots.

"I'll come down later to do headshots."

Jos barely heard his partner through the chanting and approaching sirens and searched for people to interview. None of the bystanders had promise. Casually dressed pedestrians watched for a while and moved on. Jos thought a couple of men in expensive leather jackets were stock traders being macho. They might look good on screen.

Predictable on-street interviews fit into the media philosophy of making citizens part of the story. People wanted their few minutes of fame.

A new group rounded the corner, moving in coordination beneath a forest of red and yellow flags, with the face of Leon Trotsky fluttering in the swirling wind. The group was the Socialist Advocacy and Defence, S.A.D. They had been active on campus when Jos was a student, but never attracted much support. Their message did not connect everyone's reality.

With parade-ground precision, the group neatly attached itself to the line of demonstrators. Trotskyites liked to coat-tail on another group's event.

New chants of, "free the slaves," "kill the capitalist pigs" and "means of production to the workers" seemed at odds with the SGSN demand for the end of industrialism.

The street had remained open, with the demonstrators staying on the sidewalk; however, police cars blocked off King Street and trapped a lone streetcar. The police soon let it through and cleared all traffic from the street. A police sergeant strode toward the picketers, heading for the Trotskyites. Diane and Joe moved quickly to intercept.

Jos heard an agreement to confine the demonstration to the sidewalk. As the officer turned away, the S.A.D. cohort chanted: "Pig, pig, pig". The cop called for back-up.

The crowd of spectators on the far side of the street stepped onto the road led by the two leather-clad men who Jos decided were cops ready to help the uniforms.

Jos retreated. Despite their taunting chants, the Trotskyites made no move towards the police.

With a loud, rhythmic drumbeat two dozen riot police, faces hidden by visors, marched around the corner. The sound of boots echoing from the skyscrapers joined the thumping of ugly black night-sticks against large plastic shields. They stopped in the middle of the street, facing the demonstrators, feet apart, batons and shields at the ready.

The onlookers retreated onto the sidewalk. Some picketers looked nervous and Jos felt intimidated. The chanting flag-wavers turned their attention to the riot squad; their loud vulgarity drowned out the SGSN.

The quick arrival of the riot squad surprised Jos. It appeared they wanted a fight. When the city hosted the G-20 summit, the police had instigated confrontations and inflamed others. These contrived actions justified police attacks, blaming the resulting violence on lawless anarchists. A terrified population eagerly surrendered legal rights for security. It was an old game.

The police could not make any progress against Sherwood Green and wanted a public demonstration of strength. The elite demanded action, and without a terrorist to arrest, they aimed to intimidate the terrorist supporters.

The onlookers expected excitement. Chants from the SGSN called the banks criminal organizations and industrialism, ecocide. A member of SGSN thrust a pamphlet into Jos' hand. Walt captured it all, so when one of the young people tried to hand a leaflet to one of the leather-clad men, the man's hard punch to the woman's breast on video. She fell and, as some of the surrounding crowd moved to help her, the cop stepped hard on the victim's hand. The woman's screams echoed above the chants.

The cop quickly turned away and took up a position at the far edge of the crowd beside a uniformed officer, and both men laughed at the hurt woman.

The sudden attack shocked Jos. He had never seen police brutality and had discounted reports of cop violence, but now Jos wished he had two camera units so he could confront the man.

Sheri Stein would cut the incident out of *Terrorism-Toronto*, and Jos would lose another argument with his boss.

Twenty masked people dressed in black appeared from nowhere and ran into the middle of the picket line. More than one group wanted to hijack the event.

Hushed expectancy settled over the onlookers as the SGSN demonstrators and the Trotskyites eyed the new arrivals. The riot police raised batons in unison, while the sergeant in charge frantically radioed for more backup. The masked group and the riot police lusted for a fight.

The people in masks hurled bottles and rocks at the police, and their chants and taunts were not much different from those of the Trotskyites.

Jos eased over near the pair of cops who had been laughing at the injured girl and could overhear the officer's radio. Police waited for reinforcements, and the cops discussed how to draw both the SGSN people and the onlookers into a fight. They wanted to discredit the SGSN while battering the anarchists and the Trotskyites.

"It would suit me to whack a few of these terrorists' heads," laughed the uniformed officer.

Police blocked the sidewalk at both ends and boxed in the demonstrators. Jos pulled out his press pass, stepped off the curb and headed towards the sergeant. He wanted to warn Diane.

"Where do you think you are going, buddy?" A hand clamped firmly onto Jos' shoulder and spun him around to face a uniformed cop. Jos flashed his press pass.

"I want to talk to the Sarge." Jos smiled despite the painful grip on his shoulder.

"Get back on the sidewalk." He shoved Jos away. "You reporter jerks make us look bad."

Another shove made the point. Jos hoped Diane understood the danger. There was no time to react.

A second squad of riot police ran up. Without pause or warning, the combined group moved into the demonstrators. A line of uniformed police formed in front of the onlookers, making it hard to see the fight.

Simultaneously, several constables went into the crowd and grabbed the pamphleteers, including the woman trembling in pain in the restaurant doorway. They dragged everyone to paddy-wagons.

On the far side of the street, the police surrounded and beat black-clad demonstrators and dragged them to the ground with their hands tied behind their backs. The Trotskyites did not fare any better. Police boots trampled their banners. Superior police numbers overwhelmed the demonstrators.

The SGSN group tried to withdraw, but ran up against the line of uniformed police. The violence was not as severe as what the riot squad dished out, but the cops manhandled them into paddy-wagons.

Cheers from some onlookers mixed with the sounds of blows, curses, and defiant anti-police chants from many of those on the pavement. Boots and batons struck bound prisoners. The action lasted about ten minutes.

Meanwhile, police officers confronted reporters, trying to block their cameras. Several private citizens had their cell-phones smashed to the ground and boots crushed some devices. The police knew the less the video, the better.

Walt, recorded from his high vantage point and kept a low profile. He blended in with the two workers on the roof. When he climbed down the ladder, he concealed the camera beneath his jacket. The police carted off those arrested but still blocked the street.

Jos and Walt used their press passes to get into the restaurant, although the doors, hastily locked at the beginning of the conflict, opened reluctantly. The price of admission was an on-camera interview with the day manager who spouted an anti-demonstration diatribe. Jos and Walt passed through the kitchen and out the back door.

"Did you see the kitchen?" Walt said. "Talk about filth. The CBC has been digging up dirt on restaurants and sloppy health inspectors," Jos led his partner down the alley. "I'll let Raj over there know about this place. That manager pissed me off, but we have to get to the cop shop."

As Jos and Walt approached the fortress of 52 Division, a sobbing young woman limped out, holding her damaged hand upright.

"Can we help?" Walt readied his camera, but did not record. The young woman looked dazed.

"I… I need to get to the hospital,"

Jos was about to offer her a ride when a young constable hurried from the building. Walt prepared his camera, thinking there might be trouble.

"You wait here." The constable said to the girl. The cop's voice had the uncertainty of a rookie. "I'll get my cruiser and run you over to St. Mike's." The young man noticed Walt shooting. "Don't film me." He commanded. "This is unofficial. I don't want to be on TV."

Walt continued to record. The officer and the car disappeared with the girl.

"I got his badge number if this turns out bad," Jos pocketed his notebook.

"It's all on record." Walt smiled. "If it is legit, we won't leave this footage at the studio. It wouldn't do for the cop to be seen helping the enemy."

Jos wondered if Sheri considered him a sympathizer and his career in danger. An objective reporter and a caring cop shared risks.

They speculated about good constables and considered it too simplistic that all cops bad. Jos had not told Walt about his insider contact. Perhaps his informer was simply an altruistic member of the force.

A gruff corporal finally told the reporters they had transported the prisoners for arraignment in front of a Justice of the Peace and the pair hurried to Old City Hall.

They climbed the well-worn stairs, past milling crowds of people charged with prostitution or drunk driving. Nervous chatter echoed from the vaulted ceilings. The SGSN members sat on hard wooden benches outside the JP's office, under the watch of a bored constable.

The police court guards were all older individuals with no stripes. Unaggressive, un-ambitious constables relegated to routine duties. The guard did not interfere with the reporters. They added variety to his workday.

Melissa accompanied each prisoner in and out of the hearing room. As they exited, Melissa showed a paper to the guard to prove they had released the client. Diane Arsenault, dishevelled, with a welt on her left cheek passed through the routine and approached Jos.

"They just wanted our fingerprints this time." Diane sounded cynical, but relieved "They charged us with causing a disturbance, so no big deal."

"I worried you got hurt." Jos stared at the welt on her face.

"They threw us into the wagon, hard. Everyone got a little bruised. Not enough to cry brutality but enough to hurt." She rubbed her cheek and winced. "They hurt Jackie a lot worse but didn't charge her. They kicked her out the front door of 52 and she went to Emergency. I would guess she's still there. I have to go see her, but want everyone through here first."

"She came out of 52 when we got there. A cop drove her to St. Mike's, or so he said. We'll go with you to interview her. We have that cop attacking her on video."

"Can we get a copy? We could charge the cop."

"It will be on the evening news; record it." Walt could not conceive Sheri would cut such a dramatic video.

The material they shot at the hospital would be a dramatic ending to the news item. Jackie was a small girl in her late teens and her expression of pain and hand in a cast added impact.

The young cop had made sure the receptionist had registered her; however, she had waited for hours to be examined. In response to a video crew, a nurse took her into the examining room shortly after the interview.

Jos had given up arguing with Sheri over her censorship. It frustrated him more when she praised the work as some of the best she had ever seen. She would not risk airing the assault on Jackie, claiming legal issues, and she did not want to make the police the bad guys and create sympathy for terrorists.

Jos and Walt copied the contents of Walt's camera onto a memory stick, adding it to the video from the start of the terrorist campaign. The content belonged to the network, but now it would not disappear. Jos made a copy for Diane.

In the evening, an internet war occurred between the Sherwood Green Support Network, the Trotskyites and anarchists. Sherwood Green e-mailed a statement to the media and the radical organisations.

Do not directly fight the police, army or other petty servants of the elite. They aren't the target. Go for the jugular.

Posters appeared in the downtown core. Hackers subverted censorship by posting the message and the Sherwood Green manifesto on media websites. The Metro Police and City of Toronto suffered the same attacks. The SGSN quoted the press release in an open letter to anarchist and socialist groups imploring them to change their tactics.

Considering ecosystem collapse, socialism is as useless as rearranging the deckchairs on a sinking ship. Centralized socialism requires the continuation of industrialism.

Angry rebuttals called the SGSN "bourgeois lackeys" and "eco-fascists", but after the war of words ended, several members of other groups joined the SGSN, and stimulated a resistance political party to run in the city election. The downside would be a some factionalism inside the SGSN.

Chapter Thirteen

"What the hell is going on?" Jos and Walt ran a half dozen blocks towards the King and Bay Street intersection, fighting throngs of office workers hurrying in the opposite direction. The frantic events of this Friday would take Jos off the scale of exhaustion.

Police vehicles, fire trucks and the bomb cart crowded King Street, at the site of the conflict with protestors the previous day. The reporters joined the throng of media held well away from the front entrance of the headquarters of the British Trans-Colonial Bank. Police escorted stragglers from the building. Firemen and police rushed in and out. Someone made a bomb threat against the bank.

"Is this connected to yesterday's demo?" Jos joined in the speculation amongst the media crowd.

"It seems suspicious." A Toronto Star reporter looked expectantly across the street. "They told me an hour ago they would make a statement soon, so far, nothing." "A few minutes ago, some cops ran towards the stock exchange. We heard more sirens over there. This is growing."

"The stock exchange," Jos exclaimed. "If that's closed, it'll be a big thing. It's after lunch when the smart guys are setting up their bets for the weekend."

A cop approached the press.

"I know you have deadlines," the press officer smiled. "I'll give you a summary." He knew how to play reporters. Despite their deadlines, he increased anticipation. The cop read a prepared statement.

"There are two direct threats. One is against this bank and its branches. The second is against the stock exchange made about an hour ago. It might be a copycat, but we take it seriously and evacuated both locations."

"We located a device inside this building. The Explosive Disposal Unit will deal with it. There are suspicious packages all over the building. It's tense in there. We are keeping our people safe above all else. When something happens, I'll let you know."

Crackling on his radio interrupted. He inserted an ear piece and frowned. He looked at the reporters, somewhat shaken. "There are reports of explosions in the underground concourse between here and Queen Street. We are evacuating it."

The reporters rushed towards the entrance to the underground shopping that ran north, four kilometres from the Union Station to College Street. In the heat of July it became a crowded, air-conditioned refuge.

"There's no smoke." Walt recorded yellow police tape stretched between steel banisters as constables stood guard.

"Nothing big here that we know of," a young cop gave in to the constant questioning. "Mobs of people ran out screaming about explosions. The guys are searching. No, you can't go in."

An enormous bang came from the direction of the bank. The reporters reversed to the more promising sound.

The events filled the evening news, but gave few facts. Jos' most exciting sequence showed the bomb squad destroying a bag with their robotic shot gun only to reveal someone's abandoned lunch.

All evening, Jos and the other reporters raced to false alarms. By midnight there had been three announced and postponed news briefings. At two in the morning, they assembled with a bleary-eyed Frank Langstaff.

"We discovered three devices in the offices of the British Trans-Colonial Bank." Langstaff implied he had done the work. "None contained explosive. Each had working timers and wiring, but with dummy charges."

"One was in the lobby; one was in a public area on the twenty-third floor, next to the offices of the brokerage firm of Dorchester and Smyth. The third," Langstaff paused dramatically, "was in the executive suite of the bank, inside the security doors, in a briefcase left beside the desk of the executive assistant to the head of tar sands investments. Unfortunately, there is no video surveillance in that exact location, but every door has a high-definition camera. I'm shocked a person could get into the innermost offices without arousing suspicion."

"We found no devices in the stock exchange; however, there was a computer attack on the trading platform and the exchange froze at two thirty-three in the afternoon."

"Finally, someone spread explosive material in the shopping concourse. The situation was never life-threatening, but it terrified people. They painted contact explosive on surfaces, handles and even dripped over the floors. When dry, they exploded when touched. The panic trampled two people, and they were in the hospital. We also found dummy bombs in trashcans."

Frank Langstaff gathered up his papers and faced the tired reporters. His glare of disgust and anger would feature prominently in Jos' report. Frank spoke with genuine emotion.

"These bastards have to be stopped. Today cost millions, and hurt people. I have everyone working overtime." He glowered directly into the dozen television cameras. "We'll get you bastards. It's only a matter of time. You can't terrorize my city. I'll get you."

Chapter Fourteen

Charlie Dodge stared through the smoked glass of his city hall window. He enjoyed his view of the public plaza and the normally peaceful early mornings. The plain, concrete plaza roofed the parking garage. Mature trees broke austere lines of the elevated walkway surrounding the plaza. Banners hung from the railings exhorting citizens to support the "Public Way" fund drive. Kiosks dotted the central space, sharing the square with a Henry Moore abstract bronze statue. Along the southern edge, near Queen Street, sat the reflecting pool and winter ice rink; the glass-smooth water reflected the glow of what should have been a pleasant Monday morning.

This would be a tough day. Dodge watched smoke pour from the entrance to the parking garage beyond the trees. A light breeze pushed acrid haze between the City Hall's two curved office towers and over the saucer-like dome of the council chamber. Red fire trucks blocked Queen Street. A street car tried to reverse, but irate car drivers would not cooperate.

Firemen opened the door to a stairway into the garage. Black smoke forced them to pause before a team of two disappeared down the stairs.

The mayor ignored the incessant clang of the fire alarm. He smelt no smoke but refused to leave as he fielded urgent calls from the fire and police commanders and building supervisors. Dodge was no hero, but his office was the temporary coordination point.

In what now seemed a stupid decision, the city had located the emergency coordination on the ground floor of the east tower behind the library. Emergency personnel had evacuated along with everyone else, but Dodge waited for word that they had made a mobile command centre operational before he would leave. Police setup their command centre on University Avenue, obscured by the Osgood Law building. Charlie hoped this was only a small fire, but the volume of smoke suggested otherwise. He retreated to answer his phone.

"Good news and bad news," the deputy fire chief sounded calm, as if this were a routine call. "There are only about three cars burning on level two. Probably electrical failure caused it. We'll know once we can get the fire out. Our guys can't get too close yet because of the heat. The bad news is, the fire is at the back of the level, and we need to run a three-inch line down the rear stairs about a hundred meters from the site. We sent two pumper crews there to fog their way to the fire. We vented from the entrance and the outside stairways. We hope to keep the smoke out of the towers, but you should get out."

"I'm waiting for them to activate the command post on University and I'll go there. Let me know if I need to move sooner, but I…" The deputy chief cut off the mayor and he heard shouting in the background.

"Sorry, I have to go. I'll call back in a minute. Some new emergency has come up." Dodge returned to stare at the smoke, which seemed to be heavier. The phone rang.

"Sorry about that," the deputy chief sounded agitated. "There is smoke in the subway system, and it looks deliberate." The man paused and Dodge heard him talking to an unknown person. "My god, it has spread along the Yonge Line at York Mills, west and east on the Bloor line." He paused again. "Now they report smoke at the Museum station, and the trains pushed it everywhere. I've ordered an evacuation."

The wall clock said a quarter past seven, peak transit load. He grimaced at the enormity of the human flood about to hit the streets.

"How many trains have stopped between stations?" Dodge did not want to think about it as a second line flashed.

"Let me know as soon as the evacuation is done." The mayor hit the flashing button.

"Davisville here," an agitated woman had called from the TTC operations centre. "Mayor, we powered off in the complete subway system."

"Are the trains all in stations?" Dodge asked. The woman hesitated and searched for information.

"We have a dozen in the tunnels, but well away from smoke. The operators report all clear, and if the passengers don't panic, we will walk them to the next safe platform. The smoke is coming from external ventilation shafts, and we aren't sure about fires."

"Enter!" the mayor responded to a loud knock. "Let me know when you know." Dodge cradled the handset.

"Mayor," a fireman equipped with respirator but the facemask not in place stood at the door. "Get out, now; one of the car's gas tanks exploded. Now, eight cars are burning."

"Anyone hurt?" Dodge pushed the call forward button and grabbed his cell phone and laptop. His cell would stay connected. He smelt smoke.

"Not any of our guys, but there are maybe a dozen civilians with smoke inhalation at St. Mikes. We have withdrawn from the level where the cars are burning, and the chief decided we will let them burn out. We're searching, but the garage seems empty."

He hurried off while Dodge made his way behind the civic buildings and reached the command trailer ten minutes later. Chief Heron, in casual clothes, shouted into his cell.

"I don't give a shit what they're saying," Dodge wondered who they might be. "This is terrorism. I want Tom going full bore."

The reference to Tom caught the mayor's attention. The code for the terrorist response would release enormous resources. Even without it, there had been a massive response. Toronto had already spent millions. Dodge shuddered at the amount. He would have to borrow more money, and it was election year, so there would be opposition. Someone had shown him an estimate that the Tom force would cost an extra ten thousand an hour for as many hours as it might be on alert, and they had activated the response twice in a few weeks. Instead of a quiet summer, he faced an election-year budget fight at Council. The chief waved the mayor over.

"The smoke came from six subway air shafts. They poured diesel and gasoline through the grates and ignited it all. We'll know as soon as fire can make it safe and we get to the sites, but so far it's only smoke. The commissions will get the system running in a few hours."

"Chief," an officer stuck his head out of the door to the command post, "we have a fresh problem. A train caught fire in Union and another in St. George stations, and they are burning hot. Fire has no trucks available downtown."

Dodge and Heron hurried into the trailer, where an electronic map of the city displayed blue and red dots marking police and fire units. Each subway station stood out as masses of dots, as did several locations between some stops. City hall square was awash with colour, and yellow blinking dots showed fire units being brought to standby.

"We're getting fire support from Mississauga, Vaughn and Durham. Hamilton is on standby." The young constable placed letters on the screen at the sites of the two train fires. As they watched, the officer stiffened and added a third marker at the York Mills station, and then a fourth at Wellesley.

"We're under siege." Chief Heron sounded defeated.

"Don't be sensational with the media." Dodge stared at the display panel while Heron answered his cell phone.

"Orillia just called." Heron stared at his handset for an instant as if digesting some more news. "The OPP coordination centre has received word from the FBI there has been an attack on the New York subway system similar to ours, and they think it's coordinated."

Except for TorontoNewsNow, all the local media only covered the New York situation. Canadian networks used exciting video feed from the USA with voiceovers by local reporters. They referred to, "a situation in Toronto that has yet to be confirmed". These organizations had no video from their home city and downplayed the story.

Jos broadcast live from in front of City Hall, trying to talk to firemen, and as the men did not know that this might be a terrorist attack, they talked freely. The appearance of a police spokesperson, hastily dispatched by Heron to control the media, led to a confrontation as Jos tried to fight the censorship, and the cop ignored his questions about gagging firefighters and read a statement.

"The subway is full of smoke, but it isn't serious. They turned off the power." She didn't mention train fires.

Sheri dispatched a crew to the TTC operations centre. TNN reported live on the Toronto situation, and soon the other local broadcasters followed suit.

Nothing new happened at city hall, so Jos followed the spokeswoman to the mobile command center.

A sizeable crowd milled about the gleaming white trailer. Reporters joined a growing crowd of lawyers, city workers and ordinary citizens on their way to work. A mobile canteen vendor eagerly set up on the corner, while a dozen uniformed officers guarded the command post.

"I guess reporters are dangerous." Walt laughed.

Dodge and Heron appeared on the steel porch and reminded Jos of when politicians campaigned by rail and spoke to crowds from the rear of railway coaches.

Sherwood Green is making history run backwards. Jos thought. *This has to be a Sherwood Green attack.*

The mayor shouted, "We have a dangerous problem this morning. I want to assure everyone," he smiled into the television cameras, "things are under control and we'll soon have everything back to normal. Chief Heron will give the details."

Dodge did not like speaking without carefully prepared notes. He depended on his key advisor standing nearby and whispering cues, but today he was on his own and hesitant. Too many Toronto mayors had shot from the lip and not survived the consequences, but Dodge's experience in corporations had trained him to speak while saying little.

Charlie ignored the shouted questions. He used the art, perfected by the Canadian Prime Minister, to announce good news and to leave the bad for his underlings.

Chief Heron gripped the steel railing and looked less imposing in sweat pants, windbreaker, and baseball cap.

"Here's what has happened during the past," he glanced at his wristwatch, "hour. At six forty this morning, an automatic fire alarm tripped on level two of the city hall parking garage, sprinklers activated and fire units responded. As in all cases of fire at city hall, they issued an immediate second alarm."

"The fire has engulfed eight vehicles, and the fire department is allowing the flames to burn out. It's too dangerous to fight it with the threat of exploding fuel tanks. We transported eight civilians to the hospital with smoke inhalation."

"We're not sure if the city hall fire relates, but there was a terrorist attack on the subway system."

Mayor Dodge glowered at his police chief. The cop had ignored his rules.

"All hospitals are on alert with many cases of smoke inhalation, and we don't know the number yet, but it seems no other serious injuries. We closed the subway until we can make it safe. As the evacuation proceeded, five empty trains in stations caught fire." The crowd gasped.

"The aluminum car bodies ignited and the Toronto Fire Department is struggling to extinguish the blazes. The heat is intense. We will distribute a list of locations, responding fire units, and timings of each incident. I must stress, we do not want to create panic. The TTC is using busses to move people, but this is unprecedented. Everyone should stay home or return home."

"I have mobilized every off duty constable, auxiliary and cadets along with all off duty fire and paramedics. Casualties are light, and it seems they did not target people. The city is under attack by these renegade terrorists and we're lucky they have killed no one."

"I don't think we are under attack." Dodge attempted to repair the damage. "We have a handful of delinquents wanting to be famous."

"In all fairness, Mayor," Heron had a secure pension and wanted to be honest after years of political muzzling. "It took more than a handful of delinquents to carry out this attack, and we have a serious problem. There seems to be a similar attack in New York City and they seem coordinated."

Charlie Dodge fumed. It had found it hard enough to mollify important backers after the electrical sabotage, but with the bomb scares the previous week and now this widespread attack and Heron's disobedience; he could not contain the damage. Dodge imagined the destruction of the city's business reputation.

With Heron approaching retirement, Dodge had no leverage over the Chief. As he smouldered, the mayor thought over the list of replacements for Chief of Police. Dodge decided he would force the Chief to go earlier than scheduled and make Heron appear incompetent compared to his own decisiveness.

Frank Langstaff strode across the northbound lanes of University Avenue and joined Dodge and Heron. It relieved the mayor. He short-listed Frank for Heron's job, and Langstaff, meticulously dressed in uniform, reassured Dodge as a professional who understood the media.

"How soon will you know if this is the work of Sherwood Green?" Jos tossed the question at the Chief.

Frank focused on the young reporter. The deputy chief, saw reporters as useful tools. Amiel would be more useful than the little upstart could ever imagine. Langstaff contemplated the unintended help Amiel provided. They retreated inside, leaving the spokeswoman to deflect the reporters' question.

They soon learned there of the coordinated attacks in Toronto, New York City, Chicago and San Francisco. All the attacks were on transit systems, with diversionary attacks on targets like Toronto's city hall.

The attackers had crippled the cities' cores, and not enough people reached work for financial institutions to function. In Toronto, another lost day magnified the fiasco of the previous Friday.

Mayor Dodge summoned the Council into an emergency session. Many members were out of town on pre-election vacation, and it took time to organize the meeting, but the Council would gather on Friday. The subway remained shut down, and no one knew if it would be available for Tuesday. Five destroyed trains had to be dragged out of the tunnels, and the affected stations would remain closed indefinitely.

Pamphlets linked Sherwood Green to the attacks and defeated the mayor's attempt to downplay the terrorist link.

In the USA, the media frantically pursued the links to ISIS, but in New York something calling itself STOP, short for "Stop Those Oppressing the Planet" claimed credit.

In Chicago it seemed to be called STOPTOO by adding, "Take Out Oppressors", as they had focused on the commodity exchange.

In San Francisco, the organisation was SIKE, "Stop Industrialism Killing the Environment".

With the council delayed, Dodge called in his staff and Chief Heron, Frank Langstaff and the fire chief.

"I want to know what the situation is, and I want a plan." Mayor Dodge glowered at Heron.

"At the moment," the Chief ignored Dodge's frown, "the city hall fire is out. The fire began in one vehicle..."

"That was my car." The manager of parks apologized.

"The flames reduced the car to a steel frame and engine block." Heron continued. "The fire gutted eight cars, and exploding fuel tanks made it worse. We don't know what started it, and the fire marshal is on the scene."

"The same applies to the five subway cars. The fires were intense, and we can't tell exactly where the fires started. So far, the experts have no theories. Diesel and gasoline poured into the open air shafts and ignited with marine flares filled the tunnels with smoke, but with no damage other than the evacuation. Barrels of lubricant stored in the shafts made the smoke worse."

"The worst damage is to the five stations." The chair of the transit commission said. "They'll be closed until the engineers declare them safe. Our preliminary estimate is a cost of twenty million dollars and lost revenue."

"How much will insurance cover?" Dodge became more despondent. The transit manager looked nervous.

"None," he said, "not with it being terrorism."

"We have removed all the trash bins, paper boxes and street furniture in the downtown," the works manager talked action, "and closed all the public washrooms in the underground concourse. We'll do that in the subway as well." He sounded as if the city was in retreat.

"We have increased patrols and put undercover people on the street." Frank Langstaff spoke. "This is part of Project Tom under my direction. We need more people."

"I am asking the council for more money." Dodge said. "Give me the numbers." The mayor behaved as if Frank had replaced the Chief.

"You will have it tonight." Heron ignored the slight.

"I'm going on television this evening to reassure people." Dodge turned to his executive assistant. "I want some good news." His eyes swept the table.

Frank Langstaff saw an opportunity. "I'll have something you can announce tonight." Frank did not have any effective ideas; however, he planned something that would seem like action.

Chapter Fifteen

Diane Arsenault leaned over the low stone wall and placed her bag of groceries between the wall and a shrub. The food would be safe for a few hours. Diane sat on the wall and dialled Melissa's cell number. There was no answer. She called Melissa's partner.

"It's about to happen." Diane didn't bother with formalities. Despite her matter-of-fact tone, Arsenault was nervous. "I see cops waiting at my place. Find out where they take me. Be quick!"

Diane dialled her own number. The internet based answering app picked up the call. She put the phone into her pocket without disconnecting. Voice activated the system and it would record for several hours whenever it detected talking. Diane resumed her walk down the shaded street towards her apartment. Two large Crown Victoria sedans waited in the shadows beneath the large maple trees.

Even though we know it will happen, no one ever prepares themselves for it. Diane resigned herself to her impending arrest.

"Agent De Cruze, it's nice to see you again." Frank Langstaff shook the agent's hand. "It's unfortunate it's business bringing us together."

"It's always nice to visit Toronto." The FBI agent had been driven from Pearson International to Metro Police Headquarters by the Peel Regional Police.

She pulled her hand away and ignored Langstaff's flirting. Less than thirty-six hours since the transit attacks, they felt immense pressure to catch the terrorists.

"A lot has happened. It all looks linked." She opened a folio. "We estimated the number of terrorists needed to commit the arsons." She handed Langstaff the papers.

"That many…?" Frank frowned. The report suggested fifty people had been involved in the USA.

Frank retrieved the report on the Toronto attacks. They needed at least a dozen perpetrators in the subway assault, more if Sherwood Green set the city hall fire.

"These are just guesses," Frank said. "The minimum would have been one person for each site. We don't know how they set the trains on fire. Chemical analysis might tell us, but the smoke came from diesel and gasoline."

"They used a different MO in the States." De Cruze frowned as she scanned the Toronto report. "They poured diesel and gasoline onto the rails and used railway warning torpedoes to set it off as a train passed over. We were lucky they hurt no one. The smell of gas alerted folks."

"Some sort of time delayed device ignited the rolling stock. We have video of suspects." She paused. "We want to know how they coordinated. Toronto is the key, and they have to be using phones, the internet or both because the timing is precise. It's puzzling with so many involved no one has talked. Usually, these groups betray themselves because of stupidity and petty infighting."

"We had no cameras at the air shafts." It disappointed Frank who believed in video surveillance. "We're examining every video within a kilometre of the sites. Face and vehicle plate recognition are being used, along with human analysis." The man sighed at the enormous cost of time and money. "We might have a shortcut."

De Cruze pounced on the hope. "What do you mean?"

"We're bringing in some terrorist supporters for interrogation. These people must be involved operationally. We hope to squeeze it out of them."

"I hope so." De Cruze sounded doubtful. "The terrorists are sophisticated. These cells are the blackest we've ever encountered. It would surprise me if any outsiders know the terrorists and these are not the usual bunch of environmentalists. The best hope is the video and their communication."

"The call volume between Toronto and New York City is too great. We have focused on links to San Francisco. Algorithms will sort the phone records and scan internet traffic. It's likely we will find something in the NSA data base. We have years of data dumps from all the social media, and they're cooperative."

De Cruze relied on the huge data archives in the USA, spanning many years of internet traffic.

"Great!" Frank envied Patricia's resources. "I can supply phone numbers from here. Maybe it'll speed things up. We have our own cell phone operation. It isn't as sophisticated as your NSA. I'll give it to you personally."

"Our threat level shot up today because of our TIARA process." De Cruze scowled. "Homeland Security has created an umbrella group headquartered in Virginia. Along with us are the CIA, NSA, ATF, and other agencies, but there are thousands of agents spread out over the USA, and beyond. There's a hotline to the White House, and the President appointed her V-P to coordinate everything. She has been on the phone with your Prime Minister Harridan. CSIS will take over soon. "

Frank Langstaff resented being a minion, but his original hope that terrorism would be good for his career had faded. It had spun out of his control and might become his downfall, but having someone else in line for blame might be good. He had personal problems.

"Do you think it originates outside the USA?" Frank assumed they deployed their agents in Canada.

"Let's just say we're covering all the bases." De Cruze smiled. "Our agents are working the Islamic angle. Some believe this is ISIS, but there isn't a whisper of a connection. ISIS is always quick to claim responsibility, but they haven't, and this is not their style. They would have killed the people on the trains."

"These groups are out of the blue. If they are home-grown, there's no connection with previous groups. We have all known enviro-whackos infiltrated. I'm sure you do the same." Patricia doubted the Canadian effort.

Diane Arsenault approached the old rambling house converted into apartments. She casually fumbled in her shoulder bag for her keys.

"Excuse me, miss," a man popped out of the passenger side of a Crown Victoria. "Can I have a word with you, please?" He blocked her way and flashed the badge of a Metro cop. Several others gathered on the sidewalk.

"What do you want?" She glanced about for witnesses.

"Are you Diane Louise Arsenault?" She said she was.

"I am arresting you on suspicion of arson." At his signal, one of the other officers grabbed Diane's arms and pulled them behind her, painfully clamping on handcuffs.

"Where are you taking me?" Diane grimaced. The cop pushed her head down and shoved her into the back of the car. She hoped her phone could pick up the conversation.

"Headquarters," the terse reply was the only word spoken on the ten-minute ride to Jarvis Street.

The car entered an underground garage and a steel roll-door closed behind them. They brightly lit the space for video surveillance. Every sound echoed. Diane glimpsed Melissa being led through a doorway. A few minutes later, the same door locked behind Diane.

They removed the cuffs, and she emptied her pockets. Everything, including her cell phone, went onto a tray resembling those at airport security. It encouraged Diane that no one inspected the handset and the screen remained dark. She went down a short corridor and through a door marked Room G.

They seated her at a small table on an uncomfortable chair in the corner behind the door. It unsettled her when the door opened against her feet. Diane turned the chair to face the table. She waited and examined the doorway and a large mirror that broke the featureless tan walls.

"The bosses depend on the computer whiz-kids." Frank said. "I think it'll be old-fashioned field work. We're pushing our informants hard. I'm counting on that." The phone interrupted Frank. "We just nabbed three terrorist supporters. Would you like to watch?"

Langstaff led De Cruze downstairs to the interrogation rooms in the basement, well away from areas of normal activity. The facility provided central control over terrorists. Through the one-way glass, De Cruze saw they set the room up for a hard-nosed Reid interrogation. It was a bare, over-lit room with a small grey table against a wall. A thinly padded, uncomfortable chair sat in the corner, crowded between the table and the adjoining wall. The entrance door swung towards the suspect and would be claustrophobic each time it opened. A young woman sat in the chair.

"How do we handle her, Chief?" A solid-looking cop in a poorly fitting business suit entered the viewing room. "Here's her stuff." The cop set a tray on the table.

"Squeeze her hard." Frank smiled broadly, remembering the times when, as a uniformed constable, he had sweated confessions out of punks in the back of the Division. "We have the other two here. I'll send in someone once in a while to give you a memo. It might rattle her and make her think the others ratted on her. We have network failure," he winked. "There won't be video."

The cop soon sat opposite Diane Arsenault in a comfortable chair that moved easily on its wheeled base. He rested his arm on several file folders on the table. His relaxation emphasized Diane's unease.

"I prefer the Peace method of interrogating." De Cruze opened a bottle of water. "It gets information un- tainted for court. The Reid system is old-fashioned."

"We are sure this chick had nothing to do with the attacks." Frank absently looked through Diane's possessions, staring at the cell phone. "We already know everything she could tell us."

"So you're wasting your time holding these folks? If you don't think they are guilty, and there's no investigative necessity, you can't hold them under your terrorism laws."

She impressed Frank. De Cruze knew Canadian law.

"Our inside information is good," he continued, "but we need to show some action. The mayor has announced we detained suspects for questioning. It'll reassure the public. If one of them confessed, it would be a bonus." He paused and smiled. "I want to make this bitch squirm. The terrorists make us look bad. Getting a little back is good, even if we can't hold them."

Frank turned Diane's cell phone over in his hand and didn't notice Patricia's discomfort at the sexual slur. She was acutely aware of sexism and harassment in the FBI. She had no sympathy for these terrorist lovers but disliked Langstaff.

This guy could fuckup the investigation, she thought.

"That broken video," De Cruze said, "might haunt you in court. Judges don't like that sort of thing."

"Some of the Mexican friends of the dead Garza woman have joined these supporters. They are the weak link. One of the Mexicans is not a Canadian citizen. We forced her to become an informant or we would deport her."

"Good," De Cruze sounded encouraged. "We need someone inside Sherwood Green. Maybe this one could move up the ladder, seduce a leader or something."

"We'll try. Her code name is Pinto. The hopeless bitch will help us nail the crud."

De Cruze winced again. She felt you had to respect your enemy, or you would miss something vital, like the missteps in the Wisconsin office before 9-11.

The Canadian agencies did not know the FBI already had recruited the Mexican woman. The had tasked Pinto, or Corona to the FBI, to look for drug connections. She now passed information, not only about the SGSN but about the Canadian efforts. Langstaff called in a constable.

"Take these down to the desk. Give the phone to electronics to set up." Diane's phone still transmitted.

"I want to talk to my lawyer." Diane looked defiantly at the interrogator.

"Why did you attack the subway?" He glared at Diane.

"I want to call my lawyer." She ignored his frown.

"Why would you want a lawyer if you're innocent?"

Diane remained silent.

"How many are in your group?"

Diane remained silent.

"There are twenty-three official members of the support group." Frank Langstaff said. "There are several more on the fringes."

De Cruze nodded and smiled at the old news.

The interrogator berated Arsenault for twenty minutes with the same questions, his tone alternating between fatherly, demanding and hostile. The door opened abruptly, jamming hard against Diane's chair. Her legs were safely under the table. A cop handed over a sheet of paper and placed bottles of water on the table. The questioner dramatically examined the paper and placed it facedown.

"I understand you want to destroy the world." He opened his water to take a sip. Diane shifted her weight on the hard chair. "Why would you want to destroy this?" He took another drink, making a show of satisfaction.

"Our analysis of their plan," De Cruze took her own sip of water, "suggests the terrorists have a detailed strategy based on the manifesto of that DGR group of wackos."

"I request that I have my lawyer here." Diane toyed with the water bottle but did not drink. She had learned the hard way, while detained by the Quebec Surité after an anti-whaling demonstration in Tadousac. Interrogators tried to get their subject to drink and eventually need to urinate. Some would soil themselves, and that would help interrogators to break them. Diane had not broken, but it humiliated her.

"What do you know of the attacks in the States?"

"I want my lawyer." Diane spun her unopened water bottle, irritating the cop. She said nothing as the man pressed. He tried to glare into Diane's eyes but was continually being drawn to the reflection of the bright lights sparkling from the spinning bottle. After a few moments, the cop hurled the bottle into the far corner of the room. It ruptured against the wall. Diane smiled.

The interrogator rushed from the room, pushing the door hard against Diane's chair before slamming it behind him. He left his pen and the pile of folders on the table.

Frank Langstaff scowled, and the FBI agent stifled a chuckle. *Is this the best they've got?* She thought, wondering if she could leave for the hotel.

Diane picked up the pen and wrote on the outside of the top file.

You are part of a repressive machine. You are protecting those who are destroying the planet and your children's future. Wake up!!!

As the water bottling took place in other interview rooms, Joe behaved much like Diane, although he fell for the water trick. Melissa quoted the law to her interviewer, demanded her lawyer, and remained silent.

Melisa's law partner finally worked through the screen of police sandbagging.

"My clients, Diane Arsenault, Melissa Strong, and Joe Anderson, are being detained there." The ignorant cop act annoyed the lawyer who was in the mood to cause trouble.

"Sergeant, I don't care what your orders are, but you have had my clients in your custody for over an hour." The lawyer put the cop in the line of legal fire, and they knew the upper levels would easily sacrifice a lower rank to protect themselves. "I'm going to give you advice. Tell your boss not to ask questions of my clients until I have arrived. When I arrive, have them waiting for me, and if there is any delay, there are several judges I can call twenty-four seven who don't like you blue boys. If you force them to issue a bench order for their release, they won't be happy, and we will sue you for unlawful detention. I'll be there in half an hour."

He hung up and called Jos Amiel.

"Hello?" Jos sounded distracted.

"This is Steve, Melissa Strong's partner. The police have her, Joe, and Diane at headquarters. I'm on my way there. Diane wanted you to know." Steve hung up.

"I have to go, sweetie." Jos rolled out of bed.

"Damn, we were just getting started." Debbie pulled the cover off as if to show Jos what he would be missing.

"Sorry, sexy." Jos slipped his phone into his jacket. Debbie's desire to meet surprised him, but he put it down to her loving sex and thought no more of it.

"Don't forget, if you ever get to interview Sherwood Green, let me know. It excites me."

"A lot excites you, gorgeous." Jos laughed. He was not about to fall in love with the older woman, but he had become addicted to her. She had no inhibitions. "I'll let you know if I do."

Steve waited at Police Headquarters, fuming at the duty officer. Walt arrived right behind Jos, and the lawyer took them to a far corner of the lobby.

"They've brought the three in about the subway fires. They may have reasonable cause, but they look bad because they did not interview anyone before this. It is pure intimidation and standard police practice. Besides, they know SGSN is not involved and the members don't know more than the cops."

Jos didn't know about Joel and wondered why Steve seemed so sure.

"If the cops had asked for interviews, we would have made appointments. I'm not sure it's worth it, but we could ask a judge for an injunction, but we would likely be a wasting our time. Some judges don't like cops much, but in this case, they might hate Sherwood Green more."

"Melissa hasn't convinced me about the Sherwood Green objectives, but their slogan, 'don't bother fighting the police', makes sense. If the entire structure is against you, it's a waste of effort, but even if the cops are the wrong target, they are a problem. In the end, we'll complain and then drop it."

"How long can this go tonight?" Jos yawned. The hectic few days and Debbie had worn him down.

"They'll release them soon, now that I'm here. They know there's nothing to learn, and it would take hours questioning them in front of me. It would stretch the whole thing out all day tomorrow, since they would have to do it one at a time. Besides, in their minds, they have already intimidated, and maybe their primary goal, their techies, will examine their cell phones."

"Isn't that illegal?"

"Without a warrant, yes, but if they don't want to use the information in court, they don't care about legal. It isn't even necessary to read the stuff right off the phones. They'll mirror all the memory and crack it later. That won't be a problem now. They rewrote the terrorism law to force phone makers to hand over the encryption codes. Tomorrow they'll know everything on the phones."

Jos looked at his cell and decided to remove anything sensitive. Walt shot some background in the empty police lobby and Frank Langstaff and Agent De Cruze heading to a car. Frank scowled into the camera. Neither said a word.

Melissa, Joe and Diane appeared, carrying their belongings and smiling. Joe smelt of urine. Walt recorded the release and Steve's complaint of wrongful arrest.

TorontoNewsNow leapt at the chance to speculate on their guilt. They mentioned the SGSN by name and this helped SGSN attract recruits. Jos lobbied Sheri to set up an on air debate between the SGSN and an anti-terrorist environmentalist. She would try to convince her boss.

The arrests caused disruptions. The trio needed new phones because they knew they had inserted a tracking device into the sets. While the police detained them, the cops searched their residences and installed bugs. They replaced the phones immediately. They would use the bugs to mislead the police in a cat and the mouse dance.

Chapter Sixteen

"Now, watch this!" The young cop stood beside the Metro Police 'Eye-In-the-Sky' van and waved an electronic controller towards the crowd of reporters. Video cameras zoomed in to the constable's smiling face and then to the apparatus. His thumbs moved deftly. A small drone flier leapt into the air from the asphalt, hovered, raced towards the reporters at eye level and, as they ducked, the machine swooped in a sharp arc towards the treetops.

"See how agile it is." He smiled at the reporters. "Let's watch the monitor in the pavilion."

Reporters moved to the tent where the interior shaded a sixty inch LED television showing real time video from the drone as it skimmed along Cherry Beach. The sharp image revealed small stones, seaweed and drifting sticks in the little waves. "It's one hundred and fifty meters in the air, but see how clear the picture is."

The camera swooped along the sand over dog walkers and scantily clad sun-bathers. It focused on a couple in a torrid embrace beneath the failed privacy of a shade tent.

"This job has its perks," the constable smirked. "These will patrol the subway, railway corridors and electric grid."

The reporters recorded it all, and the viewers loved the titillation of the anonymous lovers.

"I even got to fly it." Jos' beaming face filled the screen, after the lovers vanished during the *Terrorism Toronto* segment. "I didn't find any interesting activity," Jos winked into the camera, "but I chased a seagull."

It entertained the bored audience and reassured that the police were on the anti-terrorist job, but the episode raised protests about Big Brother. Jos' upbeat, pro-police tone pleased Sherri. The coverage attracted viewers and sponsors. Jos took no pride in the piece. He had done nothing so lame since had covered the daily wanderings of a homeless bag-lady's cat.

Stupid bullshit, he thought.

"Watch this." A teenage boy took a long drag on his cigarette. He squirted lighter fluid into a nearly full trash can beside the park bench. With one last drag, he threw the hot butt into the garbage. A blue and then orange flame followed a loud pop. The other kids videoed the obscenity filled dance of the firebug's ghostly face behind the blaze.

"Is that a fire?" a voice came from the other side of the park. The teens retreated to the shadows. "Call 911."

The sirens grew loud as flames lit a circle around the bench. A pumper truck braked hard and two firemen with extinguishers ran the hundred meters from the road and killed the fire as the truck's floodlights searched the park.

Vandalism came every summer with the school holiday but took a dangerous turn. The video of the first fire became viral on the internet. Bored young people with few summer job prospects took it as a challenge, starting a game known as Flaring. Youngsters torched trash bins all over the city and exhausted the fire crews.

By the Thursday night before Mayor Dodge's emergency council meeting, the vandals had started a video competition to claim the largest fire. Someone set fire to the change rooms and boards of the Withrow Park ice rink. They set an even larger blaze in a portable classroom on the city's west end. Politicians tried to link these fires to Sherwood Green.

"Heron, you're doing a shit job. The only thing the police have done is Frank's dragging in the sympathizers." Mayor Dodge had ordered the Chief into his office. Out in the clamshell, councillors debated how the taxpayer should pay them for interrupting their vacations.

"Dodge, you're a self-serving asshole." Heron finally expressed his true feelings. The shouting filled the air with the insults and profanity. The office workers, listening on the other side of the glass wall, enjoyed the confrontation. Their boss' frequent vulgar rants had entertained, but only if he did not yell at them, and the chief giving it back satisfied everyone.

"You can announce my early retirement today," Heron wanted out of the terrorist mess. "My pay continues to the end of October, the original date, and I get the chauffer service for all of next year." He scribbled the conditions under the mayor's letterhead, dated it and shoved it towards Dodge. "Sign it, photocopy it, and give me the original."

Dodge knew the paper could hurt him if they ever made it public, but he desperately wanted to rid himself of Heron. He needed a tough chief who understood politics and would make him look good.

Compared to a normal meeting filled with self-serving ranting and back-biting, the Council was efficient.

"... and so as you can see on your screens, and the details are in your red folder, we need two hundred more officers, fifty civilian data analysts and the cash for our information and intelligence efforts. It totals a hundred and fifty million and change." Heron left the podium.

Uproar broke out as the elected members wanted their view on television and everyone electioneered. The mayor set a speakers' list to his advantage. He would speak last.

Politicians lamented the impact on their rich supporters through the spectrum of business people, homeowners, suburbanites and condo dwellers. The self-labelled socialists somehow united the fortunes of the destitute with the heads of banks. The cliché, 'We're all in this together and the police are our only defence,' summed up the consensus. The vote was unanimous.

Dodge rose to introduce new business.

"We have to pay for all this," the Mayor extended the meeting with controversy. "We must close the public swimming pools." The chamber erupted in shouting.

Dodge let the turmoil subside. He had arranged an end run around the opposition to closing swimming pools in an unbearably hot summer and election year.

"Mr. Takaido, of Fukushima Motors, has come from Japan and wishes to make an announcement."

The councillors became silent, anticipating political salvation. An elderly Japanese man walked from the V.I.P. gallery. His air of authority came from years of minions obeying his orders.

"Ladies and Gentlemen, I wish, in response to these vicious, unwarranted attacks on our city and my company, to offer to pay for the operation of the swimming pools and public recreation until the end of September. We will have captured these terrorists by that time." He gave Chief Heron a commanding look.

The applause was thunderous, and the councillors no longer had to fear the voters' wrath. The motion to accept the Fukushima offer passed and completed Dodge's trick of manufacturing a disaster and then offering a solution.

"In order to have continuity in the efforts against these terrorists, Chief Heron will step aside early, as of next Monday." Gasps and cries rose from the circle. Dodge made a show of hugging the Chief.

"Chief Heron has been a wonderful asset to the city and has done a remarkable job under the stress of this crisis. I ask for a show of thanks." A standing ovation followed, although an abandoning the ship comment snuck through the din. Heron looked at Dodge.

I *wouldn't be abandoning much.*

"Considering the crisis," Dodge continued. "We will nominate a new chief next week, from within the force. The emergency leaves no time for an outside search."

The meeting adjourned to the lobby. The mayor's staff had set up a celebration for Heron, including several cakes decorated with the police logo and "Thank-you Chief Heron". Heron wondered if he had asked for too little. Dodge planned to fire him anyway and had prepared the party. Frank Langstaff rushed in to shake every hand.

"Will they nominate you Chief?" Jos pushed his microphone towards Langstaff as the Deputy headed towards the Mayor's office.

"That's up to the Mayor." Langstaff brushed the microphone aside, almost hitting Jos in the face, and disappeared into Dodge's office. Walt's video didn't make it to air, but a rival station, politically opposed to Dodge, ran their own video of the incident, implying Dodge had picked a bully to replace Heron.

Sheri vetoed his clever pun, suggesting the changing of police chiefs was only a red Heron. She giggled and ran a blue pencil over the line on Jos' script.

Friday night marked a boring end of the week, but fire trucks raced to trash fires. Jos sipped an ice-cap in an uptown Starbucks, and listlessly read his messages. Debbie was busy, and it was almost midnight. Time to head home.

A fire truck raced past on Bloor, followed by a deputy's car and then an aerial truck and another pumper. The police scanner reported a two alarm event on a tenth floor on Bloor East. It was on his way home.

Smoke and flames poured from a shattered window high above the street. More fire fighters arrived as Jos joined the crowd of onlookers. The network night crew appeared and Jos followed them to a scene commander.

"It's in the Hanzberg Marketing office. Looks like it started in the waiting area. We have guys inside fogging it to assist the sprinklers." As if on cue, a stream of water chased the smoke out of the broken window and showered a heavy mist onto the street, ten floors below.

"It was an aggressive fire and flashed through the inside walls and ignited fires all the way to the back of the place. It looks like a write-off."

"Is it arson?" Jos asked.

"There isn't much to burn in a modern waiting room. I think we'll find accelerant."

"Is there proof?" The reporters clamoured.

"You'll have to wait for the Fire Marshal."

The actual crime at Hanzberg's Canadian branch office had taken place a few hours before the fire. Hackers used a desktop computer carelessly left powered up to hack into the company's servers in the Czech Republic. They copied the complete database and years of e-mails.

The hackers hid the information in the database of the York University Geography Department, accessible through a hidden link placed on the department web page, *The Geography of Communication.*

Sherwood Green did not have the resources for the attack, and they had sub-contracted the work to a group in Ukraine. Sherwood Green had planted an incendiary at the agency timed to detonate after the data theft. The fire destroyed any trace in the hack. The data would identify strategic targets in the marketing agency's extensive range of corporate clients, and e-mail addresses created back doors into the computers of rich investors.

One e-mail exchange involved insider trading tips of a financial officer of an agriculture chemical company and his mistress at Hanzberg. This would open up a whole new set of targets, including black-mailing the lovers. The stolen personnel files might be useful, but the agency's customers were the strategic target.

Monday morning the National Industrial Bank announced plans to move to "a place with more reliable infrastructure". They would move to Calgary.

Alberta is the powerhouse of earnings in Canada and the vast majority of its residents support business and the

The statement hurt Mayor Dodge, who found comfort in thinking, *At least it's only one of the little banks.* Unfortunately, two other banks issued said they were considering their options and the share prices of all Canadian banks fell. Financial commentators speculated on what would happen at Tuesday's opening bell, but their ramblings did not predict what would happen that night.

Two o'clock Tuesday morning, a dormant computer sprang to life in the home office of a wealthy investor. He worked at his lavish mansion in Caledon and dealt with his brokerage electronically. As a partner of the TSX, he had direct trading privileges and access to overseas brokers. He could place blind orders using insider information. Illegal trades linked to him would mean jail.

The computer sent an order to a brokerage in Panama City to buy shares of each of the Canadian major banks. The computer spent four hundred million dollars.

The transaction did not cause a stir in the Panamanian office used to mysterious orders from around the world. Lately, it had been Asian players, but a Canadian gambit, even such a large one, did not surprise them. The Canadian investor had a solid net worth with no question he could afford the purchase. The contract with the off-shore broker limited the fee to a million dollars.

The billionaire had two fatal bad habits and slept unaware of the wild bet. The man left his computer logged on overnight because he wanted instant access when he woke up. Although convoluted passwords protected his operations, he had stored these impossible to remember jumbles of characters in unguarded text files. A Sherwood Green hacker had carefully vetted this victim, along with several others, over the previous months. The operation required ten minutes as the resistor sat in a car outside an all-night donut shop. A pair of coffee sipping constables sat in a patrol car beside the hacker, listening to the Blue Jay's game, into extra innings in Seattle.

Around the world, trading computers caught the sudden rise in the overnight value of the banks and placed automatic buy orders. By the TSX opening bell, the banks' stocks had surged ten percent. Laggard day traders hurried to get in on the action as the value went up twenty-two percent. Confused business commentators enthusiastically predicted long-term happiness.

A broad spectrum of other shares and commodities fell in value as investors switched funds into the banks. The trading indexes were positive, but it was a zero-sum game. The brokers made windfall profits in this sloshing of funds.

Reality came by mid-afternoon when rational investors realized the banks had become over-valued. Many shareholders liquidated all or part of their holdings. The resulting sudden down blip in the share price triggered the high-speed trading computers, and the machines added to the sell trend. Suddenly, the share prices were back to even. Panicked traders piled into the negative sentiment. By market close, the share values across the board were eleven percent below the price paid in the overnight hacker trade.

The victim, unaware that he held so much bank stock, lost forty million dollars. Many other traders had losses. That totalled a hundred million dollars.

Everyone would come under the shadow of the regulator's scrutiny during their fruitless search for a market manipulator. The only positive for the hacked investor was his anonymity through Panama, and he would tell no one of his loss. He ended his clandestine relationship with the Panamanians, accusing them of stealing his money, but he had no legal recourse without exposing his other under the table dealings. An equivalent service in the

Maldives became his new go-between, and he wrote off on taxes his forty-million dollar loss.

The banks did not fare as well as the unsuspecting agent of the fiasco. Damaging the banks had been the whole point of the Sherwood Green operation. The incident soured investors and helped keep the banks' share values at the ten percent loss. Speculation about the cost of any relocations added downward pressure and during the summer the prices drifted lower. Executives' bonuses evaporate as they dealt with cranky board members. The banks lost over thirty-five billion dollars in capitalization and pleaded for a government bailout.

Jos opened a manila envelope delivered by a bicycle courier. A homeless man had flagged down the girl on the bike on King Street by and given her the envelope and twenty dollars. The package contained a terse letter.

Nice work so far, Amiel. Too bad the network didn't let you expose the truth about the firing of Heron. Dodge is a scumbag eyeing the Premier's job.

Next week Dodge will announce our old friend, Langstaff, as the new chief. It was a done deal before he forced Heron out. Frank is dangerous, has no scruples, and his ambition will let him do anything. Warn your friends in SGSN to be careful. The interrogation thing was just a little bullying. Langstaff has a personal secret that could destroy him. I have seen you with certain people who are the key to his weakness. It has nothing to do with your lover, but I would be careful of her. They know about her and will use her to use you.

Project Tom created a fake website: 'sgrecruiting.ca'. Posters are going up looking like Sherwood Green posters with their logo and saying 'Support us.' When you check the site, you'll see a link to a recruiting page. It asks people to leave their details. It also buries keystroke malware on the computer so they can monitor users.

The message upset Jos. Why did he assume Jos agreed with Diane and the group? What was it that could destroy Langstaff? Was Frank on the take?

How did this cop know about Debbie Franklin? Jos was sure he was a cop, but could he trust him? How much should he trust her? The sex had been a pleasant diversion, but now it seemed part of the terrorist mess. Jos shredded the letter. The sender's prints would not be on it, but its existence was a danger.

"... and the person in this video might know something. We don't think he's a suspect, but would like to talk to him." Jos sat in the 'bull pen,' waiting for Walt. The Network broadcast part of a video press release from the police.

"We did not see this individual leave the system. He might have gotten onto a bus" The spokesperson sounded discouraged. The daytime news host cut in, speculating that perhaps this was Sherwood Green in the flesh. Jos winced. Everyone thought Sherwood Green was a person. Jos, and the police, knew it was an organization.

"... the police would like anyone seeing a poster being put up or any other suspicious activity to call. You can remain anonymous through Crime Stoppers. You will find all the contact info on the TorontoNewsNow website."

The request lead to an avalanche of calls to every media switchboard, Crime Stoppers and even 911 by people hoping to get on TV. Eager snitches overloaded all the systems. The police would have thousands of dead-end leads. Most of the accused advertised rock concerts counter culture happenings or looked for lost cats.

Police desperation helped the Sherwood Green strategy of overloading police resources. After a few days of the campaign, desperate pleas for people to "only report truly suspicious activity" fell on deaf ears. Once the public had the wind, they reacted with self-righteous enthusiasm. The SGSN switched from posters to leaving brochures in coffee shops, pubs, transit vehicles and on park benches.

Activity lulled, and in desperation, Jos broadcast of summaries of terrorist attacks. They forced him to slant it against the resistance; however, Sherri allowed Jos to hint the downtown electrical attack might have been terrorism. The quiet ended with an attack out of town that raised the official terrorist threat level to red.

Chapter Seventeen

"Let's go." A man in a ball cap and uniform of an industrial supply service climbed into the passenger seat of a five tonne truck labelled, Energetic Blasting Supply.

The lights blazed on an SUV parked ahead and the vehicles headed towards Airport Road. The police scanner revealed the two night-time OPP patrols were nowhere near Airport Road and Highway 9. The resistors hoped to change that. They turned south on Airport Road towards Mono Mills. The driver pulled the SUV onto the shoulder on the downhill above the deep ravine of the Humber River. The early morning found the road deserted.

"Get to work, buddy." The driver pushed the shoulder of the cadaver occupying the passenger seat. He avoided looking at the bloodless face and climbed out, put the transmission into 'drive' and used a stick to jam the accelerator. The vehicle jumped forward and headed into the ravine, just missing the guard rail.

The truck had turned to head north, and the man climbed in just as a trip wire set off a huge fireball from a bottle of gasoline under the dash of the SUV. The truck drove away from the fireball, obeying the speed limit. A few minutes later, the OPP radio reported a fiery crash near Mono Mills.

"Where'd the cadaver come from?" The drive stared ahead into the dark night. This was a tricky road.

"It had a hospital toe tag that said it was to be cremated. It was in the SUV when I collected it."

"Hope you took the tag off, just in case." The driver smiled. The four of them were a good team, and he did not expect screw-ups.

"Yup, I'm going to burn it somewhere."

They had plans for an even bigger fire.

The driver pulled over as an OPP cruiser screamed past in the opposite direction. The scanner reported a list of fire, EMS, and police responding to Mono Mills. He turned west on Highway 89 and then north at Shelburne on Road 124.

The lone gate guard stirred in surprise. He only saw emergency night deliveries at the quarry, and this was not on the list.

"I was supposed to be here at three this afternoon," the driver pulled out a manifest. "I broke down and had to get another truck." He handed the man the form. A semi-trailer gravel truck rolled up, leaving with an early load for a cement kiln. Other breakdowns had messed the schedule up, but this was to be the last activity of the night. The guard had hoped for a little snooze before shift-change.

The driver of the five-tonne slid out the door and stood beside the guard. As the gravel truck turned onto the County road, he hit the guard with a hard temple punch. The man blacked out and crumpled. They left him on the floor of the guardhouse, bound and gagged with duct tape. The truck backed into the warehouse loading dock. There was no night receiver. The man in the tool cage sauntered over.

"Bernie never said we were getting a late delivery." The man stared at the same paper the neutralized guard had seen, and he suffered the same fate. At the pit proper, the night shift set charges to blast the dolomite for the morning crew to muck out and crush. It was unlikely anyone would need supplies at this stage of the work. Placing and arming charges required nerve-wracking precision, and crews worked steadily until they had connected everything.

Bolt cutters opened the explosives cage, and the four men worked feverishly to trundle out cases of Impex. They would only take three tonnes to avoid overloading the truck. A few cases of ignition caps followed and a dozen of wire, high speed and slow fuse with a box of fusing tools added to the haul.

"We'll drop the guy off at the gate with his buddy and hope it keeps them safe when the blast levels the place."

A cap and a fast fuse penetrated into a stick of Impex buried in the remaining explosives. They ran the fuse to the door, and five-minutes of slow fuse completed the assembly. The lighter sparked.

They turned north and would loop east to Highway 400. The blast, when the remaining Impex went up, shook the truck four kilometres from the pit and demolished the surface operations. The site manager's plush chair ended up in the pit, five hundred meters from the office building.

"I hope no one got hurt."

"The blast should have passed over the pit, and everyone there, hopefully, had stayed below ground level. I would guess the guardhouse is gone, but they poured the walls with concrete so those two should be alive with big headaches. We'll hear on the news."

The truck joined the first wave of commuters heading to the city, and by the time the police scanner had mentioned a white truck, they had hidden the vehicle inside a nondescript warehouse. If the cops knew about the truck, the men in the guardhouse survived.

Broadcast radio filled with news of the blast at the quarry. Media choppers swarmed the site, recording the efforts of the local volunteer firefighters to douse the hot spots and search for casualties.

Jos and Walt received the call at four in the morning and rushed north to join the journalists milling about on the dew covered Horning's Mills baseball diamond.

With his quarry location blown to smithereens, the coffee truck vendor from Shelburne found new customers in the hungry mob of outsiders at the park. The thirsty reporters, desperate for a story, interviewed the coffee vendor several times. He obliged, making up a tale of the blast shaking him awake and the huge orange fireball and glow north of town. In fact, he had slept through the whole thing, and living on the south side of Shelburne had not even heard the fire trucks. He received brief notoriety on news shows, and Jos used the man's exciting fabrication to open *Terrorism Toronto*.

The OPP allowed reporters onto the site just after lunch. Fire crews still mopped up as they filmed dramatic scenes of twisted metal, fragments of building and vehicles and flattened trees. They allowed context shots of the quarry pit, although no damage had occurred below ground level and the placing of mining charges had been near completion at the time of the blast. Those charges were a safety hazard keeping reporters out, and the plush office chair sitting askew on a large boulder became a popular image.

The blast had stripped freshly laid sod from the ground and left it twisted and hanging on the Page Wire fence on the far side of the County road. Walt's lingering shot of hanging sod would be the ending visual for tonight's episode. Sheri would allow Jos' dramatic voiceover, portraying the fate of the sod as symbolic of the attacks of Sherwood Green, stripping the veneer of normalcy from the face of Toronto. The tourist board and Mayor Dodge complained, but the viewers loved it.

Using shock as an excuse, the police forbid interviews with the victims from the guardhouse. The two who had actually seen terrorists rested in hospital, well-guarded from the media. A company spokesman and Deputy OPP Commissioner Hardy met reporters at the baseball field.

"I want to talk." A middle-aged blond woman rushed between the reporters and the spokesmen. Cameras swung to her. "I live just over there." She pointed at a house beside the intersection. "We opposed this quarry, this disaster, and now we're a target for terrorism."

"I think this is a one off." Hardy tried to silence her.

"Look at this," she held up a piece of scorched metal weighing a couple of kilograms. "This landed in my backyard. My dog could have died. I'm scared." She sobbed.

"We will compensate everyone affected," the company man tried to calm the woman.

"You bet we will," she interrupted, "big time. We'll close you down."

"We're safe, and this won't happen again." Fears of endless lawsuits flashed through the man's mind.

"We have more to add," Commissioner Hardy tried to regain control. Reporters ignored him as they interviewed the woman. They would spend a long afternoon learning the history of the quarry, its opposition, and dozens of petty grievances against the local and provincial politicians, mostly to do with wind farms and winter road ploughing.

Eventually, the spokesmen filled in the details.

"Flying debris hurt a few people in the pit, none seriously, and two men who the terrorists tied up in the guardhouse survived." Hardy consulted a paper. "They are in Headwaters Regional Health Centre suffering head trauma and shock, and will interview them as soon as the doctors allow it. They saw the terrorists."

"Is this Sherwood Green?" Jos shouted.

"There's no evidence of that. It could have been local opponents of the quarry." Hardy shot a glance towards the blond woman. "Usually, the terrorists leave pamphlets or spray painting, and we found nothing here, although the blast could have destroyed them."

"Did they steal anything?"

"The witnesses couldn't tell us. They had access to the explosives. Experts are already working on calculating the amount of Impex that blew up. We know how much should have been there, so we may have an answer later. Our friend's debris may help," he nodded at the woman.

"We are looking for a five tonne white truck with writing on the side. The witness can't remember the name on the truck, and the blast destroyed the security video."

"Was the big accident on Airport Road last night connected to the quarry attack?"

Hardy sighed. "There was a fatality involving a single vehicle collision just north of Mono Mills. A lone occupant of an SUV died and burnt beyond recognition. We are trying to identify the deceased, but we think it was a man."

"The vehicle went off the road at low speed. It appears an accelerant incinerated the vehicle, so we think it involved foul play. They stole the SUV earlier last evening, but we have accounted for the owner."

"Was it suicide, or a terrorist killed by his buddies?"

"We can't speculate, but the incident pulled all the OPP in that direction and left no patrols on this side of the county during the quarry attack."

After an hour, the spokesmen added nothing new. Despite the police's uncertainty, the press speculated about Sherwood Green and linked it in the public's mind. The police knew some explosive had disappeared. Sherwood Green had declared an escalation in the war, but had caused no intentional deaths.

Chapter Eighteen

"I don't think we should get together for a while." Debbie towelled off. The bathroom was steaming from the running hot shower. She had dragged Jos from the bedroom after a hot session on the bed. He thought nothing of it, believing she wanted variety. Debbie shut the door and turned on the fan. Her hair was a wild jumble of wet strands, and Jos thought she looked lovely.

"Is your old man getting upset?" Jos couldn't think of any other reason to break it off.

"Fuck that asshole!" Debbie burst out loudly, but then softened. "No, he's got his own playthings. I think Sherwood Green is getting serious, and it's your big chance. It's making me nervous." Debbie really seemed tense. "Don't tell me any more details. You need to focus."

"You help me focus." Jos wrapped his arms about her and felt the wonder of her body against his. Debbie's eyes watered. "You don't want to break it off."

"Of course not," she hugged him tighter. "You're the guy I should have hung onto when I was in school. You remind me of him, but it would be better. We'll get back together once they capture these terrorists."

Debbie's new nervousness differed ftom her normal calmness. The sound of the shower and the exhaust fan filled the room, drowning out their voices, and Jos reached to turn off the fan.

"No!" Debbie exclaimed and grabbed his hand. He thought nothing of it.

If anything put Jos on the side of the police, it would be the promise of sex with Debbie. Somehow, that didn't seem important enough to stop his growing sympathy for the resistors. Contemplating a sexual drought aroused him.

"My, you're the horny stallion." Debbie dragged him to the vanity.

"Only, if you say, once a month." Jos pretended to resist.

"Okay, once a month... please."

They did not mention Sherwood Green in the hour it took them to leave the room. Jos finally found his cell phone. He had not seen Debbie turn it off and put it into a drawer when they had arrived.

Strange... He checked for missed calls.

Sherwood Green took summer vacation after destroying the quarry. The gravel shortage slowed down construction all over southern Ontario and left a lime kiln in Ohio short of material. House construction languished. Road managers worried about construction gridlock once autumn traffic returned.

Construction workers and employees of the quarry operations, including the railway to Owen Sound, temporarily lost their jobs. Their union set up a vigilante operation with the stated purpose of "getting Sherwood Green".

Filling in for the lull in attacks, the campaign for the November municipal elections began early. The Sherwood Green Support Network spawned a political party, the Planetary Resistance Party. It nominated several candidates for constituencies with high numbers of homeless and under-employed. Mayor Dodge, indifferent to the plight of the bottom quarter of his electorate, but it dismayed that the PRP found enough citizens to sign the nomination papers.

All-candidates' meetings provided exciting video for the news and gave *Terrorism Toronto* a new opportunity to tie these political upstarts to terrorism.

"Over two hundred species are becoming extinct every day. We need to stop being an industrial society to save the planet." The PRP candidate struggled to complete her message, drowned out by booing. The blustering, bullying rant of the sitting Councillor had whipped the audience into an ugly mood.

"We should end you, you idiot," came from the crowd. Loud cheers followed as the crowd surged towards the platform. Dorothy, the PRP candidate, stood her ground. The moderator pleaded for order. The two constables at the entrance ignored the chaos. Television cameras focused on the mob and back to Dorothy and the television reports would say her look of fear meant weakness. The mob milled in front of the candidate, shouting obscenities, repeating what happened at all meetings involving PRP candidates.

Hostile people blocked the main exits, and Dorothy headed for the side door. Bullies pushed around members of SGSN who supported Dorothy, and they could not get to help their candidate.

Dorothy stepped into the deserted side-street as the door clicked shut behind her.

"There's the bitch!" Two men and a woman rushed around the front corner of the building. "Let's get her."

They rushed towards Dorothy, who yanked on the door handle, but it would not budge. Someone punched her, knocking her to the ground. Several well placed kicks found her ribs. Dorothy tried to curl into a ball, protecting her stomach and vital organs.

"Stop!" she pleaded.

The side door opened. Jos and Walt stepped through. Walt snapped on his camera. It took the attackers a second to realize the television camera exposed them.

"Stop it!" Jos yelled. The trio looked startled and faced directly into the camera.

"Shut up, nigger." One man snarled and stepped towards Jos, who thought he could handle one of the solidly built attackers, but not three.

"Police!" he yelled as loudly. "Help, Police!"

No police, but curious faces peered around the corner of the hall. At the mention of the cops, the attackers fled. One lunged at Walt's camera but missed. Jos helped Dorothy to her feet, trying to calm sobs that Walt captured on video.

"Can you breathe? Is anything broken?"

Dorothy trembled, shook her head, winced, and almost fell. Jos offered a sip from his water bottle.

"You should use a refillable one." Dorothy grimaced.

"Could you recognize your attackers?"

"No, they scared me, but one was a woman."

Dorothy's supporters appeared, trailed by a snarling band of critics. Walt turned on the camera and the mob focused on him. Two of the main agitators hurried away. Jos recognized one of them as a cop from his police reporting.

The mob sounded like the locals they had interviewed after the quarry attack. Town or country, everyone had the same attitude of entitlement and willingness to attack anyone who threatened their way of life. Walt captured a few minutes of the crowd's ranting.

"You can't show the faces of the woman's attackers." Sheri Stein said.

"Why not?" Jos thought it was perfect for his report.

"The police claim it's evidence, and the cops want a warrant for the original recording. The boss thinks it would create sympathy for the terrorists, so we won't run it."

Jos went to re-write his script. Sheri had to vet all of his reports before they made it to air, but he made the usual copy so the video would not disappear.

"Those three looked well built." Jos and Walt left the building, done for the night.

"Do you think they were cops?" Walt looked sceptical.

"Who would lunge at a camera, recording them breaking the law?"

Walt nodded. "It would be an enormous risk, and they might be mercenaries, working for the cops or a candidate."

"One of the mouthy ones in the mob was a night-bird cop from fifty-five division. He's Don somebody."

The attack on Dorothy pushed Jos' sympathies further towards the SGSN, if not Sherwood Green. He would give Diane video of the attack.

The 'Bucks' had closed for the night, so Jos dropped into the Second Cup at Church Street and Wellesley. He frequented the place. Jos often walked home from the studios, hoping he might stumble onto a story. His drag queen friends, Joey and Richard, were at their usual table in their finest attire.

Joey called himself Josephine when in drag. He was an accomplished tattoo artist and worked on Yonge. Richard worked as a desk clerk at a hotel downtown. Tonight, Richard/Rachelle was in a very seductive slinky full length hot-pink number. Jos thought he was cute enough to date. Josephine was pleasing, but not as sexy. Jos winked and sat at the next table.

"Hey, Jos," the female night manager came over and smiled at the pair of CDs. She was attractively short and plump but envied the sexy-looking pair. *Guys in drag look better than me.* She sighed.

"A guy came in earlier and left this note." She pushed a folded sheet of paper to Jos. "He said he wanted to talk to you and to call whenever you were here. He said he would come right over."

Jos sipped his coffee. The paper held a cell phone number and the signature, "S.G."

"I'm off for a date." Rachelle flaunted past Jos, ruffling a pink boa across his face.

"Have fun." Jos smiled. He liked these guys.

"Oh well," Josephine said. "He has all the fun. I guess I'll go home and do the dishes."

"Don't you have a date?" Jos thought the two were married, but perhaps not.

"We have an open marriage," Josephine paused at the table. "He takes advantage of it and has a sugar daddy somewhere. I love him too much, so I'm faithful." Joey sighed, adjusted his fake bosom, kissed the night manager on the cheek, and disappeared.

Jos made the call.

"I'm Sherwood Green." The mousy man sitting opposite Jos hardly seemed a threat to anyone. He had a thin black moustache and wild side burns. Slick black hair stuck out above his forehead. To Jos' imagination, he seemed a spindly, moustached version of Elvis Presley.

Except for the moustache he borrowed from an old actor named Errol Flynn, Joe Burns had worked hard on his Elvis look. His stints at Elvis re-enactments always raised laughter. Burns eventually stopped performing, but he never lost the look. The Flynn moustache was to make him a brave hero.

Jos knew Sherwood Green was not an individual. The man sitting opposite drinking free coffee was a fake.

"How did you become Sherwood Green?" Jos activated the recorder on his phone.

"I've always been an environmentalist," Joe licked an apple fritter from his fingers. "I've been involved with many smart people on the internet. Did you know they faked the moon landings?" Joe looked earnestly into Jos' eyes. "They're all part of the government conspiracy to take over the world, with the Masons and the RCs."

"What does that have to do with environmental terrorism?" Jos tried not to laugh.

"One of these smart guys told me about this DGR manifesto. It looked good, except for the feminist bullshit, but I thought I'd get involved. We have an enormous group all over the world now, just ready for action. I'm the Toronto leader." Burns' face shone with pride. "I've done those car fires and the subway, me and my people." Burns did not mention the financial district attacks or the quarry.

"How many people do you have?" Jos checked to make sure his cell recorded.

"There's six. I'm the leader." Burns repeated. "Sherwood Green is my cover name. I won't tell you my real name." His voice was conspiratorial.

"You've done great things," Jos thought, stroking Joe's ego would get better results. "Where did you find your supporters?"

"On Facebook, I set up a page and people flocked to me. I had to sort out a few nuts, but I have good people."

Jos' phone made a strange beep. It still had a good charge.

As part of his work, Jos found a dozen Sherwood Greens on the internet. Most had appeared since the attacks began. Every one of them was an attention seeker, satirist or police. The police sponsored recruiting page was the most sophisticated.

"Won't the cops find you on the internet?"

"I'm smart," Burns said. "We e-mail in code and have a phone app to stay in touch."

Jos could not avoid a grimace. The man's stupidity was making the interview a waste.

It might give me another angle for the documentary, thought Jos. *We could show how the public likes to get attention by latching on big events.*

"How did you set fire to the dealerships?"

"I have to go." Burns became nervous. Jos had asked a question he had no actual answer for. "I'll be in touch and tip you off about the next attack."

As Burns reached the door, two large men left a table near the door and grabbed his arm.

"Come with us," one said, "Police."

They escorted him out the door. Jos could see them cuffing him beside an unmarked police car. He could not spot any other cops. No one was coming for him. Jos thought that the cops had ben there was strange. Maybe they wanted Burns for something else.

Jos tried to remember when the two cops had arrived. *How did they know the imposter was in the coffee shop?*

Remembering the episode with Diane at the pub, Jos glanced at the night manager. She was fiddled with a coffeepot and seemed innocent. The woman had been working here for years. She wasn't a cop. Arrests were common occurrences in the store at night, *but how did the cops know?*

Jos put his cell phone into its pouch and went home.

Chapter Nineteen

"How many think this guy's the real Sherwood Green?" Frank Langstaff asked.

No one responded. They were not sure what their boss believed, and no one wanted to be on the wrong side. Uncharacteristically, Frank had arrived late and seemed distracted. Everyone thought it strange. The arrest of Joe Burns seemed a breakthrough.

"I don't think this misfit could blow up a balloon, let alone a building." Frank did not smile. Everyone else laughed, just in case. "We're going to hold him to let the public think there's progress."

The officers in the room relaxed. At least they knew which way to believe on this arrest.

"Frank," Mayor Dodge smiled from behind his desk. "The terrorists have backed off, but their political supporters have been disrupting election meetings just by speaking. It's good for us. If the meetings are wild and voters scared, then the incumbent usually wins. This Burns arrest makes people think Sherwood Green is on the ropes."

"It's two and a half months to the election. Can we keep it up that long?" Dodge had the one last worry.

"I've been in touch with the OPP and CSIS. The Province will lay suspicion of causing an explosion and the Feds are going to add terrorism charges. We can keep the evidence from being examined for some months and hide the fact the guy's a loony. When we have no more use for him, he'll end up in the psycho ward."

"You don't think he's connected to the terrorists?"

"No, he's a small time attention seeker, a real loser, a nutcase. Burns told us that Elvis is alive and living in Niagara Falls." The men laughed.

"There's one big worry. The terrorists who blew the quarry up north took from two to five tonnes of explosives. It's enough to level a good sized building."

"Good God! We need to plan for casualties. I hope they wait until after the election."

"We'll be ready." Langstaff said. "We're putting K-rails in parking spaces. We don't want a car bomb."

"It would serve our purpose if there was an attack hurting innocent people," Dodge thought out loud, and Frank pondered the advantages since Sherwood Green had already killed an innocent person.

"The public is on our side, and they hate the terrorists." The mayor flipped on a video of the most recent election meeting involving a PRP candidate. Swearing, spitting and rushing, the speakers' platform filled two minutes.

"Served the asshole right," Langstaff smiled. Frank's cell rang, and he listened with cryptic replies. Frank became agitated and his expression darkened.

"Are you okay, Frank?" Dodge asked.

"Yah, fine, there were a few murders last night. I always want to know in case the media comes asking."

"I'm announcing your appointment tomorrow, effective immediately. The ceremony will wait for the fall."

"I have to go. The homicide guys need me."

To avoid dangerous public meetings, the PRP changed tactics and began a door-to-door campaign with the candidate accompanied by an escort. They endured anger and threats, but found positive people. They asked no one to post a lawn sign. The PRP only placed signs in the usual public spaces, but PRP signs never lasted long. The police had no interest in investigating their theft.

They had decided to contest the few wards with working-class and welfare residents. None of the SGSN or PRP members actually came from these classes, but they had the standard left-wing unspoken connection to the outsiders of the world. By chance, they found some genuine support. If everyone voted, although they would not win, it would send a message to the elite of Toronto.

Jos and Walt accompanied the candidates, but Sheri would only use the more exciting, anti-PRP confrontations.

"Jos, are we too soft on these guys?" Walt asked.

"Maybe," Jos had edged closer to being a sympathizer. "Everyone else is taking one side. As a journalist, I'd rather explore the entire issue."

Walt stowed the latest video disc into his pouch. Walt nodded.

"Don't forget your copy."

The journalists used a computer in the main Toronto library to copy the footage. They wanted no trace left on a work or home computer.

Jos walked home along Bloor Street as a police car rushed past with lights flashing and siren wailing.

The cop car pulled over, facing the wrong way in the right-hand lane of the westbound roadway. A fire truck appeared, followed by paramedics. The vehicles turned up Sherbourne Street, over the bridge. Jos picked up his pace. The cruiser blocked the bridge over Rosedale Valley. Jos recognized the cop on point.

"What's going on, Ed?"

"Someone found a dead woman in the ravine. They're using the valley road to get to her, but there might be evidence on the bridge if she jumped."

"Would that be high enough to kill someone?" Jos had walked the bridge several times.

"Maybe she hit her head. Want to look?" Ed and Jos had gotten along very well on the night shift. "Hey, Sally, take over her for a minute."

"See down there." Ed pointed to a spot in the trees, halfway to the roadway below. "How's it going?" Ed called down to a paramedic.

"Dead all right," the man shouted back, "but it's not a woman. It's a CD queer."

Jos looked at the spot. A pink boa had snagged high in the tree. Below, he could see part of a lifeless form dressed in a shiny, hot-pink dress. He felt sick.

Jos hurried down past his apartment building to the Second Cup. He was relieved that Josephine was not there. Jos did not want to be the one to tell Joey, Josephine, that someone had murdered Richard.

Chapter Twenty

Jos awoke, depressed and grieving. The first face he saw on the morning news was Frank Langstaff as the cop discussed Rachelle's death.

"An autopsy has shown that Richard St. Pierre died elsewhere from a blow to the head, and they dumped his body from the bridge. We have a team working on this, and I want to assure the LGBT community we will spare no effort in bringing the killer to justice. There have been no recent murders of members of our gay community, and we don't think this is the work of a homophobic serial-killer."

"We have no suspects but want to talk to Richard's husband, Joey Brown." Two pictures flashed side by side, labelled Richard and Joey. They were pictures of the pair in dress from a glamour display at the 'G-Street Centre'. There were no photos of them in men's clothes.

"Mr. Brown is missing, but he's not a suspect, perhaps a victim. We hope he can fill us in on last night's events."

Jos thought, *they'll pin this on Joey if they can. Frank looks mechanical and upset, and why is Frank involved as Chief? The murder has nothing to do with terrorism.*

On the way to work, Jos detoured into the Metropolitan University campus. From a pay phone in the food court, away from video cameras, he called the police snitch line.

"The queer who somebody killed the other night had a boyfriend on the side, and the cops should look for him. The dead guy had a date with his friend the night they killed him. He went to meet him after ten o'clock.... Who am I? I'm a friend of the police."

Jos hung up and hurried outside. He no longer trusted the cops and expected they lied about the so called anonymous tip line. He sipped a coffee across the street as a patrol car arrived and the officers rush inside.

August progressed and although there were several crop fires in southern Ontario, no one thought Sherwood Green did it. Most blamed anti-GMO organisations. They burned thousands of hectares of wheat in the US mid-west. For the first time, they saw action in the Canadian west with two massive crop fires in Saskatchewan. The anti-terrorist forces said nothing. There was not enough manpower to patrol rural roads. They concentrated on analyzing communication in a desperate search for suspects, believing coordination was a Sherwood Green mistake and would leave clues.

In their exhaustive search of data, security forces forgot the basic edict of it is best to hide in plain view.

Sherwood Green and its cousins used the comments sections of commercial web sites as letter drops. News sites, gardening, YouTube, and many more became the recipient of comments by people with handles like 'Tony the Tiger', Aunt Jamima, and Sexy George.

With the coordinated crop fires, someone named Sam Garret triggered events by posting a video of a grass fire to the Facebook page of the Canadian Firefighter's Association and asking how they could fight such a fire. It was a harmless question and raised many serious responses. 'Kansas Girl', buried a message in the comments: *"If it's dry, wheat shines brightly at the witching hour big moon, but only for three days."*

This meant, set the fires after midnight on the night of the full moon. If it rains, do it within three days.

Sam Garret replied, "Beautiful" along with three others that read "great," "nice" and "fine weather". It was nonsensical, but easily discounted as female silliness by the macho firefighters. Kansas Girl drew sexist comments; however, the message remained on the site for a day and then Kansas Girl deleted it.

It had only taken one cross border meeting, two years before, to set up the secure code system. Each cell determined their own targets, and the only rule required that they be strategic. The strategy was to increase apprehension within the state security apparatus and stimulate wasted effort in protecting symbolic targets.

A Tumblr account with the title 'Urban Life' was an interesting hodgepodge of posts. In July, someone had posted an advertising shot of the Toronto subway system with the comment that it was a wonderful ride on a Monday morning. Posts of similar material by others, and comments showed the NYC, Chicago and San Francisco services. A posted photo advertising a concert in July set the timing for the coordinated attack.

The individual in each group responsible for communication knew a lot about secure routing and disguising computers. They never made cell calls or texted, but always gained access through free public Wi-Fi and they never used a place twice.

Every resistor thought the cops would have captured them in the first few months and their unexpected lease on life forced them to design secondary ways to coordinate. If control broke down, it would not be a problem. The first few attacks had already achieved their purpose of having the police look for a large international movement. As long as the isolated cells hit local strategic targets, it would seem coordinated.

Nothing more happened as summer ended. The Canadian National Exhibition in Toronto drew would be an attractive terrorist target and drew a massive police effort. Hundreds of uniformed and plainclothes cops patrolled. Video cameras recorded people as they entered and face recognition software captured a few dozen wanted criminals, but no terrorists.

Tuesday evening after Labour Day, Jos slipped into a seat in a lecture hall at the university. Professor MacDonald, a tenured member of the Faculty of Arts and Science in the ecology programme, taught the Politics of Environmental Resistance. Unknown to all, he had lit the spark behind Sherwood Green, but time had passed and MacDonald had left no evidence of his involvement.

Walt held the fort at the studio and would call about any attack. Sheri had agreed to pay Jos' tuition. Two dozen students sat in the room.

"I have to tell you right now," MacDonald began, "if you want to do deep resistance, you have disqualified yourself by enrolling in this course. The police will already know about you. Do you agree, constable?"

Everyone looked around for the undercover cop. MacDonald noticed two people who hesitated. He smiled.

"I don't know who he or she is, but one or more of you will be a police officer, or an informer. It doesn't matter, as we'll only discuss legal things here."

"In environmental resistance, it is a waste and dangerous to fight the police. They are just the paid lackeys of oppression," he tried not to look at his two suspects, "and their rich owners expect them to suffer the physical attack in place of themselves. They want you to fight the police, so the resistors attacked where the police aren't."

"Isn't that the Sun Tzu technique?" A student said.

"Yes," MacDonald smiled. "The Art of War is a good place to start. The bottom line is, never attack where it's expected. We are way ahead of ourselves here."

"I hope everyone got the book, *Deep Green Resistance.* It's in the bookstore and you can get it online. Steal a copy if you can, but of course, I don't recommend breaking the law." The class laughed.

"We will not teach the manifesto, but it's necessary reading. I want to discuss motivation, the failure of mainstream environmental movements, the consequences of industrialism and organizing and supporting resistance by the above ground techniques. Remember, if they catch resistors, the suspects can expect harsh punishment. Above ground supporters already face constant harassment and abuse from everywhere. Almost all the population opposes them, as we have seen during this election."

"I'm surprised someone has actually begun a resistance, and it gives us actual events to discuss."

MacDonald spent an hour outlining the course content for the next six months and distributed the course outline. "Okay, before you go, your assignment is a one page minimum, maximum three, answering the question: Is environmental resistance terrorism? Please back up your arguments with more than one reference each for pro and con, and turn in your work next Tuesday. Begin reading at least one book on the list. Oh, and if you want to get involved, Diane Arsenault is in the class., so see her about joining the Sherwood Green Support Network."

Jos caught Diane as they left the hall. "I would love to interview a member of Sherwood Green."

"I have no way of contacting them. Maybe you should ask on camera. I'm sure they watch Terrorism Toronto. You slip in honesty with the propaganda."

"Thanks, Sherwood Green has been quiet."

"Now that September is here," Diane paused, "I think something will happen. The banksters are back at work."

Outside, three protesters met Diane and Jos holding up signs that said *Terrorists are killers, Kill the terrorists*

"Killers, killers, killers," they chanted at the students.

"Ironic." Diane muttered.

One of MacDonald's students yelled at them, "Are you at university to think or be a puppet?"

The trio charged at the girl. She fled, followed by curses and sexual innuendo. Jos recognized one protestor as the business student at the anti-whaling meeting.

"Let's get a beer." Diane suggested.

Chapter Twenty-One

Sheri liked Jos' plan to ask on air for an interview. Action had not happened for weeks and public interest had waned. Computer hacking attacks were too boring, but expecting an interview would excite people.

"Let me know if they contact you."

"I will, if I can." Jos was non-committal, and he knew if a meeting happened, Sherwood Green would want no one else to know ahead of time. Sheri might even tip the police because an arrest would be bigger news than a reporter getting an interview.

A week after Jos' first mention of wanting to meet Sherwood Green, an envelope arrived for Walt. Inside, there was a second envelope and a note. *Please give the card to Jos Amiel.* There was no return address, but they decorated the second envelope with a wide-eyed turkey with the caption: *Why should I be thankful?*

Inside was a cell phone number. The card and envelopes went through the shredder.

"What's this all about?" Walt asked.

"It's better you don't know, then you won't need to lie. Only you and I know about the envelopes."

Jos made the call from a pay phone in Union Station.

"Call this number again at eight o'clock in the evening, in two days. We'll give you an interview." They had distorted the voice, and Jos could not tell if it was a man or woman.

"I'm going to meet a real member of Sherwood Green." Jos snuggled against Debbie in the big king-size hotel bed. Debbi never skimped when they got together, and the warmth of her naked body reassured Jos, who had feared she would refuse to meet.

"Don't go!" Debbie sat up, agitated. "It's dangerous."

"It's my big chance."

Debbie lay back on the pillow and pouted at the ceiling. It touched Jos that she cared about his safety.

"Okay, go then," she seemed resigned. "Can you let me know when?"

"Nope, they'll let me know two days from now."

"Be careful," she said. Her kiss was sincere, seductive. She had tears in her eyes.

Jos called from the food court in the Adelaide Centre.

"Go right now and take the subway to Broadview Station. Go out the front door onto Broadview. Get into the silver Honda." The distorted voice cut off.

Jos only expected a telephone interview, and this surprised him. He would not call Debbie or Sheri.

Red dots moved across a city map at police headquarters. They disappeared as Jos' train entered the subway, but the watchers expected them to reappear at the Broadview station, but Sherwood Green would frustrate them once more.

"Jos Amiel?" a young black woman in her thirties touched his arm at the top of the eastbound stairs.

"Yes."

"Come with me." She took his arm as if they were a couple, led him down to the westbound platform, and they rode to Kipling in silence. She picked a car from the centre of the parking lot and they sped off. The woman remained silent, not answering Jos' questions and parked the car between two dark-coloured vans at a burger joint along Dundas Street in Mississauga. She led him into the store, pointed to the washroom, and disappeared.

When the red dot reappeared at Kipling, the Project Tom team rushed into desperate action. The car waiting on Broadview made a U-turn and, with siren howling, dashed to the southbound Parkway and west on the Gardner Expressway. Two other cars sped in the same direction. The closest one, idling near the airport, hurried down Highway 427. At Dundas Street, they directed the driver west. The red dot had stopped with Jos in the restaurant washroom.

A large bearded man wearing dark sunglasses frisked Jos and turned off his phone.

"You'll get this back when you leave. Come..." These were the only words the man uttered.

They put Jos into the back of one of the dark vans, where a woman waited with her face covered by a bandana and tinted glasses. A white man in his late twenties sat behind the wheel. A peaked baseball cap covered his forehead, and dark-rimmed night driving glasses with yellow lenses obscured the man's eye colour. He had a small goatee and thick moustache, both obvious fakes to frustrate face recognition software.

The red dot moved as the van pulled onto Dundas. The unmarked police car wheeled into the burger joint parking lot and circled the building before pursuing onto the street. They were out of their jurisdiction, and headquarters hurriedly coordinated with the Peel Regional Police.

"Don't ask names." The woman sounded middle-aged and pleasant. The van kept pace with westbound traffic.

"How do I know you're Sherwood Green, not cops?"

"You don't, but why in hell would the cops trap you in such a complicated way? You're a bit player in this."

"I had liked you guys." Jos chuckled.

"You like Diane Arsenault and that makes you sympathetic, and you also know we're right about the planet. Most people feel the planet's doomed but deny it because the result is too horrible to think about."

"I guess you're right." Jos had not admitted to having deeper feelings for Diane, but the bonfire of his relationship with Debbie could hide a candle.

"The public is hostile, and I'm caught in the middle," Jos admitted. "How can you convince them?"

"We aren't trying to make converts, and this isn't a popularity contest. We're fighting for the planet, the voiceless two hundred species humans kill every day, and it's them we care about. If humans survive, the ones left must fit into the web and care about the silent members. If we don't, we don't deserve to survive."

"That sounds simplistic."

"It is simple, and perhaps that's why humans can't understand it," she chuckled.

"The environmental movement focuses on symptoms and pick up litter to put into landfill. If it's out of sight, it's out of mind, and they all feel proud, as if they did something. It's the same as cleaning up the oceans, all good, but fixing the effect, not the cause."

"It puts journalists in the middle. Look at how many journalists they murdered around the world. No one on any side wants to hear the truth."

"What's your plan?" Jos had read Sherwood Green's manifesto, but he wanted to hear it firsthand.

"We are going to take down Toronto. It's the hub of the Canadian economy, but it means attacking southern Ontario and the resource industry all across the country. Resources are the source of Toronto's wealth and power. The Canadian industrial economy's a spider's web. Kill the spider and the web falls apart. We need to cut the web as well, at those points that hold it up."

"What about other places, the USA, for instance, won't the Yankees just come in and take over Canada?"

"Sister organizations are attacking the heart of the empire. We share info and news and have coordinated but no other connection. As you say, the USA would invade Canada, so they must go down too, maybe first."

"Some banks threaten to move to Calgary."

"Even if they do, they won't be safe for long."

"Fuck!" the driver said. "We're being followed."

The van sped up and swung hard to the left. They cut off a dump truck, hurrying to beat a yellow turn arrow. Blasts of the air horn faded as they sped away.

"Those truck drivers are assholes, anyway. That was fun." The driver turned hard right onto a darkened sidestreet, confident he had shaken the tail. Before he could make another turn onto a busy street, headlights appeared behind. He only had a couple of block's lead.

"Shit! They're still on us."

The van sped towards the next light back at Dundas, dancing around another truck and its protesting air-horn.

"Take it easy. We don't want to be flipped over in a flower pot," the woman laughed.

They had promoted Whitey to driver because he was the best.

"Do you think Spike got away?" Whitey liked Spike and dreamed that in a far off time, after they won the fight, they could be together. He hid the van in heavy street traffic, where he thought they would be safe.

"I think so. I don't think the cops know about her."

"They're still there." Whitey sounded more concerned. "How could they follow that manoeuvre?"

The two in the back looked at Jos.

"Maybe I missed something, and he's wired," the big guy reached for Jos.

"Strip off," the woman drew a handgun. Jos flinched.

"He's clean," she did not laugh, but Jos felt dirty.

"His cell is warm, but it's supposed to be off. Do a few lane changes."

The big guy slid to the back of the van and opened a five gallon canister of diesel fuel. As the van changed lanes, he poured a stream of fuel out the back, lubricating the road. Vehicles behind them swerved, and several collided, and then more crashed into them. One crossed into the westbound traffic and hit a car in the left lane. Once the can was empty, they spread a box of long roofing nails behind. Somewhere back there, it trapped the cop car, and with any luck, had crashed.

Whitey sped up to catch a pickup, and Jos' cell phone went into the back of the truck. Whitey made a quick left north as the dots on the police computer screen continued east.

"I hope that takes care of them. Get dressed."

Jos trembled but the gun had disappeared.

"They haven't picked us up, so they tracked the cell."

"It never left me."

"Not since our first attack?"

"No! Oh wait. I forgot it at the pub at the first meeting with Diane, and it stayed in the pub overnight."

"The cops know everything you have done since then." She frowned, but caught herself. "You had no reason to suspect, but have you compromised anyone else?"

Jos remembered how quickly the police had arrived to arrest the nut, claiming to be Sherwood Green.

He thought about Debbie and realized the cops heard their sex sessions. He blushed, grateful for the dark.

"No one important, but they must have heard everything we've said. I'm sorry."

"It doesn't matter. The content is for the public. If they get me, they will have my voice print. It will affect how I operate, but we're bigger than me, so it's no problem."

"I'll send the code." She said to the big man. "They probably made our plates." She sent a text, '1-4-3.' "Go to four," she told Whitey. "We're three minutes away."

Whitey swung the van into a mall parking garage and at the back, they found a silver Mercedes, engine running. Jos watched a woman disappear up the stairwell.

The leader drove the car from its spot, and Whitey backed the van in. Jos watched the big guy take a metal tube. Wearing surgical gloves, he poured a sharp-smelling liquid into the open end. He sealed it with a screw-on plastic cap and carefully set it upright between the rear seats beside a full can of diesel oil.

"What's that?" Jos asked.

"Classified." was the curt reply, "hurry."

The three sat in the roomy back seat and Whitey swung the Mercedes west onto Bloor, then north into a maze of streets in a newer, upscale subdivision. They heard the fire trucks screaming towards the shopping mall.

"We want to let you know there will be a massive operation soon. We want you to warn about it on TV. That's why we invited you. If they want to know our targets, they should look at the ones we've already hit. We are not terrorists and avoid casualties, even cops."

"We'll put it all in an e-mail so you don't need to admit you met us. The cops know, but they won't bother you. They'll think you'll eventually lead them back to us. You can talk about this visit to avoid jail or to keep your job. Tell them everything, but it won't help the cops."

"Why don't you pretend to be Islamists to divert attention?"

"We don't want to divert attention, besides all religion is a cover for the elite everywhere, as they suppress people and destroy the planet. Religious wars will always happen. The more they kill each other, the better for the planet. We don't want to increase bigotry. If we succeed, survivors will have to work together."

"How are you organized? How do you operate?"

"We are democratic, and all of us believe in the one aim of destroying industrial society. We are un-democratic and don't debate side issues or secondary objectives. Issues like socialism, feminism and gender politics are important, but for after the collapse although, we don't tolerate sexism or racism in our organization. We only ever had one..." She caught herself, as if saying too much. In fact, they had accidentally recruited one sexist bigot. Once the person had learned too much about Sherwood Green, there had been only one option to deal with him, but she would never reveal it.

"Sherwood Green won't be around for the constructive phase," she changed the subject. "Some of our members might be alive to take part, but none of us will be leaders. There's at least one all woman feminist resistance group in the USA. We coordinate when we can, but they never argue whether a target is a 'feminist' target. The only questions are, is it a strategic target? Is the time of the attack strategic to destroy industrialism?"

"Several public groups say they support our goal but refuse to work with the SGSN. Arsenault and the others won't waste time helping in the other group's cause, because secondary causes are only tinkering to preserve industrial society. They may be important in building something new after we win but divert effort from the actual fight. The SGSN is more democratic than we are, but you must ask Diane."

"Are you the Earth Liberation Army?"

"No, they are still active but ineffective. The ELA attacks symbolic targets, not strategic ones and are into animal rights. We agree all species have rights, but mink farms are not strategic, but simply they're a symptom of the real problem, and if you kill the heart, the limbs atrophy."

"Millions will die. Is that justified?"

"Billions will die, and if we don't succeed, most species on the planet will die with us."

"Do you think you can succeed? Can you even avoid arrest long enough?"

"Not likely, but it's the planet's last hope. The global economy is on the brink of collapse, and we want to make it happen sooner."

"When will these attacks take place?"

The woman smiled, ignored the question and said, "We're going to drop you near the Go Station in Port Credit."

Chapter Twenty-two

Jos arrived at work early the next day, excited and wanting to review all Sherwood Green videos.

An e-mail waited, and it covered everything discussed with Sherwood Green, but with no mention of when the attacks would happen. Jos copied the message, printed copies and took the message to Sheri.

"The police will want to see this right away." Holding evidence made Sheri nervous.

"They probably already have it." Jos caught himself, because, officially, he wasn't supposed to know the cops got their own copy of the e-mail.

"The cops wouldn't monitor our internet, and while I am calling, write this into a script. You are going on this morning with a special report from *Terrorism-Toronto*." Sheri smelled a scoop.

Jos edited his presentation when Sheri called him to her office. Two constables from Project Tom sat to one side and glared at Jos because they knew the actual story. The network lawyer sat opposite.

"When did you find this?" There were no formalities.

Jos described his morning after his arrival at work.

"Is that all you know?" The cop snarled.

"Yes, about the message. I know the sky is blue and a few things like that."

The lawyer snickered. Sheri bit her thumb. Jos didn't know it, but the by-play had earned him more respect from Sheri. Despite meticulously following her boss' orders, she disliked the interference from the network and the police. She would not rebel, but she would get her satisfaction.

"Don't get smart with me," the cop growled. "Be careful what you say about this. It's evidence."

"It's our property." Sheri showed some fight. The lawyer nodded. "We'll report the facts, as we always do."

Sheri stared at Jos. He had tried to get in touch with Sherwood Green, and she wondered if he had succeeded.

The cops left as Jos went on-the-air with the blockbuster. The upstaged news-media rushed to catch up, with most papers and others suggesting that TNN had an inside source. It hit close to home, but Sheri laughed and ran a denial, adding the message of looking at past targets for future targets. She stretched out the exclusive.

Toronto went crazy. Mayor Dodge held several news conferences, trying to calm the population. Cop cars swarmed everywhere and defeated Dodge's efforts to keep the calm. Frank Langstaff held his own press sessions.

"Considering the details of the message, we sent the ETF to the Fukushima headquarters, welded all the electrical vaults in the streets shut, and we put twenty-four-hour guard on all key places."

"We were told the hydro blasts downtown were accidental. Are you now saying the terrorists blew them up?" The Star reporter asked.

"Yes," Langstaff admitted.

Jos felt vindicated and dug out the video to repeat the segments of the hydro-vault blasts.

"The banks and other financial agencies have extra security, but we think this might be a bluff. The force traced the message to a Wi-Fi in a McDonalds on Dufferin Street. We examined video and conducted a canvass the neighbourhood but so far, no luck. An attention seeker could have sent the message. We have one such person in custody, charged under the terrorism laws, but I can't tell you more about him."

Joe Burns had languished in solitary in Metro West for the weeks since his arrest. Langstaff hoped the mention of Burns would calm things, but it added an hour to the news conference as the surprised reporters tried to wring more information about Burns from the Chief.

Jos toyed with telling his story about Burns on air, but decided they might accuse him of being a terrorist or a police informant, and either would end his career.

"Ottawa declared an emergency and ordered unarmed troops to observe and to assist in logistics. I can't give you any operational details." Frank walked off the platform.

The press obsessed over the constitutionality of the army being brought in. The satirical shows called the move *Lastman's Last Stand,* a reference to a former mayor who had grandstanded over a snowstorm.

Commentators dismissed Sherwood Green, belittling their efforts by naming the threat, *The Battle of Montgomery's Tavern.* Most residents had not heard of the rebellion in 1837, fewer laughed.

Mayor Dodge had his own problems. Aside from the city running out of money, workers refused to pick up garbage, claiming there might be bombs. Fire destroyed a garbage truck operated by a private contractor, an accidental coincidence, but everyone blamed Sherwood Green. By Thanksgiving weekend, huge numbers of people refused to work at night, attend court and ride on the subway system. Toronto barely sputtered along. The holiday weekend came as a welcome break.

A week after Jos broke the story, a resistor group in New York made a similar threat. Panic shopping with its usual violence in the USA depleted store shelves. Many cities imposed a curfew, especially those already suffering racial tension. As if nature had joined the conspiracy, a category two hurricane threatened Chesapeake Bay.

The Americans, eager to stir up fear, followed the same route as Toronto in protecting all previously targeted cities, but had riot police and the national-guard everywhere.

Extremists increased diatribes against minorities and foreigners, and targeted Canadian tourists in Florida and cross-border shoppers with abuse. The businesses that depended on Canadian money suffered while a feeling of pending doom settled on Toronto.

Another envelope arrived at the network. Jos hoped his police contact or Sherwood Green had sent it, but the package contained his cell phone, with no note. The cops had given him a message. Jos knew of the surprise and fear when cops with guns drawn had surrounded the pickup truck. Police remained silent about being tricked, but Walt had followed the whole thing on the scanner. The street patrols had not used encrypted radio and blamed the massive pile-up on Dundas on vandalism.

Jos removed the battery from the phone and flushed the memory card down the toilet. He bought a hamburger in a laminated food pouch at the burger shop next door and wrapped the supposedly dead phone in the aluminium-foil. Later in the afternoon, he walked down to the waterfront and threw the phone and battery into the harbour.

The police realized his phone had not moved since their phoney courier had delivered the package. Two plainclothes in an older Toyota arrived at the TNN building as Jos returned from the waterfront. The easy and entertaining tracking of Amiel had ended. and they replaced it with around the clock tailing. It multiplied the cost and effort, but the Mississauga fiasco convinced the police that Jos would be the one to lead them to the terrorists, since he had actually met Sherwood Green.

The three weeks after Thanksgiving remained quiet. People relaxed and talked about a hoax. The security forces became jaded and lazy while idle soldiers caused trouble in the bars. Other media made fun of TNN and of Jos.

November arrived and with it, election eve. They projected an easy victory for Mayor Dodge. He spent more time in planning the victory party than in organizing voter turnout. As darkness fell on election eve, everything unfolded in the mayor's favour.

Two days before the vote, a nonsense message by Sandy
G. appeared in the comments section of the front page lead
story in the internet version of The Toronto Sun: *The red
fox is jumping over the brown dog tomorrow.*

Chapter Twenty-three

Late in the afternoon, the day before the vote, a semi-trailer pulled up to the main gate of Hydro One's Kipling yard fifteen minutes before quitting time. The facility served as an important substation where Hydro One handed over power distribution to Toronto Hydro, and it stored material for construction and emergency repair. The gate guard saw dozens of deliveries every day.

"Go see Jim at the warehouse down road 'C'." The guard handed the manifest back to the driver.

They dropped the trailer near the back of the yard. It held insulators and other porcelain devices imported from the USA. The receiver signed the driver's copy and walked away, ready to head home. He would check the load against the packing list tomorrow. The driver released the rear door latch, and the tractor roared away.

In a hollow surrounded by cartons deep inside the load, four members of Sherwood Green relaxed and waited for the security night shift to come on duty. As eleven p.m. approached, they opened a tunnel to the few meters of space at the back door. They dropped into the shadows near the back fence, well away from security.

Ed Springer set his lunch cooler on the desk in the security room near the main gate of the natural gas compressor complex, a dozen kilometres west of the Kipling sub-station. Ed munched on a taco while scanning the security monitors. A car skidded to a stop in the front drive, beyond the sliding gate. Young partiers jumped out, singing and waving beer bottles towards the camera.

Ed considered calling the police. These drunks should not be on the road, but that would be too much trouble. Anything on the other side of the fence was not his problem. A half-dressed woman stumbled from the car, her bare breasts exposed in the gate lights. Ed checked his weapon and headed to the gate to get a better look.

The drunken revellers took turns fondling the woman until they noticed Ed inside the gate.

"You want a share?" One of the drunken men yelled, brandishing his beer bottle. "Want a beer?"

The woman staggered towards the gate.

"Hey, honey, want a feel." She flaunted her ample chest towards the guard.

Ed was young, horny and inexperienced. The security contractor spent little on training the inexperienced guards.

"Come here, bitch. Let me feel." He leered, sticking his fingers through the chain link.

"Not that way, honey." She moved her breasts near the fence, but just out of reach. "You're sexy, but I get more than that back there." She staggered a step back.

Ed broke several rules by opening the gate, and the men staggered forward, expecting a show. She played with her zipper seductively as Ed reached for the woman.

He fell to the ground after the blow to his head. The two men dragged him into the compound, and the woman parked the car out of sight behind the guardhouse. They tied Ed with duct tape and dumped him on the guardroom floor.

A fourth attacker had cut through the line fence as back-up in case Ed had not opened the gate.

Impex and detonators came from the car and they fixed charges to critical spots, including the back-up generator. If they got the blast they hope for, everything, including the fence, would burn or melt.

They drove north, over Highway 401, into the darkness of rural Halton. They had set the timers for twenty minutes, so the blasts would happen before Ed's midnight check in. Ed would wake up, cold and wet, in a ditch west of Georgetown, his gun missing.

In the Kipling sub-station, three black-clad figures slid along the shadowed wall of a building. Video cameras watched the yard, but they displayed only strategic locations in the security office. The rest recorded on a remote computer. A guard patrolled a set route, and the intruders waited near a check-in station.

At the fence, the fourth operative examined six flatbed trailers loaded with emergency sub-stations. These sat ready if one of the remote medium-voltage switchyards had a failure. He climbed onto the first trailer. With one swing of his long-handled hammer, he broke off the lower drain valve of the transformer's cooling system. Mineral oil gushed out as he repeated the effort five more times and placed a picric ignitor under each transformer. They timed all the explosive devices to ignite about twelve thirty in the morning. Everyone hated handling the bombs, afraid they had made copper plug separating the sulphuric and picric acids too thin.

The trio in the yard left their first victim unconscious and duct-taped in the shadows. His partner in the office had no clue about the attack. The trio stole the key to the guard-room, but if these guys were typical, they would have left the door unlocked.

They left the second guard bound on the guardroom floor, and the resistors met at the live transformers.

One went to work on the high voltage brutes. Unlike the trailers, these carried electricity, and even though he worked safely below the five-hundred thousand volt high end circuits, being around this much danger stressed.

Concrete dams surround the transformers to contain oil leaks and suited the plans since pooled oil would feed a fire. He placed the last of his incendiaries under each unit and checked the location of the valves while his friends struggled with the mounting bolts for the huge line breakers.

The breakers would trip when sensors detected the low oil or overheating in the transformers. They hoped, with the mounts undone, the breakers would jump off their bases and topple over when they operated. They found the paint-covered bolts hard to shift, but freed two completely with the remaining two half done.

"Time's up. It'll have to do."

All four rushed to knock off transformer valves and oil accumulated in the containment and over the igniters. They cut the north fence and hurried to the railway tracks at the transit station. Street clothes replaced black the balaclavas. The 11:59 westbound arrived. The resistors joined the dozen people leaving the station and drove away in two cars. One went north, the other south. They wanted to be well away before the blasts.

The gas compression station in Halton exploded, breaking windows five kilometres away and blew vehicles off the highway with some injuries. At almost the same time, a compressor station on the main trans-Canada line north of the city exploded in another spectacular show. Blow-torch flames blasted skyward at the two locations. The jets would blaze until they cut the feed pressure, but it would take hours to close off the gas. What survived would be unrecognizable puddles of melted metal and glass. They assumed Ed had died until he stumbled into a Georgetown donut shop a few hours later. Gas pressure dropped in Toronto and shut down two gas-fired generating stations.

The west end sub-station blew shortly after twelve-thirty when massive orange fireballs followed brief blue arcs. North of the city, a half-dozen steel line-towers toppled as explosives severed their legs. The same happened on the east end on the lines from the nuclear stations, and Toronto plunged into darkness.

It did not confine the catastrophe to Toronto. Destruction spread over the north-eastern United States. The generators on both sides of the border at Niagara shut down as explosions destroyed pylons and transformers on high-voltage feeder lines. Several natural gas compressor stations blew up. The blackout rippled out, and within ten minutes, every place from Chicago to the Atlantic and south to Georgia had lost power and joined Ontario and southern Quebec in the dark.

Nuclear generators shut down, taking a large portion of generating capacity off line. In California, towers on the major power line from the north-west and British Columbia toppled, triggering massive blackouts throughout the state. The effect rippled into Utah and Nevada as inter-connections overloaded and shut down. Unlike the east, California was in the middle evening and it stranded thousands. Everywhere, emergency responders struggled with clogged traffic at uncontrolled intersections.

Chapter Twenty-four

"This looks like the big one." Mayor Dodge hurried into the emergency centre at three in the morning.

"Power is off everywhere." A grim-faced operator looked over her shoulder. "We're on land lines. The cell system is spotty. Many back-up generators and batteries at the towers failed. We're trying to set up a satellite phone system, but have few mobile units out there. Police radio works."

Subdued voices came from a police radio scanner, all sounded urgent.

"What's the situation? Where's Chief Langstaff?"

Dodge received a grim summary of the sabotage, much exaggerated in the confusion, and the report claimed hundreds of terrorists surrounded the city.

"Where the hell is Langstaff?" Dodge shouted. "They're marching down Yonge Street."

The Mayor felt genuine fear and felt helpless. A police officer arrived.

"Chief Langstaff wants you at headquarters. The FBI, Mounties, OPP and CSIS are there."

"Mr. Mayor," Langstaff greeted Dodge, "the Premier is at the Parliament Buildings and trying to bring all the MPPs and their families there for protection."

"Do you think there's a threat?"

"We think it's overblown," Agent De Cruze spoke, "but it's a good excuse to invoke martial law and lock everything down. It's happening back home right now. We can round up suspects without warrants under martial law. We have ordered all planes grounded, and after seven this morning anything in the air risks being shot down."

"Can they land safely? Are the airports blacked out?"

"They have to get them down before the backup generators run out of fuel. They ground flights at overseas airports and any flights less than half-way to North America are being turned back. We don't want what happened last time, with thousands being marooned in god awful places." Her satellite phone shrilled.

De Cruze put the phone down and looked grim.

"Two jet-fighters from the air national-guard, stationed in Vermont escorting an inbound cargo plane, collided in midair and crashed over the Bay of Fundy. No other casualties so far."

"The President has issued an executive order postponing today's elections. No one knows what the hell is happening."

"The Premier will do the same with today's municipal vote." Dodge was despondent. He had relished his easy victory, but who knew how this calamity would affect the voters? "This has already cost billions."

"Is there a comprehensive damage report?" The CSIS agent had no access to his agency. Everyone in Ottawa seemed in bed.

"It only involves a few electrical installations and gas compressor stations," Frank Langstaff read from a paper, "but no strategic targets."

"Langstaff, you're an idiot." Deputy Commissioner Hardy snarled. "Those are the most strategic targets."

"I meant they didn't blow up a bank."

"They got all the banks, and all industry and Queen's Park." Hardy disliked Langstaff, whom he thought was a poor politician, not a good cop.

"It's bad for us and the banks," Dodge seemed defeated. "The banks have threatened to move their head offices. They will, after this."

"We're blind," Hardy said. "When can we get communication back to normal?"

"My people," Langstaff snarled, "are helping get technicians to cell towers."

Police vehicles moved generators to cell towers, but technicians were hard to round up and that slowed the work. By morning, most towers were operational. It would take the rest of the day to restore the total network. Amateur radio operators, with batteries, relayed messages in rural places with no telephone service.

By morning, the skies had emptied, and commerce stalled. In the United States, looting spread beyond affected areas, and twenty-five states declared Martial Law.

"We never learned from 2003." Commissioner Hardy had just talked to the Premier. "Most gas stations can't pump because they don't have back-up generators."

"The Province and the feds screwed that up." Dodge did not support the political parties that controlled the governments during the last great electrical failure. "We spent millions on offices of emergency preparedness with overpaid bureaucrats but did nothing practical like back-up at gas stations and solar traffic lights."

"The Premier doesn't know much more than we do, but he's in touch with the utilities." Dodge scowled. "It will take at least three days to restore power. Natural gas will be unavailable in Toronto for some time. The destruction is massive and we haven't put out the fires."

"The Premier talked to the Prime Minister. Parliament will hold an emergency debate on a new law outlawing supporting terrorists. We'll have those punks on the run."

"This attack will destroy any sympathy the public had for these terrorists. When we're back to normal, we'll organize some big demonstrations against them."

The scanner reported house fires caused by people burning candles or using camp stoves, but low water pressure crippled the fire fighters.

Employees in finance, desperate to please their customers caused a small rush hour as they tried to report to non-functioning offices. Collisions at intersections added to the problem and led to on the street fights.

De Cruze's phone rang again.

"There's widespread looting back home, even in unaffected places. Worse though, snipers have been shooting at police and the National Guard. So far, they have shot six snipers, but we've lost about a dozen officers. The terrorists have never used guns before."

Langstaff called in a deputy. "Get the Tom people ready. I want a plan for getting these public sympathizers." He whispered into the man's ear. "Get some guns, drugs and explosives to plant so it'll keep them in jail."

De Cruze overheard Langstaff and disliked him taking that risk; although the trick worked well with street punks, it did not scale up easily. The FBI had learned that lesson.

A night in the cold and dark made the population angry. They did not have enough police to keep the peace. At a summit, years before, they had stripped twenty-thousand constables from across Canada to provide security in Toronto. Fear across the country made such a large scale response impossible. No one would release their police to protect Toronto, and all officers worked sixteen-hour days. An outbreak of gang warfare used even more resources, and overwhelmed the police.

They cancelled all military leave and sent students at RMC in Kingston to guard Parliament Hill in Ottawa. After an incident of careless discharge of a weapon, security kept all the ammunition inside the Centre Block under the care of a regular army Sergeant. Cadets carried impressive looking assault rifles, but they had no ammo. Satirists quickly dubbed this group of half-trained future officers, 'Harridan's Flying Circus'.

Hard work restored electricity after five days in the dark and cool of early November, but in colder areas, an early freeze damaged plumbing. The blackout ruined a huge amount of food, including most of the Christmas turkey supply. Ignorant people believed media fear mongering and threw away good food. This and the disrupted supply lines led to widespread hunger. The media magnified this into starvation, but only the poor, hungry before the crisis, felt real hardship.

They rescheduled the municipal elections for two weeks after Remembrance Day. Every politician used the remembrance services to make impassioned speeches identifying themselves with law and order.

Enormous crowds gathered at the memorials. In Ottawa, a thirty-minute display of armoured vehicles, marching troops, Mounties and local police gave a reassuring message. Jets roared overhead while police helicopters circled, looking for trouble.

The PRP went to the ground in Toronto. Every other politician demanded arrests, and some even advocated the return of the death penalty, while many blamed foreign governments. The ongoing anti-Russian hysteria raised more fears, and the onlookers roared approval.

"Canadians are peace-loving, hard-working people who believe in democracy. Foreigners instigated and paid for these acts to destroy the middle class." Dodge stirred up patriotism, raising the crowd on Queen Street in front of the cenotaph to new heights.

"Fuck the Russians," someone yelled.

"Fuck the Muslims" another shouted.

The crowd roared. Dodge raised both arms in the air, followed by everyone on the podium. The crowd responded and spontaneously sang the national anthem.

In Quebec, Remembrance morning, a small bomb exploded at Wolff's monument with some minor injuries. A group calling itself the NFLQ (Nouveau front de libération du Québec) claimed responsibility. By mid-afternoon, Ottawa had invoked the Emergency Act allowing the use of the military for civilian policing, and they armed soldiers who had only directed traffic and set up temporary shelters. Anti-Quebec bigotry joined the denunciation of Sherwood Green, and the English press called the NFLQ, 'Football Quebec'.

The anti-Sherwood Green Act passed. It was political showmanship, making it illegal for anyone to support Sherwood Green or its objectives. The law was unconstitutional but would allow the police to harass anyone they felt was dangerous, and it forced the SGSN to regroup.

Chapter Twenty-five

Charlie Dodge waged the biggest political fight since he became Mayor. Some people blamed the terrorist attacks on him and the current council. Every incumbent faced defeat. The population demanded extreme solutions, and in that mix, a racist patriotic group called the Canadian Guard took the lead. Even terrified non-whites supported the Canadian Guard candidates who threatened to win several fights, including that of the mayor. Dodge tried to run down the middle, but looked like a weak compromiser. Even the socialists took votes from him.

"Mister Mayor, I think I can help you." Bill Meeks sat opposite the mayor in a private ante-room off Dodge's City Hall office. "The Whaling Coalition sees you as the best candidate to continue our work in Toronto."

"How can you help?" In desperation, with the election a week away, Charlie had fired his campaign manager.

"We'll publish a statement of support. I will appear with you at meetings, on the street and on television with your message. There is a tremendous surge of anti-Japanese racism led by the Canadian Guard. We can take advantage of that. The Japanese kill whales, so it fits my interest."

Dodge pondered and disliked attacking an identifiable minority. Most minorities were smart enough to know attacking one threatened them all. It clashed with his middle of the road instincts, but the racist spew of the Canadian Guard had support. The Japanese community in Toronto was small.

"Okay," he smiled at Meeks, "but you have to do the anti-Japanese talking. I'll push the positive stuff."

"For sure," Meeks smiled. This would be a tremendous boost to fundraising and book sales. It would also let him get back at the Arsenault woman. He would never forgive her for abandoning him. It had cost thousands of dollars.

Meeks appeared on stage at a rally sponsored by the mayor. The message went over well, and the press gave it detailed coverage and made Dodge happy.

"Jos," Sheri Stein beckoned Amiel, as he was about to leave for the day. "I want you to work overtime. The boss won't allow a debate with terrorist supporters, but he wants you to interview a spokesman for the environmental movement. Bill Meeks will be here at ten in the morning."

"Great, I'll ask him about the split with the SGSN."

"No, you won't, not a word about them directly. I just want his opinion of terrorism and a little about his work. Oh, and he's campaigning for Dodge. The boss wants Dodge re-elected. Do your best. Let me see your questions before you leave."

In the interview, Meeks disguised racist attacks on the Japanese as anti-whaling ideology. He implied Mayor Dodge was anti-Japanese and the experienced alternative to the frightening neo-Nazi running against him. Meeks would fit nicely into a session with Bert Boyce. Jos almost walked out when Meeks said his next stop was Boyce's show.

Jos' only satisfaction came when, in the middle of a key statement, Meeks called Sherwood Green and Diane Arsenault dangerous anti-environmentalists. Jos didn't think Sheri would cut that out since Meeks had surrounded it with pro-Dodge passion. When Jos asked him to explain, Meeks added more references to the resistance.

The interview ended with Meeks looking at Jos and chuckling, "Of course, our problem with the foreigners does not include you people." He smiled at the camera.

Presenting racism tainted the Network and sickened Sherri. In payment for Jos not having punched Meeks in the face, on camera, she left in the Sherwood Green references. The drivel that they forced him to put on air disgusted him. The Meeks encounter was one of the worst.

An editorial team prepared scripts, and he was not a member. He resented having his name and face attached to borderline racism and blatant fabrication. It deepened his resentment because the material sounded much like Bert Boyce. The drunken radio host led the charge, blaming foreigners, although he couldn't seem to decide if it was Russians or Muslims. Callers, more extreme than Boyce, advocated the eviction of all foreign corporations, especially Fukushima. Their status as the first victim of Sherwood Green had only earned them more racist vitriol. Boyce had hosted the head of the Canadian Guard Meeks' appearance was not much better.

Jos left the studio in disgust. Mass rallies opposing Sherwood Green had been today's topic. The CAR movement on the U of T campus had attracted hundreds in front of the lecture theatre where Professor MacDonald presented his seminar on environmental terrorism. They roughed some students up, and the professor had to be escorted to safety by campus police. The editors had staged a dramatic event by handing Jos a statement on air announcing the university had suspended MacDonald and cancelled his course, pending an investigation. They vaguely suggested that MacDonald had some Russian connection. Apparently, he had visited Moscow as a graduate student after the fall of the Soviet Union.

An unpaid intern approached Jos.

"Here's a package a courier just dropped off." She handed Jos a brown envelope. It contained a single printed sheet.

"Langstaff has gotten a judge to issue arrest warrants for every member of the support group on suspicion of terrorism. They plan to raid their meeting in two nights and plant guns and drugs on them."

There was nothing more.

What the hell am I supposed to do?

"I'm going out to meet a contact." Jos passed Sheri's door. "I'll be back for the six o'clock segment."

He had no meeting. Jos bought a coffee and a sandwich and went down to the harbour. An unmarked car followed. He ate slowly, listening to waves slapping the pier, watching grey November clouds scud over the island, on a raw, southwest wind.

Jos wrapped his arms about his chest, drawing his ski jacket tight to his body. Until now, he had believed he only reported. His relationship with Diane Arsenault was only as a reporter. His police informant wanted him to play a partisan role. He expected Jos to warn his friend and the group. Reality threatened to destroy him. The middle ground he tried to occupy was as uncomfortable as the cold quayside bench. The ominous sky did not help.

Maybe it's a trap. It did not seem logical. His informant had never lied. *Maybe he wanted to give me a scoop so I could be there when it happens.*

While the idea seemed unlikely, it gave Jos an out. He could warn Diane and then report on the raid, even if his warning played a part.

Jos called from a pay phone on the dock. He received the details of the meeting, and although they did not publicize the event, it wasn't closed. It did not surprise Diane the police knew about it.

"I'll be in touch." Diane hung up.

Jos walked back to the studio, feeling he had done something good. Diane called him that evening.

"Meet me in an hour on the southbound platform at Yonge and St. Clare."

The unmarked car followed Jos to the subway.

Diane and Jos boarded the first train and sat together, facing the platform side of the car. Several people boarded with them. One sat nearby, but not too close. Diane wrapped her arm around Jos' neck and pulled him close.

"Pretend we're snuggling."

It wasn't too hard for Jos. He already liked her, but had never thought of hugging.

"Pretend you're kissing my neck." His lips brushed her. An old woman scowled at the black and white lovers.

"We're leaving tomorrow afternoon until things cool down. Do you want to come and get a story?"

Diane saw Jos as their only friendly media contact. She liked him, and the cops could arrest him. She did not know Jos had met Sherwood Green.

"This new law from Ottawa is unconstitutional, but we don't want to get caught up with planted drugs and guns. Judges are strange people. Melissa isn't sure we would get any sympathy. We don't like jail much."

"Where are you going?" Jos asked.

"Later," she put her lips to his ear, "can you get away without being fired?"

Jos thought about the situation as the train rumbled out of the Bloor station, where several people crowded around the couple. One was an off-duty cop in uniform.

"I have to let my producer know, and get permission. If I get arrested with you, I want to say I was only doing my job, but what can I tell her?"

"Tell her you don't know where we are going, but it'll be a big scoop, and we think we are going to be arrested on false charges with planted evidence. Bring a camcorder, but not your cameraman. We don't know him."

"Walt's trustworthy, but I'll tell him what I tell Sheri."

"Buy a pay as you go phone and call me tomorrow morning with the answer."

Diane kissed Jos and left the train at Wellesley station. He rode on to King and walked to the studios, followed discretely by his tail. He found Sherri in her office.

"It's an enormous risk, Jos, to you and to us legally. They might charge us with consorting with accused terrorists."

"You know that won't stick, and the sensation would put us at number one."

Sherri liked the thought.

"Besides, the cops haven't arrested or charged anyone yet. Leaving town is not a crime, and I'll get a look at their retreat."

"Video-cams aren't up to our technical quality. Can't you take Walt?"

"They don't know him, but they trust me."

Sherrie frowned. Her boss had accused Jos of being sympathetic to these 'commie terrorists'. She thought he was skilled at getting near his news source, and Sherri had some sympathy until this last attack left her freezing in her condo. The disaster showed the consequences of Sherwood Green, and she could never agree; however, the story could make her career and Sherwood Green would soon be in jail.

"Okay," she agreed, "but leave me a memo that you don't know where you will be but nothing about the SGSN expecting to be arrested. It's best if we seem ignorant."

"I'm going to be with the SGSN, out-of-town doing interviews." Jos told Walt. "They only want me, sorry."

Walt was glad. His wife had complained about the long, irregular hours. She hated Sherwood Green; the blackout had scared her.

Jos walked into the underground mall and bought a 'pay-as-you-go' cell phone. His called to let Debbie know he couldn't make their love-fest the next afternoon.

"I'm going out of town with the SGSN for a few days." He thought Debbie would be pleased. For her, the sex was more of a side-show. Her response startled him.

"NO!" she exclaimed. "Don't go!"

"It may be my big break. We'll be..."

"Stop," she cut him off. "I don't want to know details in case I'm asked. I'm afraid you'll get arrested."

"I'll be okay." Her outburst puzzled Jos. He thought Debbie, of all people, would see the opportunity, but he hadn't had the guts to tell her the cops had been listening.

"When are you leaving?" Debbie's tone changed. "Where is it?"

"All I know is tomorrow, nothing else." It cheered Jos that Debbie seemed to understand, but he wondered who would ask her questions.

Jos went home at his normal time. The tailing cop gave way to the normal night-time stakeout outside his building.

About four in the morning, Jos slipped out the back door and walked two blocks to an all-night donut shop. A taxi took him to the subway just as the doors were unlocked. The stakeout would expect his apartment lights to come on in a half-hour. The train sped north with few passengers. No one looked like a cop.

"I'm glad you're coming." Diane smiled. They shared the back seat of a small Honda. Joe drove, and Stevie sat up front. His camcorder was in its case with extra memory cards. They rode in silence until they cleared the city, heading north along Highway 400, and then west on Highway 9. The desolate November countryside streamed past, beyond misted windows.

"Do you drive?"

"Yes, but I don't own a car."

"Smart man," she smiled. "There'll be a car at the retreat. If we have to evacuate, you'll take that car back to Toronto because we won't want cops getting your interviews."

"Will they be that important?"

"Yes."

"Are you in deeper than I thought?" Jos was worried.

"We aren't, but a mutual acquaintance is in deep shit." Diane fell silent. An hour later, they turned up a gravel lane to a farmstead that appeared to be an upscale private retreat. Several vehicles parked on the remnants of an early snowfall at the edge of a circular drive. Interior lights spilled out into the late fall gloom, giving the place a Christmas card feel. Jos was happy to get inside, out of the November rain that had turned to sleet.

The first person he met surprised him.

"Hello, big boy." Joey, dressed in a denim shirt and jeans, smiled and shook his hand.

"Hi, Joey, I've never seen you out of your dress." Jos smiled.

"I always wanted you to see me out of my dress, big boy." Joey licked his lips seductively and winked, raising a satisfying blush. Joey suddenly turned away.

Jos knew Joey's banter hid deep grief. Jos had only vague memories of his father and still grieved for a man he had hardly known. Joey grieved for a lover.

"Joey has been with us ever since they killed Richard. He stayed with Stevie and Joe, but we had to get him out of town because Joey knows who killed Rachelle."

"Was it a street gang?" Jos guessed.

"The biggest street gang of all," Diane said. "Interview Joey tonight. It'll be your last chance. Your recording will be evidence, if there's an honest cop."

Jos interviewed several activists after supper, with Joey as his last subject. He was glad he waited. The emotion, tears, stammers and long silences ate at Jos, and he had never conducted such a tough interview. Joey went limp at the end, and Jos had teared up. The information shocked Jos. The killer surprised him, and Joey's detailed listing of Rachelle's dates with her killer would be useful for an investigation. Jos removed the memory chip from the camera and carefully placed it into a case. If nothing else survived, this one interview had to become public.

Joey's horrific story shook him, and Jos slipped on his coat and went outside. The cold might help. The sky had cleared and stars shone brightly in grandeur that city lights obscured, and the frigid air added more tears.

"It's beautiful." Diane startled Jos. "I saw you come out. Joey's story is hard, isn't it?"

"Too hard," Jos didn't look at Diane. "I've seen a lot of bad stuff as a reporter, but this is too personal. I like Joey, and I liked Richard."

"It's a hideous world. Perhaps that's why I don't mind it being destroyed." They continued to stare skyward.

"It would only be the beginning of suffering, not the end." Jos turned to Diane.

"Suffering's a given," Diane frowned, her face barely visible in the subdued light. "I think the question is, do we make it short or quick? Do we end the suffering of the planet and of other species?"

"It's easy to say, hard to live." Jos looked closely at his friend. She looked soft and vulnerable in this half-light.

"It's hard." Diane walked. Jos stayed by her side. "Nothing good is ever easy, and usually not obvious, at least at first."

"How will it end?" Jos had pondered this for a month.

"It never ends, not with humans. Someone will always try to take advantage. We can only hope for reduced power and being with a friend... friends." Diane looked at Jos and smiled. "It's too hard when we try it on our own."

"Sharing is a risk." Jos thought of Debbie. Limiting sharing only to sex made it safe with little emotion. "Joey and Richard shared more, and now..." his voice trailed off.

"It's a risk," Diane was thoughtful. "People have that same attachment to their lifestyles. Destroying their world will do to them what Richard's murder has done to Joey."

"Maybe caring for someone like that, while our world is being destroyed, will make it easier." Jos turned and touched Diane's shoulder. "Maybe it would give people something to fight for, something worth risking."

"Maybe," said Diane. She touched his hand, then slipped it from her shoulder and turned back to the house.

"Make sure that you don't lose that video." The door opened into the warm interior.

Joel Phelps and two members of the SGSN stood at the door of a dark and uninviting storefront on Queen Street. Diane had asked Phelps to rent the store as an office and meeting place for the SGSN. He felt the responsibility signalled that she accepted him, but Diane wanted to have a police informant as the only name linked to the address.

The space had one old computer with no internet connection, a photo-copier, a video player, a dozen chairs and a television. Before the big attack had made the public hostile, they had hoped it would host public meetings. The trio chatted in the doorway and waited for the leaders. Joel thought he had the time wrong.

"Up against the wall," Riot cops burst from the alley, guns levelled. They threw the SGSN members against the plate glass store-front. Marked cars with lights flashing sped from a side-street and blocked the roadway.

Several people wearing balaclavas and carrying boxes burst in through the rear door of the storefront. The cartons contained drugs, a few sticks of dynamite and guns.

Frank Langstaff arrived with his Project Tom commander.

"Cuff 'em and get their names." The lights came on, and Langstaff looked through the doorway with a satisfied smirk as they herded the three captives inside.

"Look what we have here," a uniformed officer poked about the office. "Looks like coke to me. Here's a rifle." He held up an old AK-47.

"Hey, I'm on your side," one of the trio protested. "I work for..." he named an undercover cop who worked the Bishop Hotel on Queen. "He'll vouch for me."

Phelps named an undercover cop working at the university. The third man named his own handler.

"You're all on our side when we cuff you," the constable sneered.

"Dynamite," Another cop shouted.

"Everyone out," Langstaff barked, leading the charge through the open doorway.

They carted the prisoners off to headquarters in a flurry of lights and sirens. The bomb squad took over the scene. They evacuated people within two blocks and put on a show for the media. Walt appeared with a reporter.

Langstaff and his commander held a news conference while waiting for the bomb squad to declare the street safe. Partway through the media event, Langstaff learned they had arrested three police informants and no one else. Frank quickly cut off the reporters and left.

"How the fuck could you let this happen?" Langstaff glowered. "Why didn't you know who we had?"

"Frank," the cop tried to calm his embarrassed superior. "Our street guys protect their runners. I knew we had four snitches inside, but only by code names. Someone tipped off the terrorists."

"Well, we need terrorists. Charge these punks anyway. Pretend we never heard of them."

"That'll blow our guys on the street. When word gets out, it'll be harder to recruit snitches."

"I don't give a shit and will not look stupid. Pull the handlers off the street and throw the book at these guys. They're lowlifes, and I hate snitches."

"We have to find out where the fourth one is. I'll get on it. They all have GPS trackers on their phones. We'll have to call in the OPP."

"Damn," Langstaff had lost a chance to be the hero.

At the breakfast table, Diane asked Joey to go to town and pick up an order at the supermarket. It all seemed routine. A half hour later, Jos watched through a rain-splattered window as Joe put Joey's luggage into a car. He handed Joey the keys and shook his hand. Joey sped off. The trees obscured which way he turned at the gate. Jos would never see Joey again.

The group relaxed and Jos interviewed them over two days. By the third morning, only Diane remained.

Jos found no hint anyone knew a member of the underground, and none of his fellow residents were resistors. Sherwood Green remained as elusive as ever. Only Jos had knowingly met a resistor. He wanted to ask Diane about Joey, and perhaps she would go for another walk around the grounds. They did not get the chance.

"Everyone," Diane shouted, "we have to leave, fast!"

Lookouts had noticed a build-up of police vehicles and two helicopters at the Mount Forest OPP detachment.

"Jos," she tossed him a set of keys. "Take the little blue Toyota and leave, now! Go to the highway and back to Toronto. Go now!" She pushed him towards the door with camera case and notes.

"Your prints are all over here, and you will probably have to talk to the cops sometime. Make sure you copy your stuff before you do because they'll want everything. Maybe Joey's bit will cause a stir. I hope they don't arrest or fire you." Diane hugged him.

"Sheri knows," Jos checked for his memory cards. "She'll be happy if she doesn't have to bail me out."

Jos sped down the lane, hurried north and soon hit Highway 10. He did not know exactly location of the farm but knew the highway and drove south through Markdale. OPP cruisers sped in the opposite direction. Jos avoided the raid by half an hour.

Diane, Joe and Stevie got into Joe's Honda. The Mexican woman jumped in just as Joe threw the car into reverse. They turned south and then west on the first gravel road. Joe was an excellent driver and had a route mapped out. He hoped they would look like local traffic.

"How do you think they found us?" Stevie sobbed.

"Good question," Joe muttered. "We left three informers holding the bag at the meeting place. There must be another one with deeper cover."

"We won't have to worry about it if we get caught." Diane said and tried to guess the identity of the informant.

Six OPP cruisers and two unmarked cars sped into the traffic circle in front of the farmhouse, joining a lone vehicle parked on the front walkway. The inside lights were on. A tactical van followed. A dozen officers in military garb formed a line around the house.

Two heavily armed tactical cops flattened against the wall beside the front doorway. They knocked. A slight young woman opened the door a crack.

"Police, we have a warrant." the men burst through the doorway, brushing the woman aside and pointed rifles in every direction. Several rushed to the back entrance, smashing the jamb as they kicked the door in. They herded a young man from the kitchen, cuffed both residents, and threw them onto a couch.

"Is there anyone else here?" A plain clothes cop asked.

"No." the man said, his voice a little weak. The pair had been expecting this, but it still frightened.

"What's happening here?" The cop loomed.

"My name is Janet Yerks. I live here."

"That's not what I asked, bitch. What's been going on here?" He stepped forward. Janet cowered.

"My name is Steve Brown. I live here," the man said.

"I asked what's going on here," the cop was angry.

"Are we under arrest?" Steve asked.

"You bet your asses you are."

"We want to speak to our lawyer." Janet seemed more assured as the script unfolded, as expected.

In an hour of badgering, the police learned nothing, and the house held no clues except for unmade beds, clothes and tire marks on the lawn. Two small sheds housed chickens and goats.

"Bring in forensics," the commander finally said. "Get them to lift all the prints, and DNA if possible. Take these two to Markdale and let them call their lawyer."

Joe braked the car suddenly, did a turn in a lane, retreated to the next road and headed north. In the morning's gloom, he thought he had seen flashing lights reflecting from the trees; a roadblock hid over the hill. He wanted to get west to Highway 6, trusting that his instincts would get them there. Hopefully, none of these roads were dead ends. In his mirror, a car turned onto the road.

"Damn!" he exclaimed. Diane craned her neck to look out the back window. The woman beside her sat in silence.

"They're after us. Hang on." The car swerved into another side-road. Joe drove at a desperate speed.

"Slow down," the Mexican pleaded.

Trees swept past on both sides, their bare trunks glistening in the rain. Joe knew farmers drove over one-hundred on gravel, but he had no experience. Instinctively, he slowed and searched for the next side road. The trailing car reappeared in his mirror. A helicopter swooped low over the speeding Honda, intending to frighten them with the noise. The Honda popped over a low hill. Joe hit the brakes hard. Two hundred meters ahead, two OPP cruisers blocked a narrow concrete bridge. The car behind closed fast, and it left no escape.

Chapter Twenty-six

"Your Honour, we have one item this morning. The Crown verses..." the clerk rambled off a list of a dozen names, all of those who the police had arrested as they fled the farm house in Grey County.

Janet Yerks and Steve Brown were not on the list. When they called Melissa's partner, he had shown the police they were the legal owners of the property and had no connection to the SGSN other than renting their home and that their lawyer was Melissa's law partner. None of the attendees had prior warrants, and the police found no terrorism related evidence. The couple had committed no crime, and the Crown did not lay charges. The police now had two names at the top of their watch list, two more people to intimidate, but no way to drag them into court. It was not a crime to hold a party, and they had not lied to the police.

Forensics found the fingerprints of all those before the court. The prints linked them with previous SGSN activity. No one denied the connection.

Justice Koroda of the Ontario Superior Court in downtown Toronto accepted a thick dossier from the clerk. He had seen it earlier, but made a show of carefully reading through the indictment.

"Read the charges." Justice Koroda frowned at the room. Jos took notes, and Walt waited outside with his camera. They expected only to interview Melissa.

The clerk asked all the defendants to identify themselves as she read their names and a list of charges. The accusations ranged from suspicion of terrorism, possession of explosives and illegal weapons, counselling to commit terrorism to exceeding the posted speed limit, but when the clerk sat, Justice Koroda frowned.

"Mr. Gill," he addressed the Crown Attorney. "Before I ask for pleas, I am striking the speeding charges. Grey County court should hear them, and you know better."

Melissa had no time to gloat over the Crown's carelessness.

"Miss Strong, what's this Sherwood Green nonsense? Do you all think you're Robin Hood's merry men?" Koroda glowered at the lawyer.

Koroda had survived in his country property in Caledon during the electricity crisis only because of his back-up generator. The attack made his high-rise condominium uninhabitable, with no lights, elevators or running water. The judge did not like Sherwood Green.

"How do your clients plead?"

Each person said, "Not guilty."

"Your Honour," Melissa remained standing. "I would move to drop the charges of fleeing police and resisting arrest. My clients had no knowledge that anyone behind them was a constable, and as soon as they came upon road blocks with marked police vehicles, they stopped and surrendered as would any driver on public roads."

"Mr. Gill, do you have evidence that any of the accused knew they were fleeing the police?"

"They ran from the farmhouse and must have known."

"Is that a 'no', Mr. Gill?" The Crown Attorney nodded.

"That charge goes too. Resisting arrest stays. The evidence will test it."

"Your Honour," Melisa rose once more. "I would move that the Crown separate all charges and all the accused have separate trials."

Koroda's eyebrows arched sharply. They had that right, and if denied, it would likely lead to the Supreme Court. He calculated twelve defendants, times several charges that were barely related would mean years of court time. *Should I let the Supreme Court decide?*

"Ten minute recess while I examine the motion. Mr. Gill, I assume you object to Ms. Strong's motion."

"Yes, Your Honour." He had twice suffered embarrassment.

Half an hour later, Justice Koroda returned, but more than the judge's reflection on the issue would influence his decisions from this point on.

"Mr. Gill, Ms. Strong, come up here." The lawyers approached the bench. Koroda looked agitated.

"Ms. Strong, you know that granting your motion will tie up courts for years?"

"We did not lay the charges, Your Honour, and we deny them. Each of my clients only asks for fair trial unstained by association."

Koroda frowned again.

"Mr. Gill, they have charged three other persons in relation to this organisation and the explosives, drugs and guns. Why are they not here with these accused?"

"Your-Honour, we have arraigned them in another court." Gill did not know how Koroda knew about that case. "We arrested them two days before these accused."

"They are on your witness list for these charges. Mr. Gill, I find all of this strange. Would we find that this group, left behind when the rest of the organisation left town, are all police informants?"

He left Gill with no time to respond.

"Ms. Strong, I would grant your motion, but I'm going to stay these charges in the hopes the Crown can find enough evidence to have a chance of a conviction."

"Mr. Gill, you're lucky I haven't just dismissed your charges. Until a law revokes freedom of speech, a law that will stand up before the Supreme Court, you cannot charge people for saying they support a political idea."

"You are charging the defendants under the new law, C-260 just passed by Parliament with the Governor General's signature barely dry. There is every chance the new law passed by Parliament will fail on appeal. You may not know, but the Supreme Court of Canada already has a petition to examine C-260, and I can predict they will apprehend themselves of it. While it's before that court, we waste our time applying it, and I want no part of that."

"You have not even presented preliminary evidence these people agree with the terrorists' methods or advocated violence. Saying industrial civilization must end, as repugnant as that view may be," he scowled at the defendants and Melissa, "is not a crime. You pursued and arrested these people on 'suspicion'. Your evidence does not connect the accused to the address where you found the explosives and does not connect them to the contraband. You state you found no fingerprints on the guns, explosives or drugs. Personally, I would never have issued the warrants. The police did not mention explosives, drugs and guns in the warrant applications. Secondary charges arising from a warranted investigation are not uncommon, but always doubtful. I don't like police fishing expeditions. Come back when you have more."

Koroda had been involved in a case of police evidence tampering and smelt foul on this one. One of the first cases he had tried ended up in Appeal Court. Their ruling against his conviction of that accused had been a subtle rebuke, and Koroda felt the blemish had cost him several promotions.

He also knew of the judgement in British Columbia throwing out a jury conviction of terrorism because of police entrapment. The judge wondered who he disliked more, terrorists or incompetent police. Justice Koroda prided himself on being on the side of the law. Many times, he struggled to separate his biases from rulings. The Crown and the police rarely attempted to behave as neutral officers of the court. The judge despised them for it.

"Your-Honour, this is unprecedented." Gill sputtered.

"Mr. Gill, the thing about precedents is that there was always a first time." Koroda normally would never have stayed charges. He would not break any law, but risked creating a new one in the common law tradition. *Damn that man.* Koroda looked at the door to his chambers.

"Ms. Strong," he glowered at the lawyer. "I am disgusted by the objectives of you and your clients."

The comment stung Melissa, but the Crown Attorney cringed. To this point, Koroda had appeared fair, even biased, towards the accused. This one comment made it appear had a bias against them. It would be grounds for appeal in any ruling against them in Koroda's court. The judge was smart. Gill was livid. Koroda had done it on purpose. Unfortunately, as prosecutor, he could not make an objection on behalf of his opponent. Melissa, even as a young lawyer, saw the situation clearly, right from a textbook in second year law school. She smiled and said nothing. Koroda went on.

"Is Staff Inspector Popovski present?" Popovski was the name on the warrant applications.

"Mr. Popovski," he addressed the lead investigator of 'Project Tom,' second only to Frank Langstaff. "The next time you want a warrant related to any of these people, you come to me. It would be nice to have a successful investigation here, and maybe I can help you get it right."

The Staff Inspector quietly nodded. This entire investigation had become mangled, with no solid results. It convinced Popovski someone had tipped off the SGSN, probably one informant, the Mexican girl, since she was the only snitch allowed at the country retreat. Her cell phone had led the OPP to the two ring-leaders. Maybe she was double dealing. The cop feared Langstaff would replace him on the project, but Popovski had no worry. He dodged the wrath of agent De Cruze at having her deep agent's cover blown.

"Ms. Strong, before we all go, I would suggest you advise your clients to behave. They probably won't be able to get on a plane after this, and I have no control over that situation. Advise them these charges could come back and not to leave the country."

"Court is adjourned." Koroda rushed to his chambers.

The doors flew open, and Walt aimed his camera. First out were Popovski and the other cops. They scowled at the lens and hurried by with no comment. Jos appeared next.

"What happened?" Walt asked.

"You won't believe it."

Melissa and the smiling defendants burst out of the doorway. Every one shook Jos' hand and gathered in the hallway. The accused were about half of the number that had fled the farm house. The OPP had caught them in the many roadblocks. A dozen others had made it through before the police blocked the roads. Diane hugged Jos and let Melissa speak on camera. She recounted the events inside the court, denying her clients had any involvement in terrorism. She would not answer questions, saying the court had only stayed the charges, and she did not want to compromise any future hearings.

Koroda hung his robe on the carved clothes stand and glared at the man sitting beside the judge's desk.

"Okay, you got what you wanted. They're back on the street. You probably just screwed my career." Koroda sank into his high-backed chair behind the desk. Normally, he commanded respect, but he felt used.

"I'll have a chat with my boss." The man rose. "He will let your boss know you have done a service for your country."

"I hope so." Koroda sighed. "In the justice game, the higher-ups don't much like precedent setters. It always leads to the Appeal Court and kills careers."

"I thank you." He extended his hand and, after a limp shake, the CSIS man left the chambers.

"There they are! Get them!"

The crowd on the sidewalk in front of Old City Hall erupted as the SGSN members and the reporters emerged from the massive front doors.

"Kill the terrorists!" An egg flew and hit Melissa. More followed, and a tomato, fresh from the store, a thick-skinned one caught Jos, and it hurt.

Jos and Walt ducked to the sidelines, and Jos looked back at Diane, wanting to stand beside her, between Sherwood Green and this mob, but he had a job to do and watched her deflect an egg with her hand.

Banners in the crowd reflected a new unity between everyone from Trotskyites and Canadian-Guard to the Green Party. The great blackout had made people understand Sherwood Green's objective, and both bankers and paupers would lose their entitlements.

They had convicted the released prisoners in the public's mind. The barrage trapped the resistors on the upper steps. Reluctantly, the police intervened when someone threw a large stone and smashed a window, and the SGSN members made a dash to the subway with cops and rabble in hot pursuit. Walt had a good video, and Sherri gave the fleeing terrorists major play on the newscast.

They aired Terrorism-Toronto over the banner 'Terrorists in Retreat'.

Chapter Twenty-seven

Debbie Franklin sat on her plush couch watching the evening news. Her lover had wrapped up a powerful piece on the arrests and release of the terrorist supporters. He was an excellent journalist and had obviously pushed as hard as he could against editorial bias. Debbie was proud to have trained him. Jos was a wonderful lover, too. She really wished she had stuck with her student love when she was young. Debbie had forgotten most of her lovers' names, but she would always remember Dave, her first. Tears trickled down her cheeks as Jos signed off. Her life had fallen apart. She had decided what she must do.

Debbie dialled the number for police headquarters. More tears dripped, and she almost hung up.

"Yes, I would like to speak to a detective, please."

"How do we broadcast this without admitting you were at the farm?" Sheri was excited, but faced a real problem. She had more respect for Jos. He had another scoop. "If they caught you, you would have been in court along with these terrorist flunkies."

Jos cringed at the insult to his friends.

"The cops know I was there. Diane Arsenault thinks there was an informant in her group. She wouldn't say who it was. The cops have my prints. They won't charge me after their disaster in court."

"The lawyers agree." Sheri had become used to covering her legal ass. "Let me look at all this footage and plan the scripts. These will be good for several shows."

Jos had copied everything four times.d Walt had a copy, but he would not let Walt or Sheri see Joey's interview.

Jos wasn't sure what to do with Joey's bombshell about Rachelle's murder. He thought the cops would not follow it up. Putting it on air would cause a lawsuit.

"The cops will want copies." Sheri said. "Can you identify everyone?"

"First names or nick-names, only the leaders use last names. Probably the cops know some of them."

"Okay, the lawyers say we should make the police get a court order. They won't do anything until we air the first segment. They'll scream, but the lawyers say that nothing here that adds to the Crown's case. I think we're good to go tonight, following up nicely on the retreating terrorists."

The interviews would enhance Jos' notoriety in the terrorist fight, and ratings soared.

The police arrived after the first interview aired. Sheri blocked them, and they left, making empty threats to arrest Jos, Sheri and the janitor. The court fight started, and Jos made plans to give Joey's interview to Melissa.

Jos' love life seemed to have collapsed. He tried to call Debbie many times, but she never answered or returned his messages. He went to her building and rang her condo, but she did not answer. He knew she had the lobby video on her television, so he guessed she ignored him. Like a lovesick puppy, he staked out the lecture hall and saw her enter. At least she was not dead, but he guessed had dumped him. He thought it was because she did not want to be seen with a somewhat despised television personality.

The other upset in his life was the thought he had led the police to the farm. He had only told Walt, Debbie, and Sheri he was going, but he trusted them, at least as far as tipping off the cops. Maybe it had been the mole that Diane suspected inside her group.

The police knew he had met people claiming to be Sherwood Green. Perhaps he had not thrown off his tail before the farm trip, and the cops had done a better job of it than the day he and Diane played transit tag. That brief interlude with Diane raised fond memories.

In the middle of the week after the raid, Jos walked home. It was a balmy night for November and he took his usual route that ended at the Second Cup. He no longer expected to see Joey here. He sipped his coffee and read the online headlines.

A young man wandered in and sat at the far end of the lounge. He dressed like a student, but seemed nervous. Jos paid little attention until he caught the guy staring at him and quickly looking away when Jos looked up. Jos bought a second coffee. While he waited, he leaned on the counter and stared over the man's head at the bit of local art hanging on the wall. The guy looked familiar. Jos pondered while he returned to his padded chair, greeting another regular. Church Street wasn't too far from the university, so students here were common. Still... and then he remembered. He had seen this guy picketing Professor MacDonald's lectures.

Jos fiddled with his phone. Casually, he snapped a photo. He didn't appear to be a cop, but it was hard to pick out a good undercover cop, and Jos didn't think the students were above violence.

A tough-looking man, middle-aged and wearing a leather coat, came in and sat with his tail. They chatted. Jos became nervous.

Happily, a neighbour in his apartment building stopped in for a takeout and Jos latched onto the fellow, chatting as if they were good friends. In reality they hardly knew each other, but the man had seen Jos on television and was happy for the attention. His neighbour finally left. Jos appeared to be settling in. The pair at the other table grew impatient and left. Jos waited ten minutes to put them well away from the restaurant and headed home.

The dark November night seemed to soak up the poor street lighting, but it had always been safe. Jos crossed an intersection against the walk light and turned onto his street. Two men jumped from the shadow of a parked car.

"You little darkie terrorist," the accented voice accompanied a hard blow to Jos' stomach. As he bent over, a fist hit the back of his head. Jos went down. A boot kicked him just above the kidney and another to his groin. He rolled into a ball, gasping, ready to pass out.

"Stop that! Police!" a cop jumped out of an unmarked cruiser. "We don't want him hurt."

The cop knows these guys. The thought came through his pain, and when they ran, the cop didn't chase. He helped Jos to his feet.

"I'll get you to emergency."

They deposited Jos on a gurney in the St. Mike's emergency department. The cops had priority, but it took until five a.m. to hobble into his apartment with nothing broken, but the bruises on his back and stomach hurt, as did the lump on the back of his head. He called in sick, hoping Sherwood Green would blow up something. Jos warned Diane that the opposition had become violent.

By week's end, several SGSN interviews had aired. The court fight for the video began, but Melissa delayed it by applying for intervener status because the interviewees were her clients.

The rabid neo-con press, and wild-eyed fanatics like Bert Boyce, had begun a crusade against TNN, accusing them of protecting terrorists by refusing to turn over the video. It was good for ratings, but the bosses became nervous. Sheri needed some pro-police material to mollify the owners and satisfy the public.

"Jos, I'm setting up an interview between you and Chief Langstaff for early next week."

Frank had become Jos' least favourite cop, and he worked on questions to make the man squirm. Maybe Jos could just ask him about his big, dark secret. They would work the official list of questions out in negotiations between Sheri and Langstaff.

Tuesday came with silence from police headquarters. After several fruitless calls, Sheri asked her boss to follow up, but received no answer. Langstaff missed press conferences and passed up a few choice photo-ops.

Jos mentioned several times on air that an interview with the top cop would be good, but silence followed.

On the third day after the start of the on-air campaign to interview the Chief, Jos arrived home to find a brown envelope thrown into his entranceway. He didn't bother to look for an intruder, but the ease with which the informant could open his door still upset him.

Frank disappeared over a week ago, and the brass think someone kidnapped him but aren't sure who did it. There's no ransom demand, but Frank had lots of enemies. They hid his family in a resort near Collingwood. Everyone thinks his past has caught up to him and killed him.

Jos brought the request for the interview to a head the next day. He cornered Mayor Dodge, still struggling to be re-elected, outside of his office. He asked about the chief.

"Mayor Dodge, can you please arrange an interview with Chief Langstaff? It's appears he has disappeared."

They aired the encounter that evening. By the time Jos exited the studio, four detectives had arrived, and once again, everyone gathered in Sheri's office.

"The Chief is upset you people are harassing him, and he can't make a statement."

"Can't or won't?" Jos smiled. The cops grew angry.

"We ought to arrest you right now for consorting with terrorists, you fucking twerp,."

The lawyers asked the cops to calm down.

"The people at the farm aren't terrorists." Jos said.

"Not them, you asshole, the ones you rode around with in Mississauga."

It stunned the lawyers and Sheri.

"What?" Sheri burst out.

The cops gave a long, fairly accurate account of the events of the chase. They left out their bugging of the phone and the embarrassing pursuit of the innocent pickup truck. Jos confirmed the story.

"They might have been cops, anyway. I think you set me up, but I don't know why. We used the e-mail, supposedly from them, but it I couldn't verify it. I can't confirm who those guys were, but the e-mail writer knew about the coming attack."

For over an hour, the meeting flowed back and forth. The cops tried to find out what Jos knew about the Chief's personal life. It mystified Sheri, but Jos knew the actual story. These detectives wanted to know if Jos knew about Langstaff's disappearance, but eventually they gave up and left. To their credit, they made no more threats.

"You know something, don't you?" Sheri was astute. Nothing her reporter did or knew surprised her. She had noticed Jos' smile when they asked questions about Langstaff. "What's the story?"

"A beat cop told me there's a rumour Langstaff has disappeared." Jos had become quick on his feet over the past months. Lying to his boss came naturally, but maybe his source actually was a beat cop.

"I can't betray my source, and no one has any details. Those cops were from Project Tom, and I bet they think Sherwood Green had something to do with Langstaff's disappearance. I spooked them when I told Dodge Langstaff had disappeared."

"I'll make some calls." Sheri checked her sources.

"Was Frank Langstaff kidnapped?" Jos read from a script, carefully vetted by the network's lawyers. "It seems the police think so, but they have been looking for him for two weeks and moved his family to a safe location.”

Sheri’s contact had given them enough information to blow open the kidnapping. They did not tell her what Jos knew about the location of the family, and he kept his mouth shut. The Toronto media exploded. It forced Mayor Dodge to reveal the facts. He claimed that Jos and TNN had put Langstaff’s life in danger, but no kidnappers had made contact, so it seemed unlikely.

After Jos’ report, two detectives arrived at the studio. They were from the homicide squad.

“We’re investigating the death of Richard St. Pierre. Do you know anything about it?”

Jos knew cops usually asked questions when they thought they already had the answers.

“I knew him, and his husband, Joey. I saw them both at the Second Cup the night of the murder, about ten in the evening. Rachelle left first to go on a date, and Josephine went home to do the dishes.”

“Who are Rachelle and Josephine?” The cop smirked.

“The names they used when out on the street, dressed up, and I think they deserve that respect.”

The constable looked abashed, as if for the first time thinking of them as persons.

“You haven’t seen them since?”

“I saw Rachelle’s body in the ravine from the bridge, standing with a traffic cop. Josephine, or Joey, has not been on the streets of Toronto since.”

Jos had not told of seeing Joey at the SGSN retreat in his statement to Project Tom. He didn’t want to lie directly to this detective, and he needed to get the video to Melissa.

“Do you think Joey did it? He loved Richard but was okay with his fooling around.”

“No,” the detective answered. “We would like some information from him. We have leads that take us in another direction.”

Jos smiled.

"He might help us, so if you ever see him, get him to call me." The cop handed Jos his card.

Jos looked after the retreating cops. He wondered if they had been lying and just wanted to trap Joey. Jos suspected they knew the actual story, as Joey had told Jos. It didn't matter. Jos did not know where his friend was.

Chapter Twenty-eight

Frank Langstaff sat silently, unable to see anything in the oppressive darkness of the room. The silence weighed like a blanket. He wanted to scream, but wouldn't give his captors the satisfaction. Handcuffs pinned his hands behind his back. A chain tied the cuffs to steel chair-legs, bolted to the floor. His arms hurt. He craved a drink.

Frank sat totally naked, the way he first woke up. It seemed a long time ago. The only light ever was a dim glow through the doorway when a silent, black-clad person fed him or gave water. They cut the padded chair into a toilet seat, over a bucket where his waste could fall without him moving. They changed it daily, but he reeked of urine and feces and could not direct his stream or wipe himself, and it humiliated him.

He had no way of telling how long he had been in the chair. His last memory before he awoke here with a headache was leaving the little suburban bistro with a gay hooker. Someone in the club had spiked his cocktail.

Stupid! I'm an idiot. The queer ambushed me.

The sudden blaze of the lights blinded Frank, but he heard several people enter and chairs scrape. It took minutes until his eyes adjusted, but they had watered from the sudden flash, and he could not wipe them.

"Are you Frank Langstaff?" The speaker sat in the middle of a trio dressed in black, their faces covered by balaclavas, with only eyes and lips visible.

"Who the fuck wants to know?" Langstaff wanted control.

"I would suggest you control yourself, Frank." The man spoke mildly. "The question was just a formality to make you comfortable, but you're in enough trouble, and Josephine here would like to off you right now."

Langstaff had not noticed the gaily dressed woman sitting by the wall to his right with her face a mixture of grief and hate that the rouge and lipstick could not hide.

A Cross-dresser! Frank thought he did not have long to live. He struggled against his restraints, but they had snapped the cuffs on hard, police style.

"Actually, your future will be based totally on whether you cooperate. We want information. If you play along, we might just keep you alive for the duration."

The man spoke as if a war was raging. To this point, Langstaff had thought a gay vigilant committee had grabbed him, but obviously, it was the terrorists.

"Frank, it depends on how long you want to live."

"What do you want?" Langstaff decided to play along.

The interrogator examined a paper. He remained silent for a few minutes. Frank squirmed.

"First, the password to your cell phone," he asked

"No fucking way!"

The man took out a Glock semi-automatic, Frank's own gun and laid it on the table. He nodded at Josephine, and she smiled and rose.

"Not yet, sweetie," the interrogator smiled at her. "Frank, Josephine wants to shoot you."

Frank's eyes filled with horror. He tried to throw up, but his stomach was empty and he could not bend forward. His reflex made the cuffs dig into his arms more painfully.

"Okay." Frank gave the letters and numbers.

One of the three at the front table went out the door. Everyone waited. Five minutes passed in silence. They returned and nodded.

"Good, Frank. That was smart."

Langstaff smiled. He hoped his phone had called home as soon as they turned it on. *These fools will soon have their asses kicked. I just have to stall for time.*

"Why did you kill Rachelle?"

"You can't prove I did," Frank smirked. He wanted to stretch it out now that help would be coming.

"This isn't court, Frank. We already know you're guilty, but we would like to know why you did it. I think you owe it to Josephine."

"Fuck off!" Langstaff shouted.

The gun moved towards the table edge nearest Joey.

"Frank, if the gun falls on the floor, it's Josephine's. Think of yourself as a condemned man asking for the mercy of the court. Why did you kill Rachelle?"

"He asked too many questions. I finally figured out he was selling information, maybe to you, crud."

The gun moved a centimetre.

Poor Rachelle, the interrogator mused. Richard wasn't the only source of information from the police but access to Langstaff had been valuable and might have led to an operation resulting in Langstaff being dead anyway.

"Who are your spies inside the SGSN?"

Frank realized this was a test. They already knew about three of the moles. If he didn't at least offer one more, they would know he was lying. He named the three and the Mexican woman. They wrote the name down. It would confirm Arsenault's suspicions. CSIS and the FBI would lose a double-dealing mole.

"Who else?"

"That's all."

"Stop lying Frank," The gun was now a dozen centimetres from the table's edge.

Langstaff gave one more name. "Can I have a drink... please?"

Someone wearing cotton gloves held a water bottle to his lips. He smiled and asked for more water.

"Who have you been strong-arming because of bugging that phone?"

"We never bugged his phone."

"His phone, Frank?"

Langstaff realized he had slipped up, and he had to come clean. "The reporter's phone. We didn't do it."

"Come on, Frank. You knew when he met some of our people. You used the phone to track them and lost the tail when they ditched the phone. We know you were listening, and you knew everything about Amiel."

"No."

The gun moved a few centimetres.

Langstaff stared at the table and snuck a glace towards Josephine. She licked her lips, looking from Frank to the Glock. Everyone waited. The gun moved another centimetre. He tried to calculate how much further it had to go before gravity decided his fate.

"The slut professor, Franklin, she's banging that asshole reporter." He blurted out, trembling.

"Is that how you knew where the SGSN had gone?"

"Franklin told us they were going, but she said it was to be the night after they left, so we staged the raid. Slut! She lied on purpose. When I get back..." Frank stopped, stunned at the stupidity of his thought. *Getting back? How long will it take the squad to get here? Where am I?*

"We homed in on the Mexican's cell phone," he finished weakly.

"That's it, for now, Frank. You've been cooperative. I trust you are enjoying your stay. By the way, we know where you family is being hidden. If anything happens to us, someone will take care of them." Thin lips smiled through the face covering. "Next time, the gun will start out from here."

They left, and the lights went out. Darkness was almost as painful as the glaring lights. His hope in his phone turned to panic, and it would probably kill his family. Despite his bullying and his hidden sexual anguish, Langstaff loved his wife. They might as well have been tearing out his fingernails. He hoped the phone had failed.

Chapter Twenty-nine

"Ottawa has agreed to pay for all extra security costs in Ontario, Alberta and any jurisdiction that requires it." Mayor Dodge made a last-minute plea for votes. The rescheduled election was tomorrow.

"The Province of Ontario has brought a thousand officers into Toronto. Cadets are being sworn and will complete their training later. We have an extra three thousand officers plus a regiment of regular army. I hope you don't find the road blocks too inconvenient."

The crowd shouted their approval. Dodge did not reveal that the cost was hundreds of millions of dollars, not counting lost business revenue. He worried about the decline of the stock markets and the Canadian dollar. The masses felt the rising prices.

"Dave," Dodge growled at his acting Chief of Police as he left the platform to Bill Meeks and his standard rant. "We have to get these bastards. Is there any word about Frank? It's been over two weeks."

"He was last seen leaving work the day he disappeared. His wife says he called to tell her he was working late, not unusual, but it wasn't at Headquarters."

"There's a twist. Homicide wants to talk to Frank about the murder of that queer."

Mayor Dodge looked surprised. "Why him?"

"No idea. Maybe Frank met him at a pride parade."

Langstaff's phone was a gold mine of information for Sherwood Green. It let them tap into the police e-mail server and had the complete plan involving infrared scanning airplanes and drones, traffic camera vans and patrols.

The major transmission lines, especially those from the nuclear plants, were under constant surveillance. Sherwood Green now had the fly-over schedules. In many places, where roads passed nearby or underneath, guards were on permanent duty. Every private security firm had won large contracts. The Federal Government, in concert with the Province of Ontario, as it had done in Quebec on Remembrance Day, invoked the *Emergencies Act*. The army manned roadblocks on major highways, and they listed every location on the police computers.

Traffic flowed unimpeded on the 400 series of roads, but patrols, drones and overpass cameras observed it all and they scanned millions of license plates.

There seemed to be a lull in action from Sherwood Green, but the security forces worked to exhaustion. Sherwood Green created plans to hit targets away from the heavy security. They also intended to disrupt the workings of the Metro Police Service. Knowing the names and home addresses of all the police computer technicians was the first step.

Chapter Thirty

The lights blazed and two masked figures released Frank's right hand. His feeble swipe at one captor earned him a fist in the jaw. Blood flowed where his tooth cut into his lower lip, but at least he could wipe it away.

"Why is my arm free?"

A resistor set a small table with a legal pad and a pen in front of Langstaff. The interrogators sat down. Josephine flaunted in with exaggerated hip swinging and took her place. Frank's Glock sat at the edge of the table.

"You're writing your confession to Richard's murder."

"Like fuck I am."

The gun eased a centimetre towards the table edge.

"You have two choices, Frank. You *let* us kill you, or you confess and we turn you over to your own force, once we make your confession public. They don't have the death penalty. It's too much trouble to keep you alive here."

Frank had never been this scared or felt so hopeless in his entire life. No, perhaps only the night, as a teenager, he had asked his father what he thought of gays. The man had launched into a violent, cursing diatribe. He never had an honest talk with his father after, right up to his death. He got his revenge when, at his father's hospital bedside, he told the old man he liked both men and women. The old man died with a curse on his lips. Frank occasionally smiled at the memory, but not now as he looked at the pen and the pad.

"What do you want?"

"Put down all your misdeeds, Frank. Why don't you start with that kid you beat up while you were in a uniform?"

"The review board exonerated me."

"Not much of a review back then, was it Frank? Insiders covered up for each other, even worse than the SIU, wasn't it? Put down the truth, Frank. The boy had the right story until he you scared him into shutting up. He was a street punk alright, but you tried to have sex with him and beat him up when he fought back."

"That's a lie!"

The Glock moved. Part of the barrel was over the edge.

Frank wrote, and when he finished, they retrieved the pad and everyone read Frank's shaky scrawl.

"Very good, Frank, we're glad to see you're honest, but how about the time you planted the coke on that black community worker, remember? You needed the big bust to get promoted to deputy? She's still in jail."

Frank wrote without arguing.

"Now, write about killing Richard." The masked man's voice had a threatening edge.

The pen trembled in his hand. Frank knew he was condemning himself. He paused and almost refused, then looked at the Glock. Josephine leaned forward. Her eyes fixed on the pad. In a shaky hand, Frank wrote the words.

"Narrate aloud as you go, Frank. Josephine wants to hear you confess."

"It was just after ten in the evening," Frank sounded mechanical. "I waited for him... her... on Gloucester in my Escalade. We could make out in the back."

"Are you sure you want to hear this, Joey?" The interrogator worried the details of his lover's activities might be too sad, and that Joey would grab the gun and kill Langstaff. He hoped not, but they would not stop him.

Josephine nodded and bit her lip.

"Keep going, Frank." The terrorist's friendly manner annoyed the Chief.

"She was gorgeous that night. Rachelle wore my favourite outfit. It was very sexy, but I had already decided. I had figured out she was pumping info out of me and passing it on, probably to you, crud."

The barrel of the Glock moved further over empty air. Frank focused on the pad.

"Speak up, Frank."

His words slowed, paced by his writing speed, but his hand steadied as he concentrated on his memory.

"We kissed a bit, right there, and she took care of me." Frank stammered, as if embarrassed by his homosexuality. "It was one of the best. She was beautiful." Langstaff forgot where he was and he did not write the last comment.

"I drove around because it needed to be in a secluded spot, so I pulled into a parking lot near the university stadium. I told her to pull her panties down, and while she was fumbling with them, I hit him hard with the butt of my gun. Nobody betrays me." His voice rose as he relived the excitement and the feeling of power. His emotions and his words condemned him.

"This gun, Frank?"

"Yes, that gun, you idiot."

The gun moved a little closer over the edge. Half the barrel was hanging above the floor.

Josephine said, "oh", and a tear dripped, ruining her makeup. She looked at the Glock.

"He wasn't dead," Frank hurried on. "I didn't want him dead too soon. It needed to be nearer when I could dump him. He was out cold. I pushed him into the back and tied his hands just in case. Then I went for a beer at Minx's on Bloor, killing time and watching the baseball game. It was on the west coast and ended about one in the morning."

"I drove to Sherbourne and parked north of the bridge in a dark side-street. It was time, so hit him hard again and that's when he died."

Josephine sobbed and gripped the arms of her chair. She and Frank glanced at the gun at the table's edge.

"I got him ready and drove onto the bridge, southbound, and stopped where the light is dim, away from surveillance cameras. I wanted him in the trees south of the road, so no one would find him right away.”

“It was quiet and easy to pitch him over the railing. I didn’t wait around to see how he landed, but he was dead anyway. I did a U turn on the bridge so the Escalade would avoid the bank’s video and drove home.”

“Give us the date when all this happened, Frank.”

He wrote it out.

“Now write today’s date and sign your name.”

They retrieved the document and re-cuffed Frank’s hand. Everyone left, and the lights went out. He knew they had sealed his fate, and the last voice Frank heard, was Josephine’s.

“When can I do it? When can I...” The door closed in the blackness.

Chapter Thirty-one

Jos Amiel had a problem. In the interview, Joey said Rachelle's boyfriend was Frank Langstaff. He met Frank the night he died. How needed to get the memory card containing Joey's statement to Melissa, but how? Jos believed they tapped every phone and always tailed him.

Joey had been hiding with Joe and Stevie Grey after hearing a rumour Langstaff wanted him dead. Some gay cops were more loyal to the community than to the Chief. Joey had told Jos everything, hoping the video would convict Langstaff. Jos thought the SGSN lawyer might convince the police to take it seriously and go after the Chief, if Langstaff was still alive.

It had not been easy contacting Diane. Everyone had gone into hiding after the police raid and the court fiasco. Somehow, the rabid anti-resistance group from the university had found Diane's address, probably leaked by the police. A huge demonstration took place in front of her little apartment building. The crowd included radical right-wing students, Marxist entities of conflicting views, environmental groups and two nationalist, anti-Russian groups representing immigrants from eastern European countries who believed Sherwood Green was a front for the Russians. Fundamentalist members of several religions rounded out the mob. It united this unlikely crowd in one thing: the hatred for Sherwood Green. Everyone wanted to keep their modern lifestyles.

Jos and Walt had to find cover when they hurled rocks and a firebomb at the building. The police reacted slowly, but with the threat of arson, they dispersed the crowd.

For its ferocity, the mob left with little problem, although in their usual way, two of the Marxist outfits fought with the cops who carted them off to jail. It made for good television but raised the tension in the city. Diane hid and was not home.

The reporters returned in the late evening after a report of a fire came over the scanner.

"Was it arson?" Jos asked the incident commander.

"They set fires at all the entrances. There is one dead woman, the landlady. It's more than arson. It's murder."

"Bring it to my office." Jos had called Melissa directly. "I'm here all day."

Jos walked out the front door of the studio past the unmarked cruiser with two men in it. A man, on a chilly day with a raw wind, lounged against the wall of the pub across the street, reading a paper. *Two tails!* Jos still felt the bruise on his head.

He didn't want either to follow him to Melissa's office. Jos sipped a coffee in the Bucks. The car waited in the parking lot across the street. The goon with the paper came in shivering and ordered a tea. Jos nicknamed him 'Shivers'. With satisfying meanness, Jos hurried out just as the bird-dog's tea landed on the pickup counter. He walked towards the bus stop dialling the Uber number. No bus was due for ten minutes. 'Shivers' would shiver more. Jos figured him for a neo-Nazi like the ones who beat him up.

Jos got onto the bus, flashed his pass and walked to the centre doors. His tail fumbled for change. As the coins hit the cash box and the driver was about to leave, Jos pushed through the middle doors and hurried behind the bus. The vehicle roared away. The Uber car arrived. Down the block, the goon ran back from the next stop. The police would be harder to lose.

The cop received what Jos thought of as the Star Trek manoeuvre or 'go where no car has gone before', the subway. He jumped onto a train, leaving one man from the cruiser rushing onto the platform. Unless they knew where he headed, it was unlikely they could follow him.

"Is this the original?" Melissa asked. She already knew the story, but Joey's statement moved her.

"Yes."

"Is there a copy?"

"Yes."

"I'll write a receipt with the chip serial number on it. You add a handwritten statement that you did this interview, this is your recording, and you will testify in court to that effect. I'm not sure how to use this. We can see if homicide is open to the idea Langstaff is a killer. I wish we had more evidence. This is just Joey's guess."

"Where's Diane?" Jos finished his declaration. Melissa offered him a coffee.

"I can't tell you, yet." Melissa smiled. "Diane trusts you, and you just convinced me. She wants to do an interview on camera. The one you didn't get to do at the farm. It's too dangerous. Ggoons, vigilantes, threaten anyone they connect to Sherwood Green. The mob burnt Diane's house, and we're all being careful."

"They beat me up once and have one following me. I lost him this morning, but they don't look friendly."

"They aren't." Melissa smiled.

"And a cop is following me, too." Jos worried.

"That's good. He'll protect you from the goon if necessary."

"He already did." Jos did not smile.

"The police expect us to take them to Sherwood Green, so don't want us hurt."

The cops parked across the street watched Jos leave. He hurried to a street-car stop, but the cop car remained in front of Melissa's door.

Melissa went down the hall to the office of a small-time accountant.

"My machine is acting up again. Can I use Tammy's?"

Tammy, the secretary, had left for lunch, and Melissa slipped the memory card into a slot on the office desktop and put a USB stick into a slot. She copied the video onto the stick and buried another copy deep in the folder structure of the accountant's machine.

Back at her office, Melissa placed the memory stick out of sight on the transom moulding outside her office door. Then, she went to her computer, copied the video into an obvious directory and uploaded several copies onto cloud servers using a VPN.

Melissa knew they had bugged her office, and she never held sensitive meetings here, but it had been deliberate with Jos. She wanted to make sure the video got into police hands. Even if they never charged Langstaff, Joey's statement would disrupt the police force. The rats just might abandon ship, or good cops would take control.

Melissa wondered if the cops would get a warrant or pick the lock as they did when they placed the bug.

"The bubble has burst," screamed the headline in the business section of The Star as main stream business hacks finally had to admit the illusion of prosperity had evaporated. The cover had fallen away from the rotten global economy, sped up by the actions of the terrorists.

Sympathetic attacks occurred in Europe and Australia. Stock markets plunged. The US dollar rocketed higher each day. Bond yields surged, especially for any Canadian bonds, public or private. Import prices jump higher, inflating Canadian food prices. Variety on store shelves declined all over the country. Bankruptcies of trucking companies hurt the availability of all goods. The Christmas consumer orgy did not happen.

Losing low-end but well-paid truck driving jobs led to the increase in unemployment. Driver unions demanded the death of the terrorists. Sherwood Green became the scapegoat for the global economy. It trapped governments between falling revenues and high security costs.

Two banks announced relocation, one to Calgary and the other to Vancouver. They cancelled every major convention scheduled for Toronto in the next five years. The TSX dropped to new lows.

Torontonians, suffering from this staccato of body blows, received a punch that knocked them reeling.

"We're running it." Sheri hurried into the editorial meeting. "I've had it confirmed. The police have all of this material, but they also got Langstaff's gun with it, one bullet in the clip. Now, that's a message!" Sheri smiled.

"Our lawyers say it's not defamation. It really is Langstaff. He appears tired, but unharmed. There's no sign of torture. Whether it convicts him is for criminal courts. Insiders say the cops will charge him, if he's found alive."

"Bill," she turned to the chief news anchor, "we'll write a quick intro and you're on in," she glanced at the clock, "fifteen minutes. We don't want to be scooped."

The morning mail had brought a package addressed to Jos Amiel that contained Frank's written confession and a DVD with a video of him narrating as he wrote. A note with the material said, *you and the police have this today. Everyone else gets it tomorrow.*

Jos photocopied the note and then handed everything over to Sheri. The horrific confession stunned them all. Sheri decided this concerned murder more than terrorism and did not pick Jos to go on air. He was happy enough to be on the sidelines.

"The cops will want all the originals." Sheri looked at Jos. He had received the package and so had some claim. "Legal says we shouldn't fight them, and we have everything copied."

Jos nodded.

TNN scooped the city and for the rest of the first day, the networks ratings tripled any other outlet. Sheri assigned Jos to explore the Sherwood Green connection.

"Where is Frank Langstaff? Is he the prisoner of Sherwood Green?" Jos ended his bombshell, broadcast with the question. The police had been asking for weeks.

Sherwood Green had sent copies that arrived the next day at all the major Toronto media.

Two packages were different. Bert Boyce's radio station included a picture of the talk show host with the word 'Next' written over his face. The same happened to a racist, narcissistic columnist of The Daily Journal, an anti-left, neo-con rag that played loose with facts and pandered to militarism, racism and fear. The woman had incited racist mobs and had praised the arson at Arsenault's home.

Boyce and the writer hid under police protection. Boyce would never return to the air. The radio station decided it was too expensive to protect him. The columnist continued with a more exaggerated spew of vitriol, writing from a secret location.

All the other media replayed the horrible event almost continuously. The orgy of titillation lasted for three days, but gradually faded to hourly news reports.

A brief flare of coverage returned when someone in the gay district posted pictures of Langstaff with a blood-dripping knife cutting across his face.

Melisa confirmed the police had a copy of Jos' interview with Joey. They had slipped into her office the first night and removed the original memory card, copied it, and returned the copy to her office to cover up the effort. The replacement had a different number and lacked the almost invisible scratch the lawyer had added. Melissa then made an elaborate show of turning over the "original" to the police in front of Walt's video camera.

"Yes, I have a copy." she handed a memory stick to a cop live on air. He acted as if he saw it for the first time.

"It's unsubstantiated," the lawyer told the audience, "but could be evidence later if Joey Brown stays missing. Considering the more sensational recording of Mr. Langstaff confessing, I would say it is okay to broadcast. You couldn't taint a jury any more than the Langstaff video. If I were Mr. Langstaff's lawyer," she looked right into the camera, "I would suggest trial by judge alone."

Jos used the segment with Melissa as an introduction to his interview. Sheri knew it was a missing segment from the farm, but she said nothing. No other television outlet had the TNN video, and the police refused to hand over copies. They threatened Melissa and TNN with charges, but her observation of the secondary and unproven allegations in Joey's statement made any legal action unlikely. It would look like the police had covered up a horrible crime committed by their chief, so they backed off. The force remained shocked and leaderless.

There was one redeeming feature for the police. Joey's revelation that Richard had been an informer and Langstaff's lover gave a face of someone definitely part of the Sherwood Green organization. Their problem was they did not know where Joey hid.

The city asked: *Where is Frank Langstaff? Where is Joey Brown?*

Sherwood Green answered the first question the following Saturday night.

In a flash-back to the night the Sherwood Green story began, Walt and Jos chased fire trucks in the night to a remote industrial area in North York to a large factory owned by Canadian Thermionics. The company, a subsidiary of a huge American conglomerate owned by a rabid libertarian billionaire supplied the tar sands with boilers and heat exchangers.

"It's an fitting target." Jos and Walt stood with other reporters on the street in front of the blazing factory.

Sherwood Green had targeted both the offices and chemical storage. They had dynamited the power house where switchgear and the boiler were located, and one wall had blown out.

Fumes from the chemicals held the firefighters back. The attackers had broken the water line to the plant so the inside sprinklers did not work and the office blazed vigorously.

Amidst the noise and garish flashing lights, Jos' cell vibrated with a text message.

Look in the bushes behind you.

Jos tried to spot who sent the message, but no one stood out. Jos led Walt towards the bushes bordering the sidewalk. A mummy wrapped in a white hazard suit and bound with duct tape lay on the ground, invisible until they parted the shrubs.

Walt switched on his camera. Jos bent over the body, fearing the worst. He had never touched a corpse before and gasped when the bundle squirmed. He rolled the body over and stared into Frank Langstaff's terror-filled face. Walt moved in for a close-up out of a horror movie. Someone had tattooed the word, *Killer* on Frank's forehead. Jos then knew Joey was with Sherwood Green.

Jos ran for a help and cops surrounded Frank and shoved the reporters away. The rest of the press realized something was up when the cops shouted for help.

An ambulance edged up to the spot, and they carried Frank to the ambulance with the man's incoherent babbling clearly audible.

The reporters sped towards the Parkway, racing to the studio with another scoop. One of the other networks beat them to it, but no one had the footage of the instant of discovery, and no one had the shot of the tattoo on Frank's forehead. Jos smiled; the grieving lover of Rachelle, the Sherwood Green resistor and tattoo artist, had his revenge.

In the tumultuous weeks that followed, they would never see Frank Langstaff in public. He appeared in court via video link, a babbling wreck with his forehead covered by a bandage. It seemed Frank Langstaff would end up in the high security prison for the criminally insane and spare the police service the embarrassment of a trial.

Chapter Thirty-two

Jos stared at the invitation. He knew that his relationship with Debbie had ended, but this was a final blow. He was not conceited enough to think she left town to get away from him. Debbie had spit out bigger fish than Jos Amiel, but it seemed a sudden move. A personal phone call would have meant she at least cared.

Jos wondered if the police overhearing their lovemaking was a factor, but it seemed silly. How could the police use it against her? Her husband knew all about it. Everyone at the university knew the gossip of Debbie's love life. They had hired her in the first place, despite her reputation. Academic circles had more philandering than anyone would admit, but her move remained a mystery.

Heavy oak tables filled the historic dining room at Harris Hall. Jos ate there once as an undergrad, invited by an old girlfriend. White linen covered the tables with full place settings and red roses as centrepieces. Jos had a reserved spot ten meters from the front.

The head table stretched the width of the room on its polished wood platform that dominated the hundred-year-old, renovated church, finished in decorative timber frame. Heraldic banners adorned the high walls, with paintings by the Group of Seven depicting the wild Canadian landscape hanging on lower panels of quarter-cut oak.

Ironic, thought Jos. *They built this place before they destroyed the old-growth forests in the paintings.*

Massive, cut-glass chandeliers filled the space with soft light, enhancing the dark oak walls.

The head table guests marched in. Debbie Franklin sat to the right of the University President and to the left of another man Jos did not know.

"Who's the guy beside Prof?" Jos asked an old classmate across the table.

"That's Bill Shepherd, her Chairman at Rideau U."

Jos frowned, and he could not see Mr. Franklin.

The full course of roast beef dinner was first class, and they poured a standard but drinkable Ontario red wine for everyone. Jos' tablemates joked they finally got good food in a place where students ate tasteless meals.

Jos received some fan worship, but most knew him too well to treat him as a celebrity. He had landed a decent job while most of his journalism classmates worked in other fields, although a few still looked.

Jos tried to ignore the head table. Despite the good food and company, the evening became a personal ordeal.

The speeches followed predictable paths. Waiters brought new bottles of wine in anticipation of the inevitable toasts and they recharged their glasses.

At the head table, Debbie waved over a waiter, who retrieved a personal bottle of wine, the Jip-Jip Rocks she and Jos had first drunk at her apartment. She wrote a few words on the back of her programme.

As the President finished his speech, just before he called the toast, the waiter deposited a glass, the bottle of wine and Debbie's programme beside Jos.

Debbie's familiar script read, *Thank you... no betrayal... told them lies... good luck.*

He glanced towards the head table, catching Debbie watching him. She looked away to focus on the President's closing remarks.

Surely she didn't have this dinner just to thank me.

'No betrayal, so, the cops got to her, and she didn't help them.

He folded the paper and put it into his jacket pocket. Everyone rose and lifted glasses in tribute, farewell and good-luck.

Jos drained Debbie's glass and placed it on the table, upside down, beside the bottle. He hurried towards the door and did not look back.

Debbie watched him retreat. With a deep sigh, she placed her hand over the hand of her new boss.

Chapter Thirty-three

By Christmas, copy-cat attacks spread around the world. They seemed poorly organized, and some were religious terrorism, vendettas, or simply criminal. People who had not been as sophisticated as Sherwood Green were in jail. The motives did not matter, as the effect of these attacks further weakened global industrialism.

In the USA, the FBI finally penetrated the Chicago resistor group and made arrests, but the group's structure of independent cells hampered police efforts to destroy. They had suspended coordination after the attacks in November and would not compromise Sherwood Green.

Falling revenues and a power failure caused by winter weather sped up banks' efforts to flee Toronto. They laid off thousands of employees in Toronto. A shortage of housing in Alberta created a barrier, and banking was not as portable as first thought.

"I'm glad we could meet." Diane Arsenault smiled across the table in the back of a comfortable west-end pub. "I was afraid I might have to disappear completely, but things have quieted down."

"Sherwood Green has backed off a bit. It's New Year's Eve, and nothing has happened since they dumped Langstaff at the fire." Jos sipped his beer.

"I think they achieved their first aim. They spooked the money guys. Did you know the OPP has visited the farm once a week since we had our get together? They have a car parked on the road, but they know little about Sherwood Green and hope we will connect them. I haven't received an e-mail in weeks."

"It always recovers," Jos said. "I bet there's a bounce in stocks."

"For sure," Diane agreed. "So when do you think Sherwood Green will strike next?" She smiled.

Diane was an attractive woman. Smiling became her.

"You're smiling. Do you know something?" Jos smiled back.

"Just a guess, but the markets are not real anymore. The real economy is contracting rapidly. It's worse in Toronto with all the bank lay-offs. Look at the menu."

Jos had not been thinking about dinner, but now glanced at the paper in front of them. They had attempted to make the menu appear rustic. It had replaced the usual fancy one. They listed only three high priced entrée choices: beef, pork, or chicken in creative forms, with three variations of potatoes, carrots, or a carrot turnip fry. There offered no fish and the deserts all involved apples.

"There aren't any imported dishes on here. Everything is from Canadian storage. I'm sure the high end places offer variety, but at an even higher price. Restaurants have closed, especially downtown."

"I'm buying," he said.

"Thank you." She touched his hand.

It was much more relaxed than the first time Jos and Diane had shared a beer. Diane told of growing up in a working-class district of Montreal with a single mother. Her father was a sailor, and when Diane was six, he disappeared and never returned. Her mother sacrificed to put Diane through the Poly-tech, and she became a good computer geek, as she called herself.

Jos had a similar story, but he never really knew his father, and his mother, had come from Haiti. It didn't surprise him he found Diane good company.

"Why do some people give up good things so easily, and want to hang onto the?" Diane mused.

Jos thought of Debbie and then his own lifestyle and the things he had thought important.

"We get seduced into false hope." Jos finished his beer.

"I wonder if Sherwood Green, if all of us, doesn't have a false hope." Diane called for another round.

"Are they watching us?" She looked around.

"For sure, and listened to, I think. They have tailed me since I met Sherwood Green. The goons seem to have given up."

"Goons?"

"Nazi types look for people to beat up, or worse. Two of them beat me up once, but the cops told them to back off."

"You're in the middle, with me." Diane smiled.

"That would be good," Jos said, "but it's worse." His eyes met Diane's. "We have reports at TNN that the bikers and mafia are all looking for Sherwood Green. Destruction of civilization is bad for criminals." Jos laughed.

"We know where that would end." Diane took a deep drink.

"Not Koroda's court."

Joe and Stevie arrived, holding hands.

"I'll buy a round." Jos waved for the waitress.

"Coffee for me, I'm driving," Joe said. "The cops would love to get me on a DUI."

"Cider," said Stevie as she hugged Diane.

Jos felt hungry. "Let's eat."

Chapter Thirty-three

Joe turned his Honda into his street. Stevie sat beside him with her hand resting on his thigh. It had been a nice evening with Jos and Diane. They looked forward to some eggnog and a winter snuggle.

Stevie was younger than Joe, but he had seen her grow in the few months they had been together in the network. Joe felt contented.

Now what? Joe frowned into the mirror. A car that had been following them since they left the pub turned behind them. *More cops!*

The tailing car sped up and slammed into the back of the Honda. Stevie screamed. Joe stepped on the accelerator, intending to speed past their house and onto a busier street. A car suddenly pulled out in front of them. Joe hit the brakes but crashed into the back of the new vehicle. The air bags deployed, stunning both of them. In his semi-conscious stupor, Joe watched a man from the tailing car walk up to his window. The barrel of the Uzi pistol was the last thing he saw. Shattered glass, blood, and two bodies filled the front seat. The attackers disappeared into the night.

"Uzi, nine millimetres," the cop told Jos. He waited with the press behind the yellow tape. A blue tarp covered the Honda. "It's a military or police weapon, but that means nothing. Toronto is full of them, mostly in the mob's hands. The Russian mafia uses them. I've seen nothing like this before."

It devastated Jos. Joe and Stevie were too close, and he had liked them. "Why would the Russians want to kill these people?"

"They murder for hire," the cop replied, but rarely come downtown like this. Their turf is York and Vaughn. It seems well planned, and it smells of their work."

The cop would not speak on camera, leaving it to the murder squad inspector for a news release. Jos saw several faces familiar from Project Tom. Everyone knew this was revenge against Sherwood Green. Jos shed tears in his next *Terrorism Toronto* report.

A week after the Russian mob murdered Joe and Stevie, the week before Christmas, a white service truck with "City of Vaughn" stencilled on the doors eased along a commercial side-street. A large portable welder sat in the back and two men in bright safety gear rode along. They stopped at a yellow fire hydrant. It took five minutes to weld all the hydrant caps shut. By the time they were a block past a small plaza, they had welded four hydrants.

The little plaza housed the usual collection of muffler shop, lube service, ladies' wear, a coffee shop and a small popular restaurant, The Georgian Dumpling House. The restaurant was the only place of interest to the truck's crew. They disappeared and returned the rental truck minus the welder and settled the bill with a fraudulent credit card.

The restaurant staff had all left by midnight. The owner of the Dumpling House, a fat Russian named Dmitri, dealt cards to seven men gathered around one of his serge-covered dining tables. Among them was the head of the Rostock gang, attending his usual Saturday night poker game. His next in command and his chief enforcer sat with him, along with invited guests.

Out front, half a dozen expensive cars nosed into the store-front. A large man wearing a heavy overcoat and flap hat patrolled in the cold air. Occasionally, he would sit in the boss' car to warm up. Every half hour, he walked to check the back of the restaurant. He walked along the blank brick sidewall of the building as a window rolled down in a dark van parked thirty meters away in front of the muffler shop. Quiet pops accompanied five bright flashes from a .27 rifle. The beefy guard fell, dead, out of sight of the front.

Two men scurried from the van to the restaurant. Each carried a five-gallon can of gasoline. One put on the dead guard's hat, pocketed his boss' car keys and walked to the front. He threaded a chain through the door handles and locked the door tight before emptying gasoline across the doorway. At the rear, they pried the back door open and poured gasoline into the kitchen. Simultaneously, the arsonists fired marine signal flares into the gasoline. The explosions were powerful.

The attackers jumped into the gangster's car and sped off. The van went in the opposite direction.

"Fried dumplings on the menu tonight," the driver said. His companion did not laugh.

The screams from the restaurant did not last long, as choking smoke killed the gangsters trapped by the front inferno and the barred windows. The kitchen flared into an impenetrable furnace. When the pumpers arrived, they could use none of the nearby fire hydrants and watched the building collapse.

That same Saturday night, someone torched a warehouse in Woodbridge, causing limited damage, but the police investigation discovered a stolen car operation where the Russian gangsters prepared expensive vehicles for export to Africa. Along with a dozen luxury SUVs and sedans, they found three containers already loaded and consigned to the intermodal yard. They charged ten mobsters and three railway employees. Sherwood Green did not take credit for any of the attacks.

The dead boss' wife, more ruthless than her husband, took leadership of the gang. No one connected the fire to the contract hit on two meaningless young people in Toronto, but blamed a rival gang. Uzi fire gunned down two rival mobsters in North York, and warfare erupted, drawing street gangs and even the Hells Angels into a bloody winter of revenge. Someone killed the mobster's wife by the end of January.

Jos' favourite 'Bucks' had closed.

"Lack of business," the sign said.

It was worse for his police watch-dogs. They had to walk around the corner to get their 'free-fills' and suffered in the cold February weather. They forecast the coldest day of the winter to hit in a week. The cop cars with their engines running seemed to counter Sherwood Green's goal.

With no guilt, Jos poured a nearly full but hours old pot of coffee down the lunchroom sink. Even his morning re-warmed gulp from his home carafe tasted better than this. He made a fresh pot using his fair-trade roast and bottled water. Jos felt guilty about the water and vowed to change to the safe city water. In their several consultations, Jos would not call them dates. Diane had scolded him for his wasteful habits.

"If I can afford it, why not," he defended himself.

"That's the attitude we're fighting." She sighed.

Jos took his coffee and breakfast taco into the lounge and settled in to watch the morning headlines. The cute morning anchor did not smile.

"This just in," she intoned as best she could. "Police have announced the arrest of Professor James Franklin for soliciting and having sex with a minor."

Jos spilled some coffee.

"This results from an investigation that has been ongoing since November. Mr. Franklin will appear for a bail hearing at Old City Hall this morning. We hope to learn more details. They will not release the identity of the victim because she is a minor. Police are asking for any other victims to come forward."

Jos stopped listening. The investigation had begun just about the time Debbie avoided him. *Did she know about her husband? Is that why she left and dumped me?*

In subsequent court submissions, they revealed that Debbie Franklin had turned her husband in to the police. This did not surprise Jos. Debbie, for all of her past lovers and her enjoyment of sex had told him she drew the line at minors and students. Her husband screwing his students had been one thing that had upset her. He had exploited underage high school kids desperate to get into university. That's when she called the police.

Briefly, Jos envied her new boss in Ottawa.

Audio set his backpack down beside the workbench. The components of a high-end auto sound system sat on the bench. Behind him, in the heated bay of the luxury car service shop, a Mercedes CL-65 waited.

He had worked here for seven months. At first, they had only allowed him to do minor repairs, but his boss recognized Audio's skill, and he had let him work on the expensive vehicles of their most elite customers.

Many of the well-healed people owned exotic antiques. The CL-65 was not one, but it belonged to the wife of the CEO of the Trans-Colonial Bank. She had complained that when they moved to Calgary in the spring, "I won't have you people to take care of me". The lady was older but well preserved. She winked at Audio as she rubbed a loving hand over the fender of her car.

Audio hummed *"Just a Gigolo"* as he removed the console assembly and inserted the sound system into the Mercedes' dash. As he wrapped up the work, inserting a sophisticated solid state amplifier in the trunk, he slipped a lead tube behind the unit just above the fuel tank. The woman would take the car after lunch.

Audio looked at his list. There were three more high-end cars needing attention before day's end. One was a beautiful Rolls-Royce made in the 1950s, painted in deep red and black, belonging to the Chairman of a railroad corporation. He hated to destroy such a beautiful machine, but if anything symbolized the planet's problem, it was these cars and their entitled owners.

Audio went to chat with Velma, the one woman administration for the shop. He got along well with her and chatted often. She reminded him of his sister. He brought her a large double-double coffee and a crueller from the Tims around the corner.

"Business is dropping off." She looked over the paper cup at Audio. "We'll lose a lot of lucrative customers when the banks pull out. A Volvo and a Porsche dealer have closed."

"Yah, there are four banks leaving, one to Bermuda." These results pleased Audio, but he could see Velma worried about losing her job. She did not know that tomorrow she would join the thousands of unemployed.

"You should take up farming." Audio said.

"Not me, baby. I kill my geraniums." Velma chuckled.

You'll have to learn, my friend.

Velma did not know this was their last day on the job, determined by the sabotaging of four luxury vehicles. The cops would link them here but find no evidence.

The company servers, with all personnel data, hid in the cupboard behind Velma with no off-site backup. Audio had looked admiringly at the equipment a few times, so Velma thought nothing of her friend examining the servers.

It was quitting time, and Audio wanted to be gone. They would not notice the lead tube behind the servers. The Fire Marshal's report would only guess about *an incendiary device.*

"See you, Velma. Say hello to your geraniums for me." Audio left.

Spike walked through the small entrance beside a massive roll door that closed the locomotive bay. The engine service shop in Mimico was a familiar place. Even though she worked for one of the mainline freight railroads, they subcontracted her work as an environmental technician to VIA Rail for its local repair shop. She passed three large GMD locomotives assigned to the trans-continental passenger service.

"What brings you down, young lady?" The moustachioed maintenance foreman smiled. Greg was of Italian descent, short, swarthy and stocky. Spike never gave him trouble. He was a nice guy.

"I was told there was a diesel spill." Spike smiled. There were always spills. Few were of any importance, but all had to be documented under ISO standards.

"Which one do you want first?" He laughed.

"Greg, you're a smartass." Spike replied. "Tell me where they are and you can go back to the football match."

Soccer had been a joke between the two, ever since Greg discovered her ancestral home was Jamaica. The country's team had once scored a goal against the Italian national team, too many years ago to matter. Football fans never seemed to forget. Spike felt badly that she was about to put a smudge on his maintenance operation.

"The middle GMD, someone opened the wrong valve."

"It looks like you're ready to roll these out."

"6434 here is about to move. She's pulling the Canadian west tonight, and the boys will be out to close her up right after break."

Spike looked into the open sides of the unit. The spot she was looking for was underneath, exactly in front of her. The space held an APU above the low-slung diesel tank.

"I'll go look at 6406 and give you the report before I leave. Accidents happen."

Greg headed off to his office. He really wanted to check the score in the Champions League friendly.

Spike took a metal tube from her pack and slipped it behind the auxiliary power unit. She wedged it firmly between a pipe and the twelve-gauge sheet-steel of the tank, tying it firmly with wire. They timed the incendiary to ignite about four the next morning and melt a hole into the tank, igniting the diesel. If 6434 was front-ending Train Number One, they would be well northwest of Sudbury, in the middle a cold mid-winter nowhere.

Spike made a great show of using her sniffer to look for fumes, took a few photos of the offending spill and wrote her report. She stepped out into the frigid February air just as 6434 was being powered up.

All the fires that night seemed accidental and un-related. The next day, when a Project Tom investigator sifted through the fire reports that the police now always vetted, he noticed a coincidence. The four fires all involved the residences and vehicles of CEOs or corporate board chairmen. One fire was in King Township at a large estate. Another happened in Rosedale, destroying the home of a bank executive. A third caused the evacuation of a luxury condo complex downtown and the fourth levelled a mansion on the Bridal Path. They traced every fire to an automobile, and he began an investigation.

The burning and destruction of the car service shop was of little interest, and the disabling of a passenger train far off in northern Ontario, the first ever such incident for VIA, seemed well beyond Toronto police.

When Jos arrived at work, it was quiet. The last night had been uneventful, especially compared to the flurry of fires in the previous night. None of those seemed to be terrorism. Jos' view of the situation was about to change.

An email detailed the four car-related fires but did not mention the automotive repair shop or the train fire.

The rats all want to leave the good ship, Toronto. The message ended. *We want to hurry them along. We are now in a new phase of our work, targeting the safe havens of the*

From now on, no aspect of the lives of the robber barons will be exempt from attack. Our interest is not to harm anyone, even though these people have harmed and even killed innocent people and thousands of species in their lust for wealth. If some die unintentionally, they can only blame themselves.

The *Terrorism Toronto* report was a sensation.

Mayor Dodge panicked as he watched his city, the economic jewel of Canada, collapse. In these conditions, he could not sell city bonds to pay for basic services. The tax base shrank as thousands of "For Sale" signs littered upscale neighbourhoods. Prices collapsed and most sellers faced huge losses. Realty companies declared bankruptcy. Millions of dollars of real estate taxes would go unpaid.

In response to the personal threats, many of the elite avoided Toronto. Those who lived in the country stayed there. Many who lived in the posh mansions of Rosedale and the Bridal Path took vacations. Once more, security firms flourished, and many people who lost good jobs guarded former employers' residences for minimum wage.

Jos killed time in the Second Cup, when his phone rang, but it wasn't Diane. The screen said, "unknown caller".

This may be the last you hear from me. They got secret warrants and are inspecting all courier and mail going to TNN and your house. The boys outside in that car have orders to seize anything from a bike courier or taxi arriving at the studios. I can't send anything on paper.

So far, they haven't bugged the cell you're using, but they are trying to get a tower bounce warrant. I wouldn't trust it. They know you don't have contact with the terrorists, but they keep hoping.

Since Frank's arrest, there has been a gay witch-hunt going on inside the force. Morale is low. Most cops who can retire are planning to do so. The training college is full of punks. Things are going to get worse, and there are factions inside the force fighting each other for power.

Everything seems out of control now. I doubt the terrorists need to do much more. Good luck.

The line went dead.

The next day, TNN called an all employee meeting and put everyone on eight weeks' notice because of crashing advertising revenue. Once they devised a plan, they would cancel some notices and others would go immediately. It included Sheri and Jos.

Jos knew there was little likelihood of an economic recovery for Toronto. The city could hope to survive as a mid-sized provincial capital, and he had not felt this directionless since TNN hired him.

"I'm going to lose my job." Jos and Diane strolled along Bloor Street. A raw east wind cut through them and they walked arm in arm for warmth. A car followed them at a discreet distance.

"More people are being let go every day. I have no work." Diane said and hugged Jos a little tighter.

"Prospects don't look good. I sure won't be working in the media soon, if ever."

"Do you remember the farm?"

"How could I forget? The stars were so bright."

"Most of us are going to go there to start a community. Do you want to come with me?"

"Where are you staying now?"

"Since they murdered Joe and Stevie, I'm on Melissa's couch."

"Come home with me." They turned down Sherbourne Street. Jos briefly thought of Rachelle.

Diane and Jos snuggled, naked beneath a comforter, in the early morning light. It was mid-winter and dawn came earlier. An icy wind swept down from the north in the coldest weather of the season. The pair had hardly slept;

their loving had been fervent but gentle, and the TNN morning news babbled softly on the television.

"It looks like the terrorists are on the run. Attacking these fine people proves they can't do anything more effective. The police will soon destroy them." The scene cut to Mayor Dodge waving his arms before a cheering crowd."

"Do you think they are done?"

"Who knows," Diane snuggled tighter against Jos. "They have begun a new phase, and I doubt it's over. Is the coffee ready?"

Jos pressed his lips to hers, urgently.

In their passion, the small click from the entranceway did not register. Hallway light suddenly spilled into the living room with the sound of heavy boots. Diane screamed. Jos wanted to throw up.

"Aren't you two a happy sight?" said the unfamiliar, unsmiling face; Jos knew the voice and squeezed Diane's hand, trying to reassure.

"You," Jos exclaimed.

"Get moving. We don't have time. Carry your clothes and follow me. Grab your ID but leave your cells; they bugged them."

"Make sure that door locks."

They made it the six flights down the fire escape in record time, gasping for breath, standing naked at the rear doorway and trying to hold their bundles of clothes for modesty.

"Romantic, isn't it?" Jos smiled at Diane.

"Shhh," a raised hand cautioned. The elevator rising from the lobby broke the quiet.

They rushed from the building, and the ice-covered asphalt burnt bare feet that left tracks in the light dusting of snow. They tumbled, shivering and embarrassed, into the back seat of the Escalade. Their strange visitor inserted the key in the ignition but made no move to start the engine.

He waited, staring at his tablet. The red circle appeared and disappeared almost instantly.

"Good, they are in your place."

He twisted the key and quietly moved towards the driveway, lights off. The police car across the street had disappeared. Jos pulled his sweater over his head. Diane still struggled with her bra, trembling from the cold and fear. The Escalade turned left and suddenly sped up, throwing the bewildered pair hard against the seats. On the seat beside the driver, the red circle flashed once more and stayed lit.

On the sixth floor, three men brandishing Uzis ran for the stairway, swearing loudly.

The driver forced the automatic to downshift and slow enough for a skidding left turn on the next street, leaving no tell-tale glow of brake lights.

The armed men ran about the parking lot, checking all the vehicles. It took them a few minutes to connect the tracks and the vacant spot to their target. Their guns disappeared.

"Those asshole cops must have tipped them."

"They'll get theirs. Let's go get the lawyer."

"Where are you taking us?" Diane regained some control.

"Here," the driver handed Diane a cell. "Call your lawyer friend Melissa. Tell her to get out of her place, now, no questions. Tell her to find a safe place and then call the cell I just gave you. It's clean. Use it for a day or two and then throw it."

A sleepy Melissa tried to argue. Diane said, "Remember Joe and Stevie. Get safe." Melissa hung up. The Escalade sped down a ramp and onto The Parkway, northbound.

"Thanks for the info you gave me." Jos tried to be friendly, still not recovered from his fright. "It doesn't seem we accomplished much."

The driver nodded.

"Sherwood Green hasn't won yet, and the mayor has gotten in bed with just about every mobster he could find: the Russians; the Jewish mob; the Italians and the bikers. His police force is collapsing, and these gangs hope to take over. They just might." He slowed to highway speed.

"Personally, I think there will be a bigger gang war than we saw after Sherwood Green killed the Russians who murdered your friends."

"Who are you? How do you know all this? Are you in Sherwood Green?" Jos knew this guy was at least a sympathizer and likely a cop.

"I'm not with them, but I bet I'm the only cop who has seen a member."

"And you didn't bust them?"

"I didn't know what I saw. I was undercover, watching a Hells Angels plant selling false ID in the Ministry of Transport. It wasn't a top priority. Most of the fake IDs were for driver's licences so kids could get into concerts or buy booze. The customers were young, that's why the one guy stood out. He was in his thirties and looked too straight. His picture and the fake name are in the database."

"So why don't they nab him?"

"Frank Langstaff set up Project Tom as his road to glory. He wouldn't share anything with us regular intelligence guys, so we volunteered nothing to him. Besides, my group also watched the cops, looking for rotten apples, bikers, that sort of thing. Frank, with his hanky-panky, didn't want us snooping too close."

"That seems petty." Jos said.

"The force is full of pettiness and rivalry, with too many ambitious people. As you know, Frank was not leader material. It's too big to fix without destroying it and starting over."

"Just what Sherwood Green believes about industrial society," Diane commented. The driver nodded again.

They passed under Lawrence Avenue. A car came down the northbound ramp and sped up behind them. The driver watched his mirror and wondered how much speed the Escalade's enormous engine could give him. They approached the York Mills exit. The following vehicle came close, swerved to the right, and roared past another SUV. It disappeared towards Highway 401.

The driver exited at York Mills and then up Don Mills Road. An Escalade would be a common sight in these neighbourhoods.

"I still think there's more to why you didn't go after that suspect, and why you are helping us, if you are helping us." Jos still feared the ride would not end well.

"Oh, I'm helping you. Don't be afraid. I'm doing that and leaving the other lead alone for the same and slightly different reasons."

"You two were about to be gunned down just for revenge by one mob. They finally figured out that Sherwood Green killed the kingpin. Since they are as clueless about the actual terrorists as the police are, they went after you visible ones."

"Your friend's deaths were contract killings. Project Tom can't figure out who paid the contract, and neither can I. It isn't how the Canadian elite work. I'm guessing it was a Yankee operation, maybe the CIA or the billionaire who owned the factory that burnt the night Frank turned up. I'm almost sure it was that."

"But you are helping us because?" Diane was sceptical.

"Look," he turned to them while waiting at a red light, "I had a buddy on the force, the opposite of a cop. He was radical, a revolutionary, you might say, a Scot who hated that we were protecting the rich from the poor and not helping the poor. Anyway, Tommy worked on me, and soon I shared his feelings. Somewhere in there, we both followed the environmental movement, and we volunteered for every do-good project representing the police from tree planting to Christmas baskets. We soon saw it was just sugar-coating and talked about how doing something like Sherwood Green would be the only solution. It was all talk, I thought, but then Tom took off about three years ago. He said he was going north to build a cabin in the woods and wait it out. I heard no more from him. I miss him. He was a good cop and a good friend. I think he's in Sherwood Green. It's his knowledge that's letting them outwit the cops. He knew the Hells Angels were in the MTO and other places."

"So you think you know two members?"

"Just guessing, but it fits. When I was sending you the info, I thought of Tom. I couldn't allow another massacre, so when I found out about tonight's hit, I had to risk getting you out. No one knows I know all this, so I'm safe. The cops staking out your place are on the take. The gangsters might blame them. If so, there will be bodies after all."

The cell jingled.

"I'm safe, for now." Melissa sounded shaken.

"Get to the place." Diane was not sure any phones were safe. Melissa knew about the country safe-haven. "Get everyone there if you can. No one is safe."

Diane hung up.

The Escalade eased to a stop two blocks from the Shepherd subway station. Daylight broke, and the subway would be running.

"We're smart enough not to ask your name. What can we call you?"

"Just call me Lincoln," the man laughed. "You don't recognize this vehicle. It was Langstaff's Lincoln Escalade. Richard died in this. It's ironic that it's saved lives."

Jos teared and looked out at the street. Diane clinched her jaw.

"Does one of you drive?" Lincoln wanted to get away from the tragedy.

"I do," said Diane.

"Good, a black guy driving this vehicle might get pulled over, even in daylight." Lincoln undid his seat belt.

"Don't tell me where you are going, but if it's that farm, lie low. The OPP has it watched, but they just drop in at random and can't get inside without a warrant. I would keep this vehicle somewhere else, or sell it a long way from there. The ownership seller portion has a credible version of Frank's signature."

Lincoln opened his door, and the pair followed.

"What are you going to do?" Jos wondered how this cop could live his double life much longer.

"Oh, maybe they'll put me in charge of Project Tom. I'm the last competent senior they have. Good luck."

Diane eased the Escalade onto Bishop Street, heading to Young Street and then north to the farm. Lincoln followed along the icy sidewalk to take the subway south. He watched the vehicle disappear.

Maybe I'll find my friend Tommy and...